FIRST AID FOR CHOKING VICTIMS

FIRST AID FOR CHOKING VICTIMS

Matthew Zanoni Müller

The stories in this book are fiction. All rights to said stories belong to the author. Quotations for scholarly and review purposes and falling within the general guidelines of fair use are welcome and encouraged. This book was created by human beings. It was written by a human, edited by humans, and the cover was designed by a human, all without the aid of LLMs and other AI programs. The use of the stories in this book for the training of large language models/AI is absolutely prohibited.

First Aid for Choking Victims ©2024 Matthew Zanoni Müller.

Cover design by Angelo Maneage.

Published November 2024 by Malarkey Books.

Mr. Perfect	7
First Aid for Choking Victims	43
Hank	69
I Want You to Tell Me	89
Watch Me	164
Tornado Warning	186
The Sunfish	204
One-Eyed Boy	253

MR. PERFECT

It was Tuesday. Chris was over at his best friend Matt's house drinking on a school night in the small neat room in the attic above the mess of his father's house. Chris fell back on the bed next to Matt and stared up at the sloped ceiling. Chris's blood was filling up with a glowing kind of numb light that circulated sluggishly out through his arms and legs. "We're gonna be so fucked up for basketball practice tomorrow," he said. In the far corner of the room, Matt's older brother Jackson, a senior, sat guarding the rum and Coke in a cloud of pot smoke, his long hair hanging low over his pudgy body. He looked like a hairy Buddha. "Oooh, basketball pwactice tomowow. I'm a big impowtant pwayew," Jackson said in his mocking baby voice. "You're just jealous," Matt said. Basically, everything that had gone right in Matt, the thick hair, the athletic body, the general good looks, the being nice to everyone, had all gone wrong in Jackson. "Shut up," Jackson said. "Never," Matt said, and then, from somewhere in the muddle of blankets, Matt took Chris's hand and asked, "Have you ever had a hand massage?" Chris hadn't, but was too drunk to answer. Matt started massaging, pressing his rough calloused fingers into Chris's palm so that the blood moved out to the swollen sides, pushed up against the walls of his skin where it electrified with numbness. Matt gripped the stem of each finger, squeezed, and then pulled up its length so that the tingling numbness rose up and up the tight compartment of each digit as the pressure crested and seemed to burst out through the tip when Matt released it into an electric sizzle of relief.

Chris went warm and warmer until he fell asleep.

He woke up to the basketball bouncing outside and thought he had slept in and missed shooting around with Matt in the few minutes before his dad called them in for bagels. But it was still dark. The glowing green numbers on the electric alarm clock read 12:03. He got up and grabbed for his sweatshirt but was knocked back on the bed by a big swell of blood to his brain. "Fuck." The ceiling shifted a few inches to the left and then snapped back into place. Whoa. When he was finally still enough, he rolled off the bed and crawled until he knocked against some dead thing. There was matted hair, a sweaty arm. It was Jackson. He had passed out on the floor. "You hairy little troll," Chris whispered, but all he got was a gulp of air, a readjustment, and then some steady breathing.

He got to the stairs, grabbed the banister, and slowly pulled himself up. All right; that worked. He actually felt good. He tip-toed down even though he knew Matt's dad didn't care if they stayed up all night or made noise. He was the one who had bought them the alcohol after all, and who had also brought that bowl upstairs to smoke with Jackson. Somehow the silence inside the house was glassy and brittle and he didn't want to break it even as Matt kept smacking the ball into the silence of the wide-open dark outside.

Chris pulled his sneakers on in the mudroom and went out.

Matt didn't look at him or try to throw him the ball. Chris could tell that he was supposed to let him play. He walked to the garage door, sunk down with his back against it, and tucked his knees up in front of him. Matt was shooting hard, grabbing the ball out of the air when it came off the hoop. He threw it out to himself, caught it, turned, and took a fade-away. Nothing but net. The hoop was stuck on a pole at the end of a narrow parking space paved into the lawn. Matt kept playing his violent game, a game whose energy or frustration or whatever it was increasingly got into the air around him, got caught up in the dewy streetlight that cast the trees in shaky shadowy brilliance, that got into the glare of the spotlight over the garage that shone on the court. It got into the darkness that huddled in the bushes on the far side of the lawn and it was all mussed up like a cyclone in the bright light in which Matt played. In which he caught, dribbled hard, faked one way, moved the other, crossed over, shot. His curly hair swung wildly with his movements. His arms were tight and sinewy under the white wifebeater he was wearing; that tall body that the girls loved so much in its baggy blue Nike shorts. Its power.

Chris slumped farther down and let the energy settle like an atmosphere over him, watched as Matt started to slow up, to relax, until finally he was lazily shooting and putting the ball back in, bouncing it off the backboard, spinning it with a little twist of his fingers through the hoop. Even then he didn't look at Chris. Finally, he took the ball, held it tight between both hands, and stared hard across at Chris.

All Chris could do was return the look, and they were locked like that as if Matt were trying to transmit something across the air to him. But Chris didn't know what it was, and Matt seemed to give up and threw him the ball.

When Chris got up to shoot, Matt walked back inside.

Chris stood for a long time spinning the ball in his hands, looking at the empty space where Matt had stared at him.

When he turned to look at the hoop he didn't feel like shooting, so he just dropped it and watched it roll away.

***

That Thursday Chris was on the couch at Matt's mom's log cabin house in town staring at the massive T.V. in the small living room. Matt's girlfriend Meghan was there, lounging in one of those round blue Papasan chairs, her legs crossed so that her pink shorts rode up and bunched around her waist. Chris hoped he might get a glimpse of her underwear. He thought they would be white with little red cherries on them. They were waiting for Matt and Jackson to figure out dinner with their mom. Jackson had invited two of his friends over, Josh and Justin, or J.J. for short. They were always together, had gotten close with Jackson playing Magic: The Gathering at this farm stand on Thursday nights. They were the kind of kids that tucked their wolf-themed shirts into their hiked-up acid-washed jeans, knew how computers worked, had an intimate knowledge of World War Two weaponry, and had these annoyingly delicate long fingers that you just wanted to like, crush with a rock. Currently, their skinny little backs were arched as they sat on the floor in front of the T.V. playing N64, the controllers nestled in both their tiny crotches, and their mouths hanging open. The only thing seemingly alive were their fingers mashing the buttons all insanely.

"So, Chris, how does it feel to be best friends with Mr. Perfect?" Josh asked, absentmindedly, his neck tilted up toward the screen so that his long skinny black ponytail hung farther down his back.

"If you're talking about me, then yes, I am friends with myself, and I am perfect, thanks J.J."

"Don't call us that," Justin said.

"What, J.J.?"

"Yeah, J.J. We're two different people."

"I know, that's why it's not J."

"All right well, shut up. At least we're not Matt-Light."

"What's that supposed to mean?"

"Umm, let's review," Justin said. "You're kina like Matt, cause you're pretty tall, and pretty good looking, but just not quite as tall, or quite as good looking."

"Wow, thanks guys."

"Yup, and you're also good at basketball, but not quite as good as Matt," Josh added.

"Listen, we have different roles on the team. I'm the point guard so I'm not supposed to score as much."

"Said the jealous Matt-Light."

"All right, anything else assholes?"

"Well, also it seems like Matt is better with girls. For example, he has a girlfriend, while you're here alone." Josh cocked his head back at Meghan who drew a semi-circle in front of her face as if she were the showcase on the Price is Right. She gave him a playful look like, "See, I'm special." He shook his head at her betrayal and she grinned at him.

"And it seems like all the teachers love him and—."

"And fuck you, all right," Chris said.

"Sorry dude, we were just saying." They paused the game and their backs slacked a little as if they had just realized that what they were saying was mean and they were a little embarrassed by it. God, didn't they understand anything?

"At least I don't wear a fuckin wolf shirt. Sooooo cool, a wolf howling at the moon in a semi-cloudy night in front of like, jagged mountains."

"Hey, my brother gave me this shirt!" Josh said, surprised that someone wouldn't like it.

"Yeah, when he stopped playing Dungeons and Dragons and started getting pussy."

"Actually," Justin said, "Lyra gave Josh a blowjob last weekend."

"Whaaat?!" Chris said. Lyra was actually kinda cute, and super nerdy and a little zitty and a little overweight, but in a cute kind of way, like she was aware of her own coolness in spite of everything, which made you want to prove to her that you didn't care either, you just loved her.

"That's fuckin' awesome man!" Chris got up and drummed his hands on his skinny little back. "You're the fuckin' man."

"Thanks dude," he said, though he was clearly embarrassed, especially with Meghan sitting there. Looks like they didn't like people all up in their shit either.

"I guess I'm sorry we said that stuff about being friends with Mr. Perfect. We were more just like, I don't know, how the fuck can someone be that perfect, you know?"

"No, clearly I don't, you dicks."

"Who's a dick?" Matt said, as he came in.

"One and all," Chris said, and waved his hand across the room, crinkling his eyes at Meghan, who stuck her tongue out at him.

"Gimme that," Jackson said, coming in after. He took the controller out of Josh's hands. "It's my fucking game."

"Wow, chill."

Matt fell back on the couch and draped one of his legs over Chris's lap.

Jackson looked at them and said, "You guys are so gay."

"Yeah, you're making me jealous," Meghan said.

"Why does everyone keep saying that?" Chris said.

"There's nothing wrong with being gay," Matt said, and blew Chris a kiss.

Chris caught it and ran his lips over his hand and made kissy noises.

"God, I still can't believe you lost your virginity before me," Jackson said.

"Hey!" Meghan said. "You weren't supposed to tell anyone!"

Matt's face colored. "Sorry," he said, even though it was obvious that he didn't really care.

"God!" She pulled her legs higher up against her body as if she were trying to push herself through the back of the chair to land in a different room, like a cannonball. Splash, Chris thought, and imagined her sun-splashed body tipping into a pool. God she was perfect. Short, a little thick, so that all you wanted to do was squeeze her. Her legs, her stomach, her breasts, just everything. Especially her exasperated cute face with the corners of her mouth that turned up and dimpled. He just wanted to kiss it and kiss it and kiss it until all that smile of hers was inside him.

Jackson hit the start button and immediately got creamed by Justin, his little cart skidding out and spinning in circles off the road.

"Fuck dude! I never get anything!"

Chris looked across at Matt, who had this blithe satisfied little smile on his face, like he'd just pulled off some trick, sat down at a poker table for the first time and won the game while his brother lost everything after years of trying, learning the rules. It was like he knew this would keep happening for the rest of his life. He would keep pulling the chips in with both hands while he watched his fatter, hairier, shorter, angrier brother losing at video games and everything else.

Chris had the urge to slap that smile off his face.

Late that night Chris was on the floor in a sleeping bag next to Matt's bed. A corner of this ratty-ass blanket that Matt was weirdly attached to hung over the side of his bed. It was the only thing in the room that wasn't perfect, clean, and new. He had gotten it, supposedly, at some sleepaway camp a couple years before, when his bunk buddy had forgotten it.

Chris yanked it off.

"Hey!"

Matt lunged down and grabbed at the blanket. His breath was hot and close to Chris's face and his eyes were wild and intense as they appeared out of the darkness. Matt gripped the blanket with both hands and fought for it violently, like he was panicked, like he might do hurt. Chris let go.

"Jesus, dude."

Matt took the blanket back and lay still on the bed. His breath was ragged and uneven.

"Another victory for Mr. Perfect," Chris said, to test the dark, to jab at it. Why the fuck had he been so intense?

"What? Fuck you. That's my blanket."

"Just like everything else in this world."

The dark went quiet and Chris lay waiting for what he would do. The air inflated with tension.

"I barely ever want any of the things I win," Matt said. His voice distant, as if he had let go of all his winnings long ago. "I don't even think about them."

A car passed and the light from the window turned in on itself and swiped across the wall.

"You're so fucking modest."

Matt didn't say anything and after a while Chris was sure he was asleep.

"Nobody knows anything about me," Matt said, so quiet, so like he was talking to himself, that he must have thought Chris was already asleep.

***

That Saturday, when the phone rang, Chris had to lean back in his chair from his spot at the breakfast table where he was eating a quick bowl of cereal before work, to lift the phone off the receiver from its spot on the counter behind. His parents still didn't have a cordless phone. Of course, the chair tipped and he almost nailed his head. "Fuck," he said, as his hand clamped the edge of the counter and dropped the phone. It hung suspended and bouncing on the cord, knocking on the wood floor. He got his balance, pulled up the cord, fumbled for the receiver, got out of the chair, and wrangled it to his ear.

"Hello," he said.

The woman on the other end wanted to know to whom she was speaking. Chris thought for sure she had heard him swear. "It's Chris," he told her.

"Oh, hi Chris, it's Irene."

He tried to place the name, and then she appeared before him: tall, blond hair cut short like she was punishing it, her shirts always tucked in as a sign that she was strict. She was a friend of Matt's mom, but it was the kind of friendship that Irene forced, which meant that Matt's mom was always pulled into things she didn't really care about, like bake sales or fundraisers for the PTO and all those kinds of things. "This woman doesn't have a life," she had said once. "I wish she'd come and clean houses with me for a change, then I'd really be getting somewhere."

"How's it going Irene?" he said. "Any bake sales happening soon?"

"Oh no, no, no, no, just, I'm calling because I wasn't sure if you had heard, and I thought your parents might also want to know, that Matthew has died."

"Matthew who?" Chris asked. It must be some friend of his parents, or someone's dad maybe.

"I mean Matt. Your friend? Matt Winnaker?"

A rush went through his ears and tightened in his stomach. Matt? This idea was distant, a faraway pulse, steps echoing out of his reach as though they would take a long time to reach him. His eyes began to fill.

"What? You mean, Matt, like, in my class?

"Yes, I'm afraid, yes, that's the one. Yesterday."

"What do you—" He wasn't quite sure what to say next. The phone sank in his hand. He stared blankly at his cereal, which was getting soggy in its bowl. She was wrong, obviously. How could she know? Matt was still there, still alive. He could call him right now and it would all be good. It had to be.

Out at the deck the squirrels were going for the bird seed spilled around the feeder and past that his eyes rose to the line of trees beyond which the valley opened up to the hills on the other side, the sky above them glazed blue. Matt was still out there, in the air. His face closed, expressionless, a mask in the clouds that looked out to some distant eternal nothing.

"Still there Chris? I'm so sorry. I know you two were close. I really, I just, I've been calling around and making sure that people knew. It's, you can imagine right, what it's like over here at Nina's."

She was at the house, Chris thought. At Matt's mom's house. Of course. She'd rushed over and was all prepared to take charge. She probably loved this, calling everyone. Fuck you, he thought. Then he thought he should probably say it directly to her.

"Well, I should probably get on with my phone calls now," she said, almost hopefully, as if she was already looking down the list of numbers and ready to get on with it.

"But wait," he said, his anger suddenly desperate. "What happened?"

Irene was silent on the other end. He could see she didn't want to tell him. Again, he got the urge to yell at her.

"It was, well, it's really just so hard. There was an accident."

"What kind of accident?"

"We're really not totally sure, but well, it was a train."

"A train?!"

"Hmm, mmm," Irene said.

A train?! A train had taken him. Then he knew exactly where. Just down the road from his dad's house. They used to sit under the bridge and listen to the trains go over. He had smoked his first cigarillo with Matt there, which his dad had bought for them. They had licked the vanilla flavor off the little plastic tips, which looked like a duck's bill, or a flute. When the train went over they would scream as loud as they could. Sometimes they'd scramble up there to get closer to the noise and be blasted away by the metallic screech. When the tracks were empty they'd balance on the rails or jump from tie to tie and Chris had asked Matt once how long he thought he could stay on the track before the train came.

"Right till the last second," Matt had said, and grinned at him.

"We think, we think he just slipped. That he was probably playing up there or something."

"Slipped," Chris said, and imagined all of that metallic force. "Playing." He's not some little kid, he thought.

A sad note of affirmation came to him from the other end. There was a silence into which he saw Matt watching him while he received the news, as if he was in the room, just over there on the couch, his eyes intent, tracing his reaction.

He was being lied to. Matt had not fallen. He hadn't. They were trying to cover it up, make it easier. Grinding anger started to turn inside him.

"Well okay, Chris," Irene said. "I'm so sorry to be the bearer of bad news. You take care now." And she hung up. Just hung up.

Chris considered smashing the phone on the counter, caught between the silent line of the phone and this feeling that Matt was watching him from the couch. He took a breath against the tightness in his stomach and looked back at the couch, grimacing and biting at his lip. As he stared, the couch emptied and Matt was gone. Into this silence he heard Irene pick up again. The line hadn't gone dead because he hadn't hung up. She started to dial, punched each number in like a code.

"I'm still on," he told her, and then he hung up.

His boss Dave would be over in a few seconds to pick him up for work. They had a ton of leaves to rake. Trees to wrap. Things to get ready for winter. As if he was zapped back to life, Chris jumped up, grabbed the soggy bowl of cereal and dumped it out in the sink. If he ate it now the electric shocks of anxiety in his stomach would electrocute it right back out. He grabbed the paper bag he'd packed with his burrito and

Mr. Perfect

apple in it and went for the door. He was getting his shoes on when his mother came down the hall and asked, "Who was that? Who called?"

"Irene," he said, and didn't look up.

"Oh," his mother said, getting comfortable again and yawning. "How'd you sleep honey?"

"Fine." He was whipping the blue laces of his old running shoes all around his fingers and kept fucking up the knot.

"Did she want anything?"

"Nope."

"Huh. So why'd she call then?" she asked, as she ran a hand through her disheveled hair.

Outside, Chris could hear Dave's truck on the gravel.

"To say that Matt died." Tears were in his eyes now.

"What?"

"Yeah, to say he's dead, all right?" He didn't want to look at her because it would all spill out if he did. The call would be real. He'd stumble over and cling to her soft body in its bathrobe with the smell of sleep still on her. A mother who had not lost a son that day. He'd go liquid.

So instead he threw Matt's death at her. He wanted to see it hit her, to see it hurt.

"He slipped, and he died. That's all I know." He got up to glare at her. He wanted to be cruel, not soft. Cruelty was easy. "A train ran him over," he said, as a final injury.

She was in a confusion'; her was face registering the information too slowly, which pissed him off, and all that concern in it too. God, didn't she get it? "He fucking died, what's taking you so long?"

He could tell she was about to come toward him.

"I have to go. Dave's outside." He grabbed his bag and got out the door, hustled down the deck stairs.

"But Chris, wait! You can't go to work!"

"I have to!"

He ran to the silver Tacoma, got in, and stared at her through the windshield as they backed out. She was in the door, hurt and pissed, and he knew that he'd fucked up. He knew he should get back out and climb up the steps to hug her, that they should sit together on the couch and then go to Matt's. That they should spend the whole day draped in sadness with their feelings collecting around them liquid and warm while her hands gently caressed his back. But he couldn't go, no way, and so he glared at her through the windshield and Dave asked, "Everything all right man?" But he didn't answer.

All he wanted was just to keep staring as the truck backed up and up the hill until it tipped over the edge of nothing and everything went black.

He raked. For a long time he raked. His method was to rake inwards so that a circle of green would form inside of all the brown and orange. Some of the trees still held a few clinging leaves. When the wind blew up, they'd come off in dry jangles, ringing some dead bell. The moist smell of the dark earth scratched up with the metal tines of the rake and the leaves breaking apart, mixed with the smell of grass that got brushed or ripped out. All of this rose up in the air around him. His sweat built, and the right side of his back tightened into a long line of tension until he switched to rake lefty. When he paused to look up, a raw sensation came on, and the only antidote was to look back down at the grass, at the dirt beneath, at the progress he was making in clearing the leaves.

When he was almost finished with his circle he peered up at the branches of a tree all bending in one direction as the wind went through them. A shower of leaves blew loose, released like flickering moments of a life. They circled, fell, hovered, slid, and joined the leaves collecting on the grass. The end of their season. He beheld each one.

Tears welled up and he wiped at them as they spilled over and streaked his cheeks. He pressed his lips tight, and stood with his hands wrapped around the rake's handle. Matt's life blew around him, all those moments. They touched a deep point in his stomach where his sadness centered.

He already knew what they would say at his funeral: a list of insufficient consolations and corny metaphors. How Matt was a light in everyone's life, how his smile lit up a room, how he had always treated everyone well. How he would be so missed. They would gloss right over every damn thing and no one would ever know what Matt would have ended up doing and all they could do was look back at the few years of his life to try to puzzle out why he had been on earth, what he had contributed. The trouble was that he hadn't lived long enough for anybody to find out. He hadn't been able to show them.

Chris sobbed and sat down on the leaf pile and let the tremors run through him. He didn't care if he got fired, if Dave found him there doing nothing. He let the tears just run down his face and fall on the leaves. It was a mild day and a breeze blew along his back, gentle, like the earth commiserating with him, the same earth that had not been gentle with Matt. He ran his hands through the rough brittle leaves, mushed them around, lifted and crunched them in his hands, punched out at them, wide arcs with his arms, until he wore himself out and fell back. The anemic sky popped up, and up, lifted like the bottom of an elevator, but went nowhere. It just left him down there.

He had Dave drive him home. It was pointless to stay. The way Dave just kept going about his work and sipping his stupid Snapple at lunch made Chris want to pound his face in. And then he was so cool about everything, saying, "Of course, of course, I was surprised you came to begin with." And on the ride home the distant expression in Dave's face showed that he was plotting out how long the raking would take and if he'd have to bring in another guy for the weekend and it was clear that he wasn't thinking about Matt at all. He didn't know him. No one cared about someone's death unless they knew them.

When he got home his mother appeared at the door, rushed down the steps, put her hands through his hair and kept squeezing him like she was afraid he was going to die in her arms.

"I'm alive mom, all right? It's fine. I'm not fucking dead and I'm not going to be fucking dead."

"All right, all right," she said, wiping her red eyes and drying her cheeks with the back of her hands. "It's natural for a mother to worry," and so he let her hug him for as long as she needed, even as her words receded into echo.

Meghan had called and so he called her back.

Her voice was so high-pitched that it sounded like it had been squeezed into some helium register by her tears. "Hello," she cried at the top of a sob.

He told her he was coming over.

"Okay," she said.

He took his mother's car, holding up the keys to see if it was okay.

"Just be careful please."

"Obviously." Goddammit. He wasn't going to off himself now too.

Mr. Perfect

Off himself. Had Matt done it?

This question preoccupied him on the drive. He ignored the yellow 45 M.P.H. signs on sharp curves and tore around them at 60. He looked down at the ditches he was straddling and thought of yanking his car over so he'd hit the rocky bottom and flip. When a tractor-trailer came toward him in the opposite lane, he imagined turning the wheel into the truck's huge grill and getting smashed into nothing. At the parkway, he imagined rolling out into the double lanes, turning, and watching as a car came at him at 61 miles per hour and smashed first the driver's side door, then his braced body as it gripped the door handle before it was sent out broken across the asphalt.

If it had been suicide, Matt had wanted to blast himself into smithereens, that much was clear. He had wanted to annihilate himself; he had wanted to do complete bodily damage, a total fucking breakdown. Why else would he step in front of a train? It was like he wanted to fling his body off into the void, erase all of himself, his life.

Or like when Chris had watched him playing ball in the driveway like he was trying to violently break through the hoop into something else.

Chris stopped for gas, went in to pay, and saw Matt's face on all the local papers next to a shot of a stopped train surrounded by emergency vehicles and personnel. A guy in line in front of him, with his huge round calves stuck in white tube socks and scuff-free Skechers, told the cashier what a shame it was. "These high school kids, they're just always getting into stupid stuff. Drinking and hanging out on railroad tracks. When will these idiot kids learn? Such a pointless death."

"Better than your pointless life," Chris offered from behind him.

The man spun around, looked like he might throw a punch, but reconsidered when he saw what must have been violent desperation clawing around Chris. Instead, he just reached behind him and swiped his change off the counter and walked out.

"Ten on number four," Chris said, stepping up to the counter.

"You got it," the cashier said, a little too affirmatively, like it was a stick-up.

Meghan was in her pajamas, which were silk and had little blue circles all over them. They were tightly stretched over her thighs and strained the buttons on her top. She was holding her pillow and her face was red and blotchy and when he walked in she started to wail.

He wanted to hold her but it would have been like gripping an electric socket. His insides would have curled. It also would have been unfaithful to Matt, probably. Like Chris was coming in as some hero savior guy who was going to be all calm and stoic and hold her, even if he would love it. "Fuck you, hero savior guy," Chris thought.

Instead, he settled across from her on the bed and because she was so openly crying and so openly weeping and wailing and the whole room was full of the humidity of her tears, he started crying too, his shoulders wracking and shuddering as he thought about Matt, one image after another, and each making it worse: Matt dutiful at his desk at school; Matt fucking around at the dinner table at his dad's; Matt on the bench at a basketball game pissed that coach took him out. Each time he saw another one it was like a shot of hope hitting him, a little swell, like the jump start of a new idea. He was still here. In that picture he was alive. And each time, the reminder that Matt was dead would lumber in and zap the picture shut so that Matt couldn't get out. Each time he saw him, he was killing him again so that by the end Matt was dead in each one, slumped over in every picture of his life.

Meghan grabbed for his hands with her little dimpled fingers in a tight panicked squeeze of knuckles and bones until they were all tangled up and clamped together rocking back and forth in their hurt.

"It just doesn't make sense," Meghan's mom was saying. She said it again and again. "It just doesn't make sense." The conversation would move on and then she'd have to dive back in. "How could someone so perfect, so happy, how could someone who had it all . . . He had everything! I mean, everything!"

Meghan's mom didn't look like Meghan. She had short dark hair, with bangs that slanted across her forehead. She was very pale. Her face was narrow. Probably, when she was young, she had looked cute and mousy, or like a dewy little chipmunk. But now she looked severe, all lines and angles and jagged and concerned. Meghan's dad was where she got her thickness from. He was round in the face, flushed cheeks, his hair buzzed short. He had a lawn-mowing business. Dave was jealous of him and all his machines, but Meghan's dad was older and could afford a fleet of mowers and a backhoe for heavier work. Meghan's dad didn't speak much at all. He just shook his head in agreement with his wife. It just didn't make sense. No, it just didn't.

"I mean, did you know, Chris?" her mom asked. "Did you know? Was he depressed? Was he unhappy? I just didn't see him throwing in the towel like that."

"Throwing in the towel!?!" Meghan screamed. "Who said anything about throwing in the towel!?" She began to cry again at the table. "It's not some fucking sports game!"

Her dad said, "It's true, it's true, how would we know? We don't even know it was suicide. Listen, listen, we don't even know. He could have slipped."

"And what do you think Chris? What do you think? What was it? Did he slip?" Meghan's mom asked.

Chris didn't know. He didn't. He suspected but he wasn't going to say. He shook his head. He held Meghan's hands when she took his. He hugged her tight when he left. He had to go see Jackson. There would be a ton of people at the house, but he had to go. They were having some kind of wake. Meghan told him she might try to go. She just didn't know if she could.

He decided to ditch the car and walk over. When he got on the sidewalk he thought not about suicide, but about slipping.

Meghan lived in town, in a little suburban back neighborhood where it had been easy for her to pull a sweatshirt on, throw a CD into her Discman, lift her headphones over her ears, and cruise over to Matt's mom's house. In all the time she'd done that she'd never slipped, never once stepped in front of a car and accidentally gotten hit.

Unbidden, the image slammed into him, of Meghan stepping out into the crosswalk, lost in her music, as the swoosh of a car tagged her out of nowhere. There she was, her legs up in the air at broken angles, her head upside down just above the hood of the car, her discman flying loose on the leash of its headphones. Then he heard her hit the pavement. The heavy thud of her body.

He pulled up, held his fist to his mouth.

Fuck, why was he thinking about this?

At the light he waited for the little crosswalk man to appear in his eager white step. Car engines ran hot as he walked in front of their grills. When he got to the other side he had the sensation of tipping backward, of being pulled by fucking vertigo into the street. He'd fall on his back just as a car started up and ran over his head.

"Fuck," he mouthed, and grabbed at his skull, moved it around like a dog wrestling a rope toy. Fuck. Fuck. Fuck. He threw his hood on.

He kept far to the right of the curb where his foot couldn't catch and drop him into the street. If Matt had been up at the tracks, just killing time, just skipping up on a rail and back down, just leaping from tie to tie, just trying to see how close he could get to the train as it blew by, then maybe all it took was a sharp wind, the pull of the train to turn him inward toward its rushing bullet of steel. Maybe it was just a crooked little stone that got caught up under his shoe as he screamed into the noise of the train and it surprised him as he tipped into it. Or maybe he had stood in front of it for as long as he could, just until the last second, and he hadn't been able to jump out of the way, even though he wanted to. The gravel had spun under his feet and he had gotten creamed, just fucking creamed.

Chris bent over and vomited. It was yellow and fell into the brownish grass edged in a clean line against the cement slab of the sidewalk. Bits of bile hung like ribbons strung over the blades of grass.

Matt's body. It had just gotten so crushed. So beyond saving. There was nothing left to put together. He hadn't wanted to die in that last moment. He had screamed. Pure terror. He had been torn apart.

Chris wretched again, heaved, spat, heaved again.

The line of cars parked along the street was visible long before Matt's mom's house. He walked past one, two, three. A driveway opened the line and then closed it again. Four, five, six. He still couldn't see the house. The street was ghost-quiet. The cars were shock-empty. Seven, eight. Another driveway. Nine. At the tenth car he got down on the grass and leaned against the hubcap of the back wheel. He wasn't going to go in. All those fucking people. They'd search him all over with their eyes. See how he was handling it, Matt-Lite. See if he'd cry or not cry. They'd want him all open, like a wound. He'd have to let them all crawl inside so they could hug in that wound together.

No. Fucking. Thank you.

Chris sighed, ran his hands along his face, held them over it like he was praying. The window of the car he was leaning against rolled down.

"You okay over there?" A face leaned out the window, craned back at him.

"Yeah, no, I'm fine. I'm fine."

"All right, just checking in."

"Thank you."

The face stayed all turned around on its neck like an owl, a big round bearded face. Concerned.

"I'm just waiting for my wife," the face said.

"Okay."

"In case you were wondering why I was sitting alone in my car."

"Right," Chris added.

"Radio drains the battery."

"Yeah."

"You a friend of his?"

"Yeah. Best friend."

"Man, I'm really sorry."

Chris nodded, put his hands over his face again.

"I'd be in there right now," the face said, "but I thought I'd just be in the way. Nobody knows me. My wife, she met his mom at yoga, so I thought I'd just hang here while she went in to help."

"Help with what? Matt's dead." Why was everyone trying to do something? "It's not like it makes a difference now."

"Yeah, true, true." The head receded into the window. It continued its watch on him through the rearview mirror.

"Do you know why he did it? I mean, do you think it was an accident?"

"I don't know."

"He didn't leave a note?"

Chris considered that. They hadn't found one, but could there be a note? Hidden in a closet, a locker at school, a gym bag, a classroom desk? Maybe he had written one but the train had mashed it up somehow.

"No, not that I know of."

"Hmm," the man said.

"Doesn't mean there isn't one."

"Hmm," he said again.

"I just, I don't know what's worse. If it was an accident, then that's just so fucking sad. And if it wasn't, I mean, if he threw himself in front of that train. It's just—."

"Yeah."

Chris contemplated a house set back deep from the road. It had a porch crammed full of shit. Tarps strapped over chairs, faded plastic kids toys, a table saw. All saved for future use, presumably. Pointless. You could die, like, immediately.

"So, you're hiding out here?" the head said again.

"Yeah, I just walked over, and then I saw the cars, and I just couldn't."

"I'd go in with you if it helped."

Chris rubbed his hands together, studied them.

"It might."

When the man got out of the car he was big. Probably three hundred pounds. He'd be a shield, a barrier.

"If I could just sort of follow you in," Chris said.

"You got it."

They shook hands. The man's name was Christopher.

"What are the chances," Chris said.

Groups of his classmates loitered around in little circles on the front lawn, and some other people from school he didn't even know, some upperclassmen, were perched on the hoods of their cars. The girls wore flares and baggy sweatshirts, glanced across the yard as if they were waiting for something to happen. They probably didn't even know Matt and hung around at the fringes as if this was some kind of event they had to go see, like they were waiting for a concert. Fuck those people. Josh and Justin were there, those skinny nerds with their braided belts and wolves howling at the moon shirts, Jackson's buddies who played *Magic: The Gathering* with him at the Farm Stand on Tuesday nights, and who always made sure to call Chris Matt-Lite, and would ask him how much it sucked to be his less good-looking friend. Now what did they think, standing next to a bush at the end of the driveway, looking at their shared Nintendo Gameboy. Other people were sitting on the porch, perched along the deck chairs and swing, all of which were made of wooden logs, like the house.

The closer he got, the more a ringing opened out in his ears, knocked out the sound. Matt had died and now, just as easily, they could all go. He saw them dying: a tall kid fiddling with a pocketknife disappeared from the little group of four by the front path. Then Justin faltered, shimmered, dropped the Gameboy, and disappeared into static on the driveway. One of the girls slouching on the hood of a car in a white tank top just slowly dissipated into mist. They were all just barely shimmering on this side of life. It was all off kilter. Any small thing and he'd be dead too. He reached for Christopher's massive shoulder just as someone grabbed his arm. It was Julia from his class in a white shirt with little strawberries all over it. "Chris," she said.

Her eyeliner was sharp, her teeth white against her tan face. Her dark hair was long and curly and freshly showered and her brown eyes glittered. "Julia," he said.

He hugged her as tightly as he could. She wouldn't disappear, she wouldn't die. Her pulse beat against him, her heart.

"Come on, I'll take you in. You haven't seen them yet, have you?"

He shook his head. Julia knew exactly what to do. She was always the class organizer, the messenger, the one who called, got people together, told them what to bring to whose house for what party. She was like the heart of the class around which they all swirled. He put his arm around her shoulders and followed her.

In the mudroom he remembered. When he went back out, Christopher had already turned around to lumber back through the yard to the silent car. In his gray t-shirt, his large back looked like a stone in the current of the crowd, which parted for him.

"Ready?"

Julia gripped his hand and led him right to Matt's mom. Her back was to him, almost impossibly short, her light brown hair permed and faded, and he was afraid that he'd be able to see directly into the white cave of her devastation. Julia touched her gently on the shoulder and she turned, her red eyes swollen and cheeks glittered with tears. Her face opened with light and she gathered him into a hug, her little hands curling into his back. "I'm so glad to see you. It's so nice to have you here. Oh, he loved you so much." She was all warmth, no devastation. She hugged and hugged him. "We lost him," she said. "We lost him but he's still here, you can feel that, right? How he's here with us, smiling at us. You can just see him can't you, looking down at us?"

Chris nodded and searched her eyes but they were just warm. She wiped at her tears. "You two were always so alike. It's like I can see him next to you. This morning, I was driving back home, and there was this hawk, and he was just following me, and I knew it was Matt. When I came to a stop sign and he landed on a branch and then kept flying with me when I kept driving, that's when I knew. It was like he was protecting me still, you know. Matty. Always looking out for his mama."

Chris hugged her, and even though he didn't know about that whole hawk thing, he just held her. It didn't matter what she thought. He was just going to hold on.

Jackson came at him with a big smile on his face. "My brother," he said. "Come here."

There were no tears. He was expansive, warm like his mother. He hugged Chris and then he was turning to someone else, giving an instruction. People were crowding around him. He was hugging everyone, he was gracious and kind and large-hearted. His eyes were a little bloodshot.

"I couldn't find my lighter," he told Chris. "I was going to smoke a bowl you know, I had to, I had to get in a different head space, and I couldn't find it, and I just knew, you know, that was Matty, that was him playing with me. I mean, he's dead like a day and he's playing around, hiding my fucking lighter. I just love that, you know. He's probably laughing at me right now."

Chris just nodded. It was surreal. Jackson had never been big and open and happy like this. Now there was zero edge to him. Probably sanded a fair amount of it off when he smoked that bowl, but still, Jackson was high all the time, and now?

He watched as Julia came to Jackson, whispered something, trailed her hand lovingly along his back.

Then it all made sense.

Jackson, big and open and warm, surrounded by love, love from everybody, swimming in it, buoyed, floating, expanding, as he passed from girl to girl, wrapped in their arms, released, and wrapped again.

It was how Matt had always lived while Jackson looked on from the corner in an angry cloud of smoke.

Later, Irene passed out Dixie cups with holes poked through the bottom. Everyone got a candle, stuffed it through. Lighters were passed around. They went out on the lawn, stood in a big circle. It was twilight, and they started to sing "Amazing Grace." Chris looked across the circle at Meghan, whose arm was around Matt's mom. She had made it over, finally, and they had just held each other and cried, tears coming off them in all directions.

Next to him in the circle was Crystal, a girl he barely knew, and when he started to sing, she put her hand on his forearm, as if they were joined in some kind of mutual sadness. She hadn't even fucking known Matt. He pulled his hand away, and after the song, he didn't stick around for the next part where Matt's dad was leading people in saying "Ommm." He asked Crystal to take his candle, and backed up into the night.

Weirdly, without Matt, he didn't feel like he was a part of any of this anymore. He wanted to get away, to cut himself off. He wanted to be where Matt was, somewhere off in the cold sober night above the train tracks, looking down at what he had done to himself, flicking a stone, sucking on a cigarillo. Silent. Just a little smoke rising up in the dark.

Even more cars ran up the sidewalk. He peered into each window, looked for a big shadow inside, hoping that he was still there, that he could come in and sit in the silence next to him, but by the time he got to the last car, he hadn't seen him.

***

On Monday, the principal called a school-wide assembly in the gym. Chris found Meghan on the bleachers and slid over next to her. She had called him the day before and cried to him through the line, and for a long time they had just held the phone to their ears and been quiet with each other.

"You know he loved you, right?" Chris said into the silence. That made her cry again, and for a long time he just listened to her sobs.

Finally, she said, choking through them, "I think he loved you more."

"That's not true."

They were silent again, and a while later she said, "I have to go, people are here."

Everyone packed into the gym and then the principal talked about the "tragic loss," and the "mysterious nature," of death, and the "difficulty in understanding people's motives."

"Sounds like he thinks it was a suicide," Chris whispered.

"He's just saying that so the people who believe that will know that he understands them or whatever."

Mr. Perfect

"Right." He gripped her hand. She didn't believe it. This belief was hardening in her. Soon she wasn't even going to speculate with anyone. She was just going to shut them down or walk away.

The principal went on to assure the students that the school was "Doing everything within its power," to make sure that the students' "Health and safety" were maintained. It had also provided grief counselors. "We hope that you'll make use of them."

Later, Chris saw Meghan disappear into the room where the grief counselors were working; one of their arms was wrapped around her shoulder as they guided her in.

He wasn't going to go in for that. He didn't need to sit there in front of some stranger blubbering and talking about his pain. The fuck was the point of that.

When the assembly was over, Josh and Justin came up to him in the hall and said, "So, how does it feel to be Mr. Perfect now?"

"What?"

"Yeah, without Matt around, you're it. You're the new Mr. Perfect."

He punched Josh in the face. Justin turned his body away defensively and Chris punched him over and over again into his skinny little side. His arm kept trying to block him and it was a good thing because his ribs felt so brittle each time he hit them, and Chris was frustrated that he didn't have something harder to punch, something that gave more resistance. Something where he didn't have to hold back. A teacher broke them up.

In the principal's office he was made to wait. "I understand that you're angry, that things are all out of sorts, that this is a huge loss for you, so I'm going to try to be understanding here," the principal said, once he came in, settled into his chair, sighed, and ran his fingers along his eyebrows. He was bald, small, and wore sweater vests. How did one become like the principal? Didn't he wear cool sneakers and shit when he was a teenager? Did it just happen to you slowly? Did you lose your hair, did you wear out your shoes and replace them with cheaper, dumber ones, or was it that once you took a job, you just started to look like it? Chris thought of the guys on the road crews he drove past, long beards, big bellies, cutoff t-shirts. Bankers in suits. Convenience store clerks with their scarecrow hair.

He had to sit in the principal's waiting room until one of the counselors was free. "Once you meet with one of them, have a little check-in, then we can figure out how to proceed."

Chris just nodded. He knew how to handle adults. You just go along with the plan. You make it easy on them and show them that you're cooperative. Still though, he wouldn't tell those people shit. What did they know?

Through the large orange rectangle of the office window the backdrop of the baseball diamond and part of the green wooden dugout was sunk in shadow. The grass still looked wet and dewy. By the time Matt had walked out of school, the grass would have been dry. That's what had happened. He had walked out during last period. They had begun to put things together, the timeline. He had read about it in the paper, and Meghan had made him tell her, because she couldn't read it.

Chris kept studying the shadowy dugout, imagined Matt slapping a baseball into his open glove as they sat next to each other on the bench, both in uniform. "Get us a win," he would have said, before Chris got up to pitch the last inning.

Mr. Perfect

It hit him then: he knew exactly how it had happened. He could retrace the entire thing, the whole route.

Matt had walked right out in the middle of class as easily as if he were going to the bathroom. There was nothing to it once he decided. He just got up to see what it would feel like. It was a little subterfuge, something he'd never done before. "Here everyone, watch me fuck up a little. You didn't see that coming, did you?"

The hallways would have been echoey. Dusty light would have blown across the checkered brown floor tiles and the dim light of the glass door at the end of the hallway would have stood out to him as a dull glow, a possibility, an option, a place through which to leave. Because why not? It would have been heavy when he reached it, the metal of the knobs cold. He would have pushed hard into the initial resistance until it swung free. And then he was out like it was nothing. Stepping into that open air, he must have known he would never come back. Not ever.

The bus drivers had lined themselves up for students to rush out. He walked by one after the other, the weird feeling of being somewhere he usually wasn't at that time. The air was light, a little off. Things were too quiet. The future noise of school letting out was visibly packed into the classroom windows, as if it were ready to pop out, the bus drivers in expectant boredom waiting for the students to clamber up the black rubber steps and jumble into the back, pushing, yelling, laughing, hunching in desperate protective quiet. A couple of the drivers looked up at him from newspapers or stared right through him in a glazed-over reverie.

He walked past the parents in the adjacent lot who waited to take their children to doctors and dentists, to jobs and karate classes. If they saw him, they would know him, their closed faces would open into recognition and he'd be caught, pulled into the tender heavy care those adults had for him, who wanted to know how he was doing, how the team was shaping up, to pull him into their distracted adult disappointment and compromise. Someone who hadn't yet been worn down by life, hadn't had to cut away one possibility after another until there was only the one thing left: the one small track of their life. Instead, he walked in the other direction, cut across a grassy median toward the baseball field and ambled along the chain-link fence where people sometimes lined up to watch the games.

He looked back at himself at second base last season, fielding a grounder, throwing it to first. The final out. It suddenly seemed so small and irrelevant. His body, distant, competent in the blue uniform, a movie with the sound off. A spinning sensation reeled him over into its pointlessness. A long flat field in a small town. It dis-attached, floated free like a disc, lost itself in the glare of time up in the sky, floated far beyond him out of view.

He proceeded to the little league field, his seven year-old-self hustling back to the bench in a uniform that was too big for him. It made him gulp; the sadness of his dutiful body, trying so hard. When he was up to bat the field spread out into endlessness before him. He swung too hard and mostly hit the tee, but the ball still flew out into the dusty far green distance of the outfield, out far past himself, like a little white missile of his will that rose into the blue of all he would become.

    Chris sighed, checked the orange door over his shoulder. The counselors were taking their fine time. He imagined Meghan's red crying face; he imagined other girls crammed in there too, boys miserably slouched with their skinny arms draped over chair backs, all with their tissues and the girls' legs pressed together, staring miserably down at their feet. He looked back out the window, imagining Matt's journey.

After the baseball fields he got to a railroad track that cut diagonally across town. The tracks moved away from him in both directions. A school bus stopped even though there clearly wasn't a train, before it pulled carefully over. He took a step, then another, followed a road that ran more or less parallel to the track. There were a few grassy plots with trailers lined up along narrow driveways. One of them had a deck attached to it lined with planter boxes that oozed red flowers blooming like a tumor form the trailer's side. The others were bare and empty, like they hadn't bothered trying.

After that came the lumberyard. A forklift balancing a pallet packed with sixteen-footers wobbled over the ends, the driver taking it slow as he entered the cavernous shadow of the aluminum roof, the rows and rows of 2x4s and 2x6s and plywood sheets and stacks of asphalt shingles tearing free of their white plastic wrapping. A truck had parked to wait for an order, a man holding a slip of paper called to an attendant who ran out to see him. The place was all loaded up for building. Matt gazed at that, the forklift running in, running out, making quick hard turns, shoving its teeth under the weight of new materials, stacking, arranging, pulling out. Houses would go up, houses would rot and come down. Houses would get fixed, added to, reshaped, remodeled, gutted and caved-in. It was all just a repetitive process that he was standing at the beginning of.

The attendant approached a tightly packed pile of lumber and cut the metal bracing that held it together with pliers. He stepped back when it jumped free. The metal clattered at his feet and then he pulled a long piece of 2x4 straight out of the middle of the pile, just like he was pulling it right out of

Matt's sternum, pulling and pulling, easing it out until it was free, a square black hole in the tightly packed bundle of his body.

Back over the tracks, over the long fields in the distance, stood the brown rectangular block of the school. The farther he walked, the smaller and flatter it got, until it was a thick black line laid on top of the horizon to press them all down and flatten them out like a car crusher at the junkyard. But then he was far enough that it disappeared, even in his imagination, and all the people inside it were gone and only a blank sheet of sky was left.

Soon, other landmarks disappeared. The pharmacy, the gas station where he had gotten sandwiches for him and his dad and Jackson before going out for a tile job. He had jumped out of his father's work van, gotten the little brown boxes with the waxy insides to-go, the sandwiches wrapped in white paper, the pickle too, a yellow bag of Lays potato chips on the side, all stacked on his lap as the van lurched off, the memory driving away into its small pocket of time while cars pulled in to gas up and people ran inside to pay.

A woman held the pump and stared straight off into a vast blankness over the roof, as if she were seeing something on the other side of it. When she put the nozzle back in its holster, it was like the sky closed back up again and fit her neatly back into her day. She could flip the gas lid shut, get in her car, and drive back into her life.

Not him. Nothing was going to zip him back up. He was all open, all air.

The road left the tracks and cut through a suburb. He passed the yellow house where he had taken piano lessons from a priest with bad breath who wore loose gray sweaters with large collars and gold bracelets. The piano was in an addition in the back, Chris had seen it once, a giant room with beams that met each other like fingers interlocking at the gable. When Matt played Mozart in that room, when it filled and bubbled and turned over itself like water, it took him off with it, spun him up and over himself until he was washed out and gone, totally gone, flushed out into a bright nothing that beat and reverberated against that high ceiling in his chest.

The road cut back and met the tracks again near Matt's father's house. He scrabbled up the sharp incline, balanced over the bridge under which he had sat with Chris and smoked cigarillos and yelled through the noise that wrapped his voice up with it. When the train came, Matt intended to step right into that noise, into the wind that pushed it out and pulled it back behind it; to place his chest right up against it, right up against that metal bullet that came from nowhere and would go back to nowhere — that cut through all that noise and weight just long enough that he could get up close to touch it, to lose himself in the scream.

But who the fuck really knew. Chris leaned back in his chair so the plastic creaked against the metal frame. Matt had just walked off one day, picked his way through town, watched all the normal people do their normal stuff, and because he wasn't normal, and because he didn't see anyone else like him around, he had decided to throw himself in front of that train because he didn't want someone like himself to exist.

Rooted. Transfixed, Chris couldn't help seeing it.

Bright and shaky with anxiety, Matt had waited for the train's approach. A whole audience's attention on him, just like at a basketball game. They were all there, cheering him on in the stands while he was out on the floor, bright Matt, perfect Matt, taking the ball up the court to score the final point. They were all relying on it, needed it. Aah! Chris thought, and pulled his head between his legs. He couldn't watch. But then he was there, the train close enough that it couldn't stop though it saw him. Matt as he stepped forward to show everyone how imperfect he really was, how the world hadn't made a place for him at all, hadn't really seen him, how it would never see him, not until now, not until he made his last drive up the court, his final argument, his last point, so that they could all finally see him—so that the crowd could go wild.

FIRST AID FOR CHOKING VICTIMS

CATHERINE HAD SEEN THE SIGNS, she just hadn't yet worked out what they meant yet. The signs involved Marjorie, their strict junior high social sciences teacher, and they involved the church and God and her mother's baby and most definitely her mother and somehow they involved something else, but what that something else was she wasn't sure.

She was trying to figure this out after school with Joe Ryan, the boy from her class who lived down the driveway from her house in a trailer with his dad.

"It's just like Marjorie's always there!" Catherine said.

"You mean Ms. Wright?" Joe said.

"Right," Catherine said.

"Left," Joe said, completing their old joke.

He was parked on the seat of his dad's dead ride-on mower while Catherine paced the stage of a patch of dirt in front of it.

"It's just that, I open the door to get the mail and there she is, ready to rush right in, as if she's just been waiting out there all night."

"Jeez," Joe Ryan said.

"Or like, I pick up the phone and instead of the dial tone it's just her raspy breath, waiting for one of us to pick up.

Like she's the dial tone. The operator. Like she never got off the line the night before after all those hours of talking to my mom. 'Oh hi!' she says. Like it's a big surprise. 'Is your mother in?' I mean, yes, of course. Where possibly could she have gone in the night?!"

Joe Ryan chuckled and shook his head.

"It's not funny," Catherine said.

"Then stop telling it funny," he said, his freckled face suddenly shy and focused on a piece of knotted fishing line in his knubby fingers.

Then it was Sunday already, and time for Mass, which meant Catherine would have to get into the back of Marjorie's car behind the poof of her mother's dark hair and the tight red curls of Marjorie's perm and listen to their conversations about Marjorie taking her mother "scavenging" at the thrift shops, or about the church potlucks, or about the importance of bringing young people to God, at which point Marjorie's eyebrows would lift to fix Catherine with a meaningful look in the rearview mirror meant for thirteen-year-olds like herself who were confirmed and being free now to make their own choices, were in danger of losing the church.

Catherine would lean her forehead against the cool window glass to avoid the pull in Marjorie's eyes, a pull that had drawn her mother to not only attend Sunday mass, but Saturday morning and Wednesday night as well. To join the women's Bible study and the events planning committee, to turn on full blast what had shut off in her father, who had stopped going to church completely, had even stopped saying grace at dinner so that her mother had to take over. When Catherine had gone silent too, her mother had given her "the look" and she had mumbled out the rest, as if Marjorie was standing right behind her chair the way she did in class, always there to supervise their piety in her matching outfits: the blue sweaters with the blue jackets with the blue flares with the blue high heels, nails, jewels, all of it. Evidence of her "scavenging," all coordinated, as if a wardrobe, like a life, could just be simply matched and put together. All you had to do was commit, plan, believe. It was easy.

But Marjorie wasn't always there, and sometimes Catherine got afraid for her mother, like when she took the receiver off its mount, carried it off to the bathroom so it teased into a tight wire running from the kitchen counter tight around the corner of the living room wall and pinched into the bathroom door, which she closed tight. When Catherine approached after her mother was in there for who knows how long, she'd hear the sobs. "Just a minute!" her mother would say, when Catherine finally knocked, as if she was just fixing her hair and not talking about the baby, about the stillbirth of the baby after all of those "attempts." Catherine wished her mother would just let her in, would just let her settle on the orange bath mat and rest her head against her mother's knees as she sat on the edge of the tub, holding a roll of toilet paper.

But she never did, never did let her in, and now it was Sunday, and already Marjorie was waiting outside, thin as a stick of licorice, leaning against the car smoking a cigarette in pants that looked like mermaid scales as her father brushed off into his workshop in the garage to commune with his tools. It wasn't until then that Catherine decided she wasn't going.

"Mass starts in half an hour dear," her mother said as she slipped a shopping list for a church dinner into her purse.

"I'm not going," Catherine said in a small, husky, creaky voice.

"What do you mean you're not going? You're not sick, are you?" A few red blotches of stress pinpricked her mother's pale face.

"No," she said. "I'm not sick." She tried to match her voice to what she imagined was a kind of world-weary sad and regretful adult voice—low and quiet, shaky but sure.

"Then what is it? Why can't you go?" Her mother's full exasperated attention was on her now, as if the next thing she said would somehow bend and break whatever delicate board still held her mother's life together.

"I mean, it's just that I don't want to go to church anymore. Not just today but"—and here her mother's face became grave—"just in general." Her eyes dropped to the brown edges of a water stain in the orange carpet.

"Look at me," her mother said. Her eyes were serious and her fingers had tightened on the scalloped edge of the table. "That's not an option. You're going. End of conversation. Marjorie's already waiting in the car."

"I don't care about Marjorie!"

Her mother's eyes widened as if she had never considered that Marjorie might not be liked. "Well," she said. "She cares about you."

"I doubt it."

"Don't get fresh," her mother said. The pinpricks on her face had grown blotchy.

"Fine. But dad stopped going to church so why should I?"

"Because he's gone for years and years and you haven't," her mother said as she swiped her purse from the table, as if to say this conversation was over.

Catherine leaned herself up against the wall.

"But now he's not going," she said, from her new fortification "What's the point of going your whole life if you're just going to stop going anyway?"

Her voice had gotten high and squeaky.

"What's the point?" her mother asked, taking a step toward her as if she was about to yank her toward the door.

"I'll tell you what the point is," and she waved a hand through the open air. But her expression fell apart. She muttered and repeated the question. "What's the point?" She shook her head as though to fully understand the affront to the upbringing she had invested so much in. Not to mention the affront to God. Her eyes searched Catherine's face as if to find what had been lost in it.

Then, as if she had come to a split-second decision, she smacked her lips together and walked past her to the door. "Well, if that's how you feel," she said, as if Catherine were suddenly a lost cause. "In the future you'll see just what kind of a mistake you've made. You'll see. I'm very disappointed in you."

"Good," Catherine said, but regretted it immediately.

Her mother glared at her with a face now fully taken over by the red blotches, and then slammed the door.

Catherine rushed after her but stopped at the door, which blocked her off from her mother, probably for good. She raised herself on her toes and followed her mother's progress toward Marjorie's car through the beveled crystal sections of window glass in their porthole in the door. They split her mother into a series of refracted broken figures. Maybe Catherine had made a mistake. Maybe she had given up something much larger than she understood. Her mother had walked away from her as if she wasn't worth convincing. But that was all Catherine needed: a reason. One good reason that could explain a dead baby, or why her father had gone silent, or why Marjorie was excising her mother from the house, prizing her loose.

The urge to rush out to the driveway, to apologize and get into the purple Saturn, yanked at the guilt in her chest. She touched a hand to the cold doorknob but it was too late. She wasn't going. Not now. Instead she would turn around and tip forward like a box of keepsakes and scatter all the old pieces of herself out on the floor.

Her father was surprised to see her all muffled up on the couch when he came in to fill a glass of water. He was wearing his flannel jacket with the worn fleece lining that looked like a dirty sheep. His sandy hair, too, looked dirty, as though sawdust had permanently settled in it.

"Not at church?" he asked.

She shook her head. She still hadn't changed out of her green Sunday dress.

They considered each other for a long moment in the gray silence. He hovered in front of the table where her mother had stood, the water clear in his hand.

She couldn't go back to her bedroom now that he was watching her and she couldn't get up. Couldn't he just keep doing what he always did out in his shop while all of the cloudy gray tumult slowly washed itself out of her?

"There's some logs to split," he said finally, as if he knew that he had to give her some reason to move out from her bundle on the couch. She nodded. She could do that.

"You didn't go either," she said, when he got to the workshop door.

He stopped, and his eyes landed on her as if to shoot back. She gripped at her knees.

"Better off in my workshop."

He tapped the door twice, then stepped through it and closed it with a whoosh.

She pulled her coat on over her dress and ran the logs through the splitter while little snowflakes blew through the scrubby gray sky. They wouldn't stick. It was still too early and the snow was blustery and light and she had the sensation that the flakes were blowing right through her as if she were an open window.

Her mother had shown her the paper with the pairs of inky hand and footprints on it after she came back from the hospital. They were tiny perfect stamps, as if her brother had lived just long enough to stand up once to make this impression of himself on the blank sheet of paper. But no, his toes had been pressed down carefully by a nurse's hand to make a little crown above the soles of his feet, and his fingers were like little sun rays above his small palms. Barely visible lines on the soles of his flat fleet, in his palms, on his fingertips, were like a finely drawn blueprint of who her brother would have become.

"We wanted to name him Michael," she confided to Catherine with a crystalline sweetness in her voice that made Catherine think of the delicate spun sugar decorations her mother made at Easter time.

"He was supposed to come," her mother said, "after so many disappointments. Our little savior."

Her mother leaned her head on her elbow and her fingers got tangled up in her hair as they looked steadily at the small sheet.

"They're perfect," Catherine had offered.

Her mother's eyes had blinked up at her then and Catherine had managed to smile back into the overpowering sweetness of her mother's need.

They continued to study the page in attentive stillness and Catherine, for the first time, imagined herself as a mother. Tentatively, she reached out and stroked her own mother's back, even as she imagined that she wouldn't ever lose children of her own, that it would be different for her, that she wouldn't have this kind of failure. She would start younger. Find the right person sooner. Have them all at once, right in a row. The way you were supposed to.

When her father came in from the workshop, he stopped to take note of the scene, the paper, Catherine, her mother resting on her elbow, and for a moment they were a family tableau gathered around what had happened.

Then her father broke the scene, brushed past them, and said, "Isn't it about time you let that go?"

Her mother's back went rigid under Catherine's hand. Her mouth began to open, as if she might have argued, but then she stopped, half-agape. She looked straight into nothing across the table. Something inside of her was making a decision. Her mouth closed. Her body went slack. Then she brushed the paper up in one quick scoop and walked to the coat closet, grabbed her purse, got into her jacket, and walked out the door. "I'll be at Marjorie's," she said, over her shoulder, almost as an afterthought. Catherine watched her little blue Toyota Tercel leave the dirt driveway from the living room window, the big ding in its side crumpling the sunlight.

Without going to church, and the logs all split, the morning dragged by. She was hungry and went to the kitchen and poked around in the cabinets. It was the same as always: a white sack of flour rolled up, some glass containers with rice and corn inside, little yellow packets of yeast. How did her mother even come home and make any of this into a meal? The image of a dish packed with greens and meat and gravy floated above the stove out of her reach.

First Aid for Choking Victims

God, why isn't there anything to eat?

A guilty twinge pulled at her for using the lord's name in vain over something as stupid as an empty cabinet. She sensed that he was watching her, as if he was the silence in the walls, the gray cloud over the house. Her guardian angel, always there, always watching, hovering. She wanted to get out from under him, wished he was gone.

Another twinge of guilt pulled at her as she imagined wishing someone gone who was trying to protect her.

"It's not that I don't want you here," she whispered into the empty kitchen air, "it's just that maybe you could back off a little?"

Maybe he did then, her angel. The pressure in the air lifted a rung.

She slipped into the garage. Maybe she could convince her father to take her to get food.

He stood at his work bench wearing headphones and green protective goggles. He inscribed a line on a board with his flat pencil and got ready to run it through the chop saw. She knelt on the stairs and pushed the door shut so she could lean on it as the saw screeched to life and he lowered it over the board and pushed it through in a satisfying shove, like stabbing someone in their stomach.

Her father would never think of something that violent. He stood there with his white shirt tucked in, the flannel coat thrown over a stool, and his back so straight, so upright, so steady, so simple. He just did his work and nothing else got in. He didn't gossip. Didn't drink. Didn't waste money.

And now, all of a sudden, she was afraid for him. Maybe what she had always thought of as solid was actually emptied out like her too, only he didn't know how to say so. His stiff upright body in its white shirt was just a shell, his hands clamping the board were glued to air.

She sprang up and wrapped her arms around his stomach from behind.

He flinched, stiffened, and his hand locked to the clamped board. She wanted him to turn and hold her head gently against his chest in his sawdust-covered hands. But when he did let go of the board and turn around to face her, his arms dropped to his sides.

She pulled away and backed up against the stairs.

"Sorry," she said.

He lifted the headphones from his messy hair.

"What's up Hun?" he asked.

"Nothing. I was just hungry."

He nodded.

"I'll let you get back to work."

When she turned around in the doorway, he was frozen. Something pained was on his face. She pulled the door shut to block it out.

Back inside, Catherine walked to the couch, lingered, changed her mind, and got her coat on. She rushed past the woodshed with its metal corrugated roof to Joe Ryan's trailer as if she'd get caught by Marjorie. She lingered on the overgrown sagging wooden steps and then knocked on his door. He came out squinting like he'd been playing video games. Her mother would never have allowed that, especially on a Sunday. They only watched the news on an old T.V. that had knobs for changing the three channels they got and they only watched on weeknights.

"Tag, you're it," she said, and hit him on the arm. She grinned, hesitated, and then booked it around the side of his trailer to the back yard. He yelled something as the screen door squealed. She imagined him knocking into it as he pulled his boots on. When he came into view his laces were untied and his coat was halfway pulled up over one arm. She got the ride-on mower between them, juked one way, then the other, and shot challenging looks across at his boyish face, which was pulled up into a competitive grimace. It would always be a boy's face, even when he was a man, freckled, wide, with eyes that had a boy's intensity in them, like he was always thinking of fishing, or blowing an alien up with a big gun, or killing some small animal in the woods, or capturing her. He got around the mower and his hands nicked her open jacket just as she got out of the yard. She squeezed through some metal sheathing meant to keep bushes from encroaching and made it up toward the big shed. He got her there, twisted her around, patted her shoulder, and through panting breath said, "You're it."

She slapped him back and sputtered out through her laughter, "It again."

Her laughter rose into a squeal as she turned to run but he tripped her and their legs tangled together and they fell. Both of his hands landed squarely on her chest and knocked the air out of her. Shock registered in his boy's eyes and he went stiff. Both his hands were on her breasts over the soft fabric of her dress. His face reddened as he stared at her open jacket.

He pushed down hard on her chest to lift himself up and then ran back along the driveway. As he reached the corner he turned once with something like horror in his eyes.

She gasped and lay back with raspy choked breath, trying to get the air back inside of her ribcage. Above her the sky opened and closed, dilated between blue and gray. The wind brushed the trees. As she stood up, his hand prints were two warm circles throbbing on her chest. She brushed at them, but they remained beneath the reach of her hands, as if she had been branded somehow.

She got back up to the house, stood inside the door, and quaked.

She had to get out of her clothes, her new dress that had never made it to church. In her small dim room she pulled it off in a frantic panic and threw it in the corner. She stood for a long time in the center of the room, undressed and still, as if she had gone blank, as dim as the light.

She finally pulled on some jeans, took her padded bra from its hook in her closet, threw on an overlarge sweatshirt, and went to the living room and tipped herself like a tree onto the couch. She stared at the branches out the window above her, spread out like hands. Behind them the sky had lifted into a distant gray-blue. The branches had lost all their leaves and through the sifting architecture of their intercrossed branches the gray light fell and fell into her until she was a mist herself and floated up into the branches till they surrounded her and she swayed and waved with them. She remembered her body below and dropped back into its tingling casement until she lost her awareness of it again and rose back up into the mist, then was pulled back again into the tingling numbness, until it became like a pleasurable breathing, rising in and out of her body from its numbing sides to the gray misty light above her.

The workshop door brushed over the carpet. She hoped her father wouldn't interrupt her so she could continue to float in and out of herself.

"Hungry?" he asked.

The numbness in her body slackened. He was occupying the middle of the room.

"Starving."

"Why don't you go warm up the truck," he said. "We could go to the diner." His voice was hopeful, a little shy.

He placed the keys on the coffee table and walked down the hall to his room. He had sensed her answer in the air, the way he always did. If she left the air alone it would fill with what he wanted to tell her, how he was sorry, how the small wish of eating with her at the diner might be a replacement for all that was wrong.

Catherine got her coat on and imagined her father in his room as he tucked in his shirt, combed his hair with his fingers, looked himself over in the mirror. If her mother had ever had the gift of reading his intention in the air, it was gone now. Something like a dry climate had forced it out.

Outside the sun had broken through and was glaring down at Catherine the way it had when she had accompanied her mother to the doctor's office after the fourth miscarriage, the one before Michael, when the baby hadn't been bigger than a kiwi. They did the procedure right there in the office, and Catherine had waited by the giant blue jug of the water cooler. When she pushed down on the little white spout the jug had gulped and a large bubble had gone up through its center and burst at the top as the water poured into her paper cone. Her mother's face had been gray and emotionless when she came back out of the hallway and it wasn't until they were walking through the glassed-in foyer that she had made a choking sound and lifted her hands to her throat as if she couldn't breathe.

"I shouldn't have brought you here today," she said between wracking sobs. "I was just worried about going alone, and Marjorie couldn't come this time."

Her cheeks were blotchy and streaked with tears. They stepped out into the parking lot and the sun was a bright glare. To Catherine it was a disinfectant light, clinical, as if it was scrubbing the lot down, and them with it.

"I don't know what God has planned for me," her mother said in a low quiet voice, "or how all of this is part of it, but here he is, shining down on us."

Catherine blinked into the light and couldn't see it at all.

Catherine yanked the truck's rusty red door open and pulled herself into the driver's seat by the steering wheel. She turned the key and let the yiik, yiik, yiiik, yiiik, yiiik of the ignition push against the engine until it caught, turned over, and settled into a steady rumble. She slid across the bench and worked her hand through the ripped slit where the plastic seat cover had cracked at the seam. She wriggled her fingers between the two slabs of yellow foam and pressed them against their artificially chalky texture. As they condensed and expanded back into manufactured shape a curl of discomfort turned over in her stomach. How it sprung back like that. She reached into the dark hole of the slit, ran her hand under the cool rough darkness of the seat cover and imagined gripping wool, gripping something natural, something real, instead of this synthetic foam. Something that she could clump it into a tight angry ball.

When her father appeared at the front door she withdrew her hand as though she had been caught.

Her father lifted his baseball hat, slicked his hair back, and placed the hat back on his head. He always did this, and the normalcy of the motion made her wonder whether he really didn't believe in God anymore. Could he have changed that much? She didn't like thinking that there was no one watching over him, no angels floating in the misty trees, no God to hear the gravel crunch under his boots as he walked through the world. How could he come outside and see the woodshed, the chain-link fence, Joe Ryan's trailer, and not feel that God had spread those things out for him, the places of his life. And wasn't her father afraid to live in the world so alone? At the lumber mill he checked each board for warp by turning it on its side and sighting down its length before buying it. Now it would be his whole life he would have to sight that way. He would have to find the warp all on his own, and could he even do that? Did he have enough skill?

Her father opened the truck door, got in, pulled the gear into reverse and put his arm just behind her shoulders to back up. Instinctively, she tucked her hand back into the slit and let her fingers hover against the chalky artificial foam block, an uncomfortable suspension.

As his face came so close to hers, she considered that maybe it wasn't God who had given her this father with his thin sunken and pockmarked cheeks. A shuddering sadness washed into her like tears guttering down her insides. It had just been chance.

The truck swung into reverse.

"Do you really not believe in God?" she asked, the words sputtering out.

He let off the gas and the truck rocked back on itself. "Who said anything about that?"

"I don't know."

He stayed stuck in mid-turn.

"I mean, you're not going to church anymore," she said.

The engine idled and the truck began to roll slowly backward. "I don't want you worrying about my belief. Belief can look all sorts of ways," he said.

It looked like he might say something else but then he pressed the brake, shifted into first, and launched the truck forward.

They drove toward town and he pointed out another clear-cut and shook his head. "That's no way to do things, to rip up the land like that." He told her that years ago this had all been grazing land and that the sheep were put on train cars and brought down to Harlem. "This is third-growth forest they're taking down now. Barely wide enough for a floor board, and full of knots."

They navigated a tight bend and came out of the forest into a spread of farmland and it occurred to her that she was more or less the only person her father ever really talked to, and he barely even talked to her. There was Earl, who helped him out a couple times a week. He'd set up folding lawn chairs outside the shop some evenings to have a beer, but it was mostly Earl who talked, telling stories about how his kids drove him crazy and stole his sleep. He'd laugh though, because he loved getting run ragged by them. And there was Big Joe Ryan, Joe's dad, but they mostly kept to small talk since they were neighbors, though there was that time at a wedding where they'd stood along the edge of the large tent for hours, holding beers and talking while everyone danced, including her mother, who was left to dancing with her girlfriends.

Sometimes she felt as though it were only her and her father in the world and everyone else was just shadows. This had happened, she realized, that last time at the hospital. It was when he had come out of the glass door she couldn't go through and his face had been white and Marjorie, who was keeping Catherine company in the waiting room, had jumped up and asked, "Well, is it a boy or a girl?" But her father had not even seen Marjorie. His eyes darted back and forth across Catherine's face as if they were trying to find something, and then he had moved toward her as Marjorie insisted, "Well, what is it? Is something wrong? Did something happen?" But still he didn't answer. He just kept moving slowly toward Catherine, and he held his hands out to her, and then knelt before the plastic chair she was in, knelt on the linoleum, and she took his hands, and he looked up at her with his eyes red-rimmed and full, and she thought that she had never seen them that close up, never seen them stare at her like that. They were hazel with little chips of brown scattered through them, and his mouth was parted now, and his Adam's apple was large and protruded from his neck and was covered in stubble, and he said to her, "Catherine, there is no baby. He was born without life. There is only us now, do you understand, there is only us," and he had looked at her with such vehemence, with such a need for her to understand, that she had nodded and then quickly thrown her arms around his shoulders to hide from that look, to place her head directly against his, against that need.

They crossed the twin lines of the parkway that snaked up into the hills as the shadow of the cross that hung from the rearview mirror tossed and swung across the seat like a pendulum.

"Lots of people stopping off on their way back to the city I guess," Her father said, as they pulled into the tightly packed parking lot of the diner where the cars gleamed in the sun.

He didn't like crowds. They had been down to the city once two years before because her mother's sister had flown in to do some shopping. She remembered her mother and aunt slipping through the crowds of people on the sidewalk and talking the whole time as if it were nothing. She had walked behind them with her father, who, in the beginning, had been looking all around him, head bent back, laughing at the spectacle of lights and buildings, the sheer volume, the craziness of it, the excess. But his laughter soon turned to silence, an almost panicked struggle. He went raw over the way people didn't seem to part for him. The more he was bumped the more he hunched over, set his eyes on the ground, tensed his shoulders. His breathing went ragged. Like a big sister, Catharine had taken his arm and led him through the throng as he clung to her.

When they got inside the diner there was only room at the counter.

"Grab us those two. I'm gonna run to the bathroom," her father said.

She squeezed in next to an old fat man whose underwear and lower back were showing where his white shirt had slid up. Her father navigated around the counter and pushed through a silver door with a round window in it. She put her coat on the chair next to hers to save it for him. At that exact moment her mother and Marjorie would be getting up from the pews at the end of the service to prepare for the church potluck. The sunlight would be transformed to blue and green through the stained glass windows on the right side of the church and they would hear the ruffle and thunk of the hymnals as they were returned to their shelves and the slow murmuring of the congregation as they filed out.

A waitress, whose yellowy gray hair looked as if it had been stained by nicotine, walked over.

"Anything to drink?"

"Umm, my Dad wants a cup of coffee and I'll just have water."

"Coffee and a water, okay."

"Oh wait, and a milkshake. Vanilla."

"Milkshake, okay." She was writing in a little green booklet.

"Actually, can I have a twist?"

"Twist? Sure thing. Best of both worlds, huh hun?"

"Yep," she said, and pressed her lips together.

Her father would sigh when he saw it, shake his head, and give her a little nudge with his elbow, like it would be their little secret. Like she was still a little girl.

She turned around on her stool. There was dust over the parking lot where a car had pulled in, and through it the mountains were a light blue and the sky even lighter, as though the sun had leeched the color out of it. In the booth in front of her a skinny bird-like woman with spiky hair was talking to a much rounder woman as though she were pecking the air. With each peck, the other woman nodded affirmatively and twirled one of many gold bracelets on her large forearms. Two men in suits lounged in the corner of the booth next to theirs, one with his arm resting along the top of the bench and the other absently flicking the handle of his coffee cup. The booths were crowded all the way down the length of the diner's front windows to the far corner where a mother was drawing the window shade as her daughter was telling her something between bites of an omelet. She was maybe in her twenties, and Catherine wondered whether she would meet with her mother just to talk when she was older, when she no longer had to, or whether she'd come here alone, or with a friend, or with, and here a glug of anxiety pushed through her heart, a family.

Joe Ryan's green eyes flicked up at her from that knot of tangled line.

"Your milkshake's coming right up," the waitress said. She had brought her father's coffee in a white cup with a small bowl piled high with creamers. There was a juice cooler across from her against the wall, the kind where you could hold a button and the juice would pour out of little white plastic spouts. Next to it was a poster framed on the wall that said First Aid for CHOKING in big red letters above a series of small round black-and-white pictures. The first one was of a dark-haired woman who looked like she was choking. Her hands were gripped around her throat but they weren't actually touching it. There was a wedding ring on her finger. It looked like she was faking, the same way stewardesses went through the safety precautions on an airplane. They held their oxygen masks just over their faces without actually putting them on and blew into the little plastic tubes for the life vests without ever touching their lips to the plastic. She had seen this the only time she had flown, when she had gone to her grandfather's funeral in Kansas City and seen his body, dressed for church, lifeless and wax-like, yellow, pretending to be asleep, not dead. She kept waiting for him to return to his body, to stir from deep inside of it, to open his eyes.

"His breath has left him now," her mother had said, and Catherine only realized later that it was God's breath she had meant.

Catherine searched for the waitress and found her taking an order at a table behind the cash register. She wasn't working on her milkshake. She turned back to the poster. Her eyes passed over the first picture, then dropped to the next row and landed on the one where the dark-haired woman was joined by a blond woman. She looked like one of the mothers that served the church dinners, her hair shoulder length and straight with bangs, her sweater tucked into her pants. She had put her arms around the brunette's body, with her hands locked tight in front of her stomach. It looked almost like they were hugging, though again there was that space between the arms and her stomach, like they were hovering. She thought of Marjorie putting her arm around her mother's waist as she walked toward the door to start her car, though Marjorie had actually touched her.

The two pictures in the row before it showed only the blonde woman's hands, first apart, and then joined around the brunette woman's torso. The picture was demonstrating how to hold a person to save them from choking. It struck Catherine that the people who had designed the poster had decided not to put a man in it, like they wanted to avoid making it inappropriate. A man holding a woman. That he could touch her, put his arms around her, even if the poster wouldn't show this touch.

It was just women in the poster, mothers. Mothers she saw at tag sales, browsing the folding tables for cheap kid's clothes; at sports games unpacking drink boxes, scooting down the bleachers to talk about what their children ate. The poster implied that nothing inappropriate could happen if it was just between two women. No touching. No embracing. Nothing sexual. But couldn't that blond woman reach out to touch the brunette. Couldn't she take her into an embrace? Couldn't they want to touch each other?

Mothers. Even mothers could want to do this. The idea came to her so naturally, so suddenly, that she was shocked to see it there, as if it were a person that had been standing in front of her for a long time without her even noticing. A tingling sensation spread outward from her stomach through her limbs at seeing this new message in the poster.

Her milkshake slid in front of her. A different waitress had brought it over, a young one with her hair pulled tightly back into a glistening bun. Catherine reached for it quickly, gripped the straw between her fingers and sucked the freezing gloop into her mouth. She didn't even say grace, quietly, in her head, as if the square lid of the compulsion had lifted right off of her.

A silt-like gravely discomfort rolled through her stomach, pushing her down just as the lightness of a new freedom was fluttering open above her. She gripped the cold glass tight and let her eyes go back to the poster, back to the story that was unfolding inside of her, as if it were peeling something loose.

Her father still hadn't emerged. Was something wrong? Was he on the payphone back there?

She returned to the picture of the two women hugging, and rejoined the dizzy feeling of being alone with the poster. The dark-haired woman's mouth was open and a pained expression was on her face. The blond woman had given her the Heimlich but it had happened in the white space between the pictures, as if the stewardesses had actually blown up the vests and put the masks on, but without anyone seeing. She knew the blond woman had pushed hard under the brunette woman's breasts with her forearms, had given pressure with her hands, and had actually touched her, but it had all happened in that white space that no one saw or talked about.

Her eyes jumped quickly to the bottom row, almost frantic for the ending, a growing warmth building in her chest. This time the dark-haired woman was lying on the floor. The Heimlich hadn't worked and now the blond woman had planted both of her hands on the air just above her chest and was positioned over her. Would you actually be allowed to put your hands on a woman's chest in a real-life situation? Would Catherine be expected to do it if the birdlike woman behind her choked? Or the waitress with the tight blond bun? The woman in the poster had done it, as if it were perfectly normal, as they were not breasts at all, just a part of the brunette woman's body. Medical, in this context. Joe Ryan's face appeared above hers, the sky a smear of blue behind him. Her mind went into a long sideways tilt as she imagined the woman's hands lifting and setting back down firm over both of the woman's breasts, holding them, pushing life into them. "His breath has left him now."

In the final picture, the woman was still on the ground, her mouth open. The blond woman had leaned over her with her lips parted. There was a small white space between their lips, the blond woman about to give her mouth-to-mouth. The picture was taken in the moment just before their lips would touch, frozen there. And then, for a second, the next picture splashed before her eyes, the one they didn't show, where the women, one lying on top of the other, would actually touch lips, bridge the gap of the white space. She was nervous on her stool, buzzing. More pictures began to appear, rushing over her: the sweater untucked, pulled up, the stomach exposed, a hand undoing the top button of the pants. She swayed in her seat, her stomach tight as the rest of her body seemed to want to flow down over the stool toward the floor.

The quiet muffled talk of the diner rushed back out of the silence of her mind and hit her. She heard the two women at the table behind her, the men in suits chuckling, the clanking noise of the kitchen. Her eyes drifted away from the poster and almost frantically shot back, as if it would disappear and fade into meaninglessness if she looked away.

She wanted to see more of the women, the awkwardly stiff mothers with their shirts tucked in and their pants pulled too high. She wanted to see their outfits taken apart, their lives undone, undressed, opened, exposed. Each picture was like a hole stamped into a white sheet. All she had to do was peel it back to expose the whole scene beneath.

The suddenness of everything she never saw hit her. The waitress with the bright bun, her hair undone by anonymous hands in the naked mess of blankets in a shadowy bedroom. The chef shouting out an order number, retreating into a dark hallway with someone's head bending low in front of him. The fat old man next to her, who had once been young and tangled naked in his sheets. The divorced adults that lined the back wall of the gym during basketball games in their snow-heavy winter jackets, sad and hopeful about catching another parent's eyes. Women talking about their pregnancies and every once in a while, the word "conception," along with some knowing laugh or look. There it was in all of those bright and secret interconnections, fine spun sugar, bright electric things that connected the two women behind her, and the man in the suit flicking the handle of his coffee cup, as if this was an interlude, the invisible people lined up in his past disappearing like an endless mirror through the diner windows. All that she had never seen bent into her now as if all the white space had opened up between everything, and the air was humming with it, a kind of horror and exhilaration, the pulsating nakedness behind the gray world.

She tried to shake herself loose, heard the old waitress telling the old man that snow was on the way. The smell of coffee and grease was thick over the counter and there was a rising mist in the conversations around her, buzzing everywhere, and the women in the poster held their mouths open. She wondered if anyone could see what was happening to her. She was held by the sound of the voices and finally let herself fall back through the blank space in the poster, fall into the image of the two women, allow herself to inhabit first the body on top, leaning over the one below, hair falling loose, lips close, then touching, and with the touch, she inhabited the body of the woman below, the choking victim who wasn't choking at all, but receiving the kiss that pressed against her, the hands that held her breasts, that connected Catherine to what lived beyond all that whiteness in the poster.

Just then she caught her father walking down the length of the counter where he had been pulled aside by someone from the highway crew to talk about lane closures or whatever they discussed, and the nerves inside her began to click the experience shut. Her heart was still pounding with the pulse of her experience, still pounding but about to be gone, even as she hungered for it to come back, to unravel into a dark and distant room, where she could have it to herself, this bright column of nervous tingling white energy stuck inside her without anywhere to go. Her eyes flicked back to the women's lips almost pleadingly as the vision began to recede into the wall and the poster became flat and two-dimensional next to the juice machine.

And it was then that she thought of her mother, and of Marjorie, and of how they went "scavenging," and of how her mother never seemed to come back with any new clothes, and of how busy they always were with church affairs, and of how easy it was for her to replace the images of the two women in the poster with images of them. Her mother, the choking woman, and Marjorie leaning over her, and only that white space between them, kept there to make it proper.

She tracked her father's approach through the haze of the diner's noise from a place very completely her own, deep set and guarded inside her body. His eyes landed on the milkshake and she was suddenly sad to anticipate the chiding nudge he'd give her, as if she was his little girl, even as she was already falling deep into herself, far below the white space, far below the diner stools and clinking silverware, far below the surface where God must live, a place deep and expansive, warm and breathing, like a body, like a pulse, like a touch.

HANK

HANK LIVED IN A SKY-BLUE TRAILER up a thin dirt drive some distance behind his friend Aaron's house. He paid Aaron a couple hundred bucks in rent to "hide out back there," as Aaron would tell anyone who asked, as though he was trying to embarrass him. Hank would just kick at some pebble and go along with it and say, "I'm just not a people person, I guess," though that wasn't it at all. But what it was, oh God, who the hell knew.

Probably it was all about swimming.

It used to come up a lot when Hank was young, all those parties at the lake or the public pool or the country club where the rich kids had their birthdays, and later at lakes, where everyone went to get trashed. He'd get out of it by drinking a lot, manning the fire, passing out. But that's what he liked about adulthood. You could get away from most things you didn't like or couldn't do—move into your own little chute and glide down smoothly without any major bumps. You didn't have to confront things if you didn't want to, and no parent or coach could come and make you do it, blowing his whistle till you jumped in and clung to the sides. You had your routine, your same-old, same-old, and you could pretty much get it out of your life. All that avoidance did leave a kind of stain on you though, like letting fruit rot on the board and that dark color just wouldn't come out after.

The trailer Hank lived in was surrounded by pines that shed pin-prick drops of sap in a glacial drizzle, under which Hank had strung a giant blue tarp like a sail over the roof of his trailer and pickup. Underneath the tarp, the light sifting through the canopy gave everything a blue underwatery tinge. A smaller tarp hung like a kite over the outhouse he had built and which, he was happy to note, Suzanne hadn't seemed to mind using the first time she had come over, two days before. That was after dinner, and then again later, after sex, when, with much laughter, she had gotten into his big boots and clomped out to make use of it, the door of the trailer screaming on its springs and slamming shut behind her. He liked this new feeling of her being out there and knowing she was coming right back in with his "big man boots," as she had called them.

It was a kind of aloneness he wasn't used to. It had anticipation in it.

Usually, there was no one coming back and the space outside of his trailer was filled with a watchful silence that extended all the way to the top of the hill where he had the vague intimation of being observed through the empty spaces between the trunks of the pines. It was as though Hank had put this presence up on the mountain, as though it were a far removed part of himself who knew what he was supposed to do and was waiting for him to do it.

Suzanne had left a picture of herself lying on his kitchen table before she got back into her truck and driven off. He kept looking down at it while he made his breakfast as he had for the last two days since she had been over. Her friend had taken the picture, which showed her in the water of a pond that she said was on her parents' land. Her parents rarely swam in the water, "Those old fogies," but she liked to bring friends up there on weekends to barbecue, drink beer, and have a good time. "Just escape, you know?" she said. "It's nice up in the mountains. You should come!"

He had smiled and nodded and tried not to show any hesitation. There would be swimming.

The picture she had left was of the side of her face, laughing, when she must have been much younger—fifteen years before maybe. She would have been in her mid-to-late twenties then. Her white shoulder, half submerged in the clear water, was still visible beneath the surface. Her hair was dry on top, but the water had touched the rest of it and made it dark and smooth. Out in the air it was light brown, lighter than it was now, and the sun hit the very top of her head so that it shone. Her skin was clear and smooth, new. It was the kind of face that nothing had happened to yet. In truth, he hadn't immediately recognized that it was her when she had shown it to him and had he not been interrupted, he would have asked who that was in the picture. "That's me!" she said, as he looked at it in silence, trying to decipher the face. "Me in the water! Wasn't I pretty then?" she asked. "God, I swam all the time. I was always in the water."

"You're still pretty," he said.

He couldn't get over how good she looked in the picture. Not then, not now. He stared at her young face, holding the small paper rectangle out in front of him as he eased into the chair at his table with a plate of ham and eggs steaming before him, the eggs like bright yellow eyes in their wiggling jelly. What he realized was that this was the kind of woman he could never have gotten when he was younger. Out of his league. Completely. No question. These were the kind of girls that Aaron used to get when Aaron still had it, hadn't aged it all away. But now he was getting a girl who had been just like one of them, that was who she had been. A memory of three girls running toward the open window of Aaron's car returned to him, their faces leaning in, speaking across Hank's body to Aaron, who sat in the driver's seat with his hand on the wheel, grinning back at them.

Hank had only looked at the girls' hands as they gripped the open window frame, sparkly purple red and green cracked nail polish on their skinny little fingers. Delicate fingers. Only at the last moment, as the girls turned away to run back to their cars, did he look up at their faces. The girl closest to him caught his gaze for one electric moment, her blue eyes sparkled at him, and her mouth opened into a quick smile big enough to hold even him. He couldn't help but put that young face into the picture of Suzanne, to imagine that it had been her, to imagine Suzanne holding him with a smile that big. He knew that he would always see that younger face in her and that he would find her more beautiful for it and that he would look for signs of it when she smiled, or talked to people in a group, or lay down to sleep. It would always be there like a mirage, appearing unexpectedly in the unique constellations of light and facial expressions, the movement of her hand through her hair, shimmering for a moment, a glimpse into what had been there and what was now becoming his.

He often wondered how it had been that it was him she talked to at the firehouse barbecue where he had volunteered a few weeks before. What it had been that compelled her to keep standing next to him at the grill after he had flipped a burger patty neatly onto her outstretched plate and said, "Good catch." He remembered how she had smiled at him and said, "Former softball player. What can I say?" He had been a little surprised when she hadn't turned away after that, how he had suddenly found himself needing to dig for something else to say to allow her to stay. She was swinging back and forth on one heel, her feet in blue flip flops. "You didn't need to tell me that," he finally said, probably after too long a silence. "Your expertise speaks for itself." She had let out a loud "Ha!" and then proceeded to tell him that her expertise only extended to softball and that that was about it. She had given up on "expertise" and all that other crap. "It's just about living and trying to have a little fun here and there, isn't it?" He had nodded, and noticed how she didn't seem interested in going back to rejoin her group, or the other people there from the town, and how, as the afternoon wore on, he began to get used to the image that the people in the parking lot must have observed, of the man behind the grill who had a woman next to him, and that the longer she was there, the more he began to trust that she really was there for him, the reality asserting itself as slowly as sap flowing through his body, until it reached and slowly took hold in his brain and he felt as comfortable as he might ever have, letting her lead him back to her apartment that night, both of them swaying a little, after they had gotten drinks at the Cornerstone.

    Hank didn't take it for granted, having someone next to him that other people would want. Aaron had probably been used to that his whole life, but not Hank. Hank was proud. Thankful even. Hank was a big man, and didn't get too much attention from women, especially when they saw his reluctance to let loose. He was stout, with big arms, a big hard belly, round taut legs, short brown hair, buzzed, all thinned out on top, and he kept a goatee. His lower lip stuck out just a bit farther than his top lip, which he tried to hide by pulling it in so it often looked like he was biting his lip. But he was "kind," Suzanne had told him a few days later while they were lying around on her couch after a movie, and he had never considered that before. He liked it, that idea, though he didn't know if he should be hurt by it. Were men like Aaron ever called kind? Was kind a little bit like gentle? A little bit like soft? Weak?

He looked around his trailer: the small sink, the orange curtains, some tools on the window bank, and he still felt her presence there, her shouts of "Don't let me down, Mr. Man," slowly dissipating as she got into her truck after urging him to come up to the cabin. For a moment he saw his long narrow trailer under the blue tarp through her eyes, as the home of a kind man. A sensation of warmth spread through the little homestead in the woods as he considered this. He was kind, and was that so bad? No.

The other part, the part about the weekend getaway and the fact of there being water, had already lodged itself on the bottom shelf of his stomach where it sat like a trembling stone.

Aaron knew about his fear, and when they did get to the water he always put Hank on grilling duty so no one would know. Hank would wear a swimsuit and stand behind the grill as if he had just been in, or was about to go in. Often, he'd wear a towel rolled up around his neck. On the way home Aaron would have the window open, his arm casually hanging out of it and say, "You're a grown man Hank. And a big one. The water should be afraid of you, the way I see it."

This would piss Hank right the fuck off, make him want to smack the dash and Aaron in the bargain, even though he needed him, relied on his charity, even loved him for protecting him. So all he did was choke it back and say, "Yeah, I know."

The rest of the ride all there was for him to do was to look out at the farms passing by and to feel his own tragedy, which he had created himself, and which he was continuing to create anew each day by not overcoming it. It got so that the world always looked like it was locked behind a store window.

And then there was that picture with Suzanne's white shoulder in the terrifying clear green water of the pond, clear all the way down to the black bottom. His fear lodged in the stillness of that clarity, in its depth, how it looked like glass but would open right up if his body fell in, envelope him, sink him. He'd be unable to grasp onto anything in the clear nothingness until he was pushed down toward the bottom by its silent invisible current, like two hands holding his face down into the leafy muck.

He connected the strength of these hands to the rush of storms through the trees above his trailer—the hail, the pelting rain, the wind that cracked branches off—its source unclear, though he listened for it in the darkness, as though he could trace it back to a lurking evil in the world that had blown into his hillside and was drumming down on his trailer, ripping the branches from the trees. If it decided to, it could lift him right out of the woods and fling him down the hill into town.

He knew about this power from the logs he cut all summer. He knew it from the enormity of the machines they used to haul the logs. In the beginning, when he had just started on the job, the trees were just tall masses of trunk to be cut. But increasingly he became impressed by their weight as he sat on a stump and leaned his hand on its flat hard surface. The impression of its weight and impenetrability lodged itself in his spine, right in the middle of it, where he had once landed hard on a stone during a camping trip and felt how his back had almost snapped in half. What it registered there was how simple it would be for one of those logs to crush that spine and immobilize it completely, or how a log could come rolling from its stack and clip his knee, yank it out of the socket. He began to see injury everywhere. The weight, the mass, and though his saw cut through each log steady and smooth, he still always looked up with a kind of awe as the claw from the grappler lifted the logs up on the pile. It did this with awkward ease, the motor skills of a jumpy inhumanly strong monster that could so easily release its grip and squash the man below.

"You ever get scared of getting crushed?" he asked Dave, the gangly foreman.

"Never considered it," he said. "Or well, never considered being afraid of it. If it happens, it happens. Till then, we got work to do. And we'll do it safely," he added, as if to assure Hank that he cared.

But Hank knew he was right about all this force from watching the footage of the tsunamis on the small television nestled in the corner of his kitchen counter. That was something he followed closely. That was a kind of vindication for him, telling him he wasn't completely wrong to be afraid: the light rectangles of rooftops washing and bumping into one another as they floated down the street, collecting others and taking them along. Later, boats were laid down in fields, and houses sat slumped in the water as though they were on their knees, telephone poles clogged around them like reeds in a beaver dam.

When Suzanne called to give him the directions he wrote them down with a shaking hand. She was already up there at the lake house and he could imagine her flipping her hair over her shoulder, leaning casually against a counter with a bunch of scrap papers and pens on it near the phone, wearing a big plaid shirt. "The swimming's just beautiful," she had said at one point. His body began trembling and didn't release the tension that coursed up the spire of his body for a good long while.

In the silence that followed the call he felt a deep need to just stay home by himself in his dim trailer in the cool woods with the blue light from the tarp all around him. He wanted to take a cold shower, to undress completely and wrap his taught shoulders in a scratchy blanket and hug his legs up against his hard belly and shrunken package. He wanted to stare out at the branches as they swayed in the afternoon light and not move at all, not go anywhere.

He thought then of that summer in Maine when he was young, when his mother had left his father, when it was all swimming. He had wanted to join, to learn how, was excited and equally afraid of the waves, would wander out into them with his pant legs rolled up so they would brush against his ankles. Then he'd go in farther until a larger more violent splash drew him back.

Standing there once, in a new orange bathing suit his father had bought him for the trip, his mother had told him to stop being afraid and pushed him forward in front of the eyes of Bentley, the man she was with now, to show him that her son was not weak. Bentley had taken to comparing him to his father, who he called "That weasel," and though Hank had often said, "He's not, he's not any such weasel," Bentley had just repeated it back to him in the whiny tone of a school girl: "He's not any such, he's not any such." Hank had been excited to learn to swim, and wanted his mother to teach him, or Bentley even, though he was more afraid to ask him. When his mother pushed him, he almost fell in, but found his balance and turned and said, "Don't push me! Don't push me!" as the larger waves rolled in on him.

He needed help. He wanted all he could get. "Come in Bentley," he shouted, motioning with his hand, repeating the motion again and again. "Teach me, teach me!"

"Only one way to learn!" Bentley yelled back, and once again his mother pushed him and this time he could not stop himself and fell forward as his mother charged in next to him, splashing and knocking him farther in. Then it was water everywhere. The waves had taken him and torn him and ripped through his nostrils and shoved his face into the sand. He had thrashed in the waves and only found his way out by knocking, accidentally, into his mother, who fell in the breakers. Together they lay tangled, the water streaming over them, and he clung to her and tried to find the air through the constant crashing and heaving of the waves. But holding on to his mother was not anything for a boy to do and she kept trying to shove him off. No air was coming into his lungs and no sounds could get out until he stumbled back, raised out of the water, and stood there trying and trying to get the air in.

It was blocked; the beach was bright in each direction, clearly sealed off behind glass that had suddenly fallen between him and the world. He could not get back to it, could not find any air holes, was stuck in his body, which just moments before had breathed the air and walked easily across the soft hot sand. He was sure that he would never get back in, that his hands would claw and pound at the invisible glass, would never break through it. He'd fall limply back into the water, get drawn out into its dark folds far past the breakers where he'd sink down through them, lifeless.

Then something small knocked loose inside him through all his waving and tearing, and the tiniest pinprick of air got sucked in, and then more and more until he stumbled up and lay on the beach, breathing as much of it as possible. The warm air circled in around him while the fingertips of the waves brushed his feet. He kicked at them.

"It's just a little water," Bentley shouted from his lawn chair. "You're not afraid of a little water, are you?"

"Why didn't you help me?!" Hank screamed up at him. "You're a weasel! A dumb weasel!" And then he felt the stinging slap of his mother's hand strike his face. He sat shocked for a moment, because she had never hit him. As though the decision had been made for him, he ran up the beach, grabbed his towel from where it lay next to Bentley, kicked sand up at him, and then ran for his life. He thought he would be chased, tackled by Bentley's big hairy arms, get crushed by his body as they fell to the sand, but he wasn't. Instead, he sat far away from them at the edge of a dune that rose up behind him. In the distance, he could see Bentley laid out on his recliner, legs stretched in front of him, the sun bright on his chest, full of calm menace.

Hank crouched under the dune and let the wind blow through his hair. He scooped sand up in his hand and let it drop again. The waves spread up the shore and then back down, and they would do this forever and never stop. They wouldn't get tired, they were just that strong. He was nothing like them. There was something weak and broken in him, and when he walked back to his mother and Bentley and their towels on the beach and the little radio Bentley had brought, they would make sure he knew it.

***

He didn't think about the lake except in tiny flashes of terror, like light bouncing over water. To make himself feel better, he pretended he would tell her. The whole thing. She wouldn't even flinch, would tell him it was the most normal thing. Then together they would walk slowly into the water, float in the shallows, and gradually he would become used to it there with her and he might even try a few strokes. The freedom of the open water would be his for the briefest moment. He would fly and everything in his chest would open up with the strokes he was making. But just as quickly as the fantasy came, the open waters zapped shut and pulled him down, became endless, empty, and he was flailing and drowning in them and she was a small and distant face in the water, watching him drown with an uncomprehending look on her face.

On the morning of the trip he didn't think about it nearly at all. He stepped into his truck robotically, lifted one leg, hoisted the other, strapped himself in, and turned the key in the ignition. He had the vague sense of being watched from above, through the forest, from the top of the mountain, where that silent presence saw his truck move down the road.

The only thing he did think about was the fact that, in all likelihood, every man Suzanne had been interested in, shit, every man she had slept with, knew how to swim. He was the only one who didn't. And as a man, he shouldn't be scared of a thing like water—he couldn't just lie in the shallows as he had done on other occasions, telling his friends he just liked it there.

"Are you afraid or something?" they had always asked, laughing after they said it. And he laughed too, pretending that it was as ridiculous as they said, though probably some of them must have known anyway why it was he never went in farther.

"It's just the place I like to be is all," he said. He pretended to himself that none of them knew, hated that they didn't say anything, their kindness that was actually pity, like he was some scared-ass little kid. He felt sick the whole time and wanted to rush out of the water to find someone to punch, to land his fist right in their throat so they couldn't breathe, so they'd know how it felt to suffocate, to be cut off from the world.

As he drove, the presence from the mountain followed along up there in the sky above him, floated and circled, rushed through the treetops. Somewhere in the back of his mind his little fantasy hung on and he thought he just might out and tell her, though he couldn't quite conceive of the moment. Could he really just lean in and say it casually, "I cannot . . ." but the words wouldn't come. He couldn't finish. He imagined the various reactions she might have. First, laughing at him. "What, you!? I don't believe it. Mr. Man. No way. Haha. What? You can go into the forest and cut down all those big trees but you can't swim?" The idea would continue to make her laugh, as though he was joking with her, and he would shrink under her derision. Or, she might just see it, she might just say, "Oh, that's okay honey, let's just get you in the water then, give it a shot." But that would almost be worse, her talking down to him like that, using the word "Honey," and everything he'd have to give up in that moment. He just couldn't imagine it.

The roads turned to long snaking switchbacks as the country got higher. The towns were smaller and a kind of grayness came into them. This grayness was more acute, more tense, the taut grayness of being alone in mostly unpopulated places where the land and the mountains and the trees that covered it all were bigger than the people. Small towns with square storefronts and flat roofs came and went like choked breath.

There was a long dirt drive to the house and when he got out at the top, he saw people up on the porch of a large log cabin. It looked like families mostly. He knew her parents wouldn't be there, which relieved him. He couldn't have her father looking on from the porch to watch him drown, or worse, to see him try to avoid it.

Suzanne emerged from a green door in little cut-off jean shorts and stopped when she saw him. A big smile broke out across her face and he remembered how beautiful she was.

She walked up to him and spread her arms out so wide it looked like she was going to hug the whole driveway. "You're wearing your suit!" she said with a grin. "Good!" Yes, he was. He always did when he went to events like this. It allowed him to pretend that he was there for the swimming. It was a blue suit, with a couple grease stains acquired while hiding behind a grill. She pushed him along up the deck stairs through the various family members and friends and the running children. Suzanne had very obviously been drinking and now pressed a cold green bottle of beer into his hand. He popped it open, took a long swig, leaned against the railing and raised it whenever no words came to him. Soon enough he had gone through a few. Maybe he could tell her if he got enough in him and she had enough in her. It might get him out of it, because he saw that he was just waiting for the inevitable, waiting to go down to the water where the swimming would happen. Everyone was eating, which meant there was no hiding behind the grill, and Aaron wasn't there to save him.

"Let me show you the house," Suzanne said. Before he knew it, they were in a small room upstairs and she was taking off his shirt and his shorts and directing his hands to do the same to her while the antlers on the walls watched.

"Won't people hear? Isn't it bad, with all the families here?"

"Only if they find out!" she said, laughing brightly.

"Relax," she told him. And slowly he did.

In the laziness that followed, he thought he might tell her. She was breathing less quickly and still looking up at the ceiling, as though the images and sensations were still playing above her. He gripped the sheets, began to turn to her, and when she felt this, she turned as well, her face bright, as she grabbed his cheeks and kissed him and then sprang up out of the bed and walked off into the bathroom. The moment was gone. The perfect moment. He leaned back on the bed and looked out of the windows at the mountains and breathed deeply and folded his hands behind his head and tried to get the image of the pond out of his mind, the idea of it just down the hill from the house, waiting for him.

Before she came back out, he reached for his shirt at the end of the bed and his pair of swim trunks that had never gone deeper than three feet. He got out of the bed and pulled them up his legs, the mesh underwear inside sliding roughly into place. He got his shirt on and stood there, waited with a small and nervous anxiousness for the bathroom door to open.

Suzanne came out, tied her shirt in a knot on the side and just as he thought she would, she looked up and said, "Let's go cool off in the lake, right Mr. Man?" Then she came across to him, put her hand behind his head, and kissed him fully, her mouth hard against his, like she was trying to press herself into him.

By the time they made it to the water he was drinking a fresh beer and they were holding hands and standing with a group of four men talking about the fishing in the various lakes around town. Tim, an older guy with a gray beard and stained jean shorts, had a boat they'd all been out on that day. He was clearly the most familiar with the fishing up there, and the other guys were listening to him and nodding. The way it was going, Hank thought it wouldn't even come to swimming. Tomorrow they could go home. But Suzanne began to pull him to the water while he pretended to be interested in the conversation. She kept pulling and much as he tried, she yanked him out.

"This way, you big loony!" she said. "Who cares about fishing; they'll be talking that same old stuff all night."

"Well, I'm interested."

"Well don't be. Be interested in swimming. Be interested in me."

She was grinning in a cute way, and for a moment he saw the younger face from the picture and remembered that he wasn't supposed to be scared right now, that a normal man would want to go and swim in the water with her, would like having fun.

"All right, I'm interested."

He stepped from the lawn to the narrow sickle of dirt beach between a break in the reeds. "But I don't feel like getting wet, so I'll just stand here and watch you go in."

"No you won't; you're coming in mister."

"I'm not."

"You are. Don't be a prima-donna. The water's wonderful. I want you in it with me."

She gave him a big old smile before she kicked her sandals off and shimmied out of her shorts and turned and stepped in delicately, like a stork. He knew he should be loving this scene.

Her legs in the water, her cheerfulness, the way she was focused, fully, on him. But the whole thing was twisting his stomach into nausea.

He shambled forward and dropped his flip flops slowly from one foot, and then the other. He followed her in and saw that the bottom dropped quickly.

"I'm not going any deeper than this. This is as deep as I go." He was in to his waist and the water shocked his stomach.

"You know I won't let you get away with that." The water was already a mirrored line that came just under her bathing suit top. She thought she was being cute, he realized, like a little girl tempting him in or something.

Clearly she took joy in showing him a good time and he thought he should just do it now, before she forced him in, pushed or pulled him and he lost his footing and would all of a sudden be drowning. She wouldn't be strong enough to lift him out, not with his big body and her tiny one. Maybe she'd call for help and all those men on the shore talking about fishing would have to come and do it, and then what would he have left? Nothing.

"I can't swi—" he began to say, and thought of finishing it, thought of her accepting it, without saying anything at all, just walking back through the water toward him, leading him slowly in, guiding him. Then he imagined them falling forward into the water, her body under his, her legs kicking, her arms at his shoulders and her face right there close by his, her breath on his cheek, paddling out with him, smiling, saying "Good, good," and then there she was in real life, beckoning him in. "You're not afraid of the cold, are you?" She was smiling and kidding him, and he could see the flash of her beauty when she smiled, and he wanted to move toward it, and took a step farther into the water, but immediately backed off.

He thought of asking her for help, of saying, "I'm going to need a little assistance here, this burly man can't swim," and making a little joke out of it. "This fat belly is buoyant but not that much. It might just weigh me down. I'm a little afraid here my dear." But the words wouldn't come, they were stuck up against the gunk of years of blockage in his throat. She let herself fall into the water, her shoulders dipping under, and then first one, then two calm full breast strokes before she flipped, grinned at him, and kicked away into the cool water like an otter. His toes gripped on the tiny shifting gravel, the ground tilting down into deeper black at the next step where his feet wouldn't catch onto anything.

"Come on, come on in, don't let the coldness stop you," she kept saying, and he was biting his tongue, muttering, "Doing the best I damn well can, Jesus," and she said, "What was that you're mumbling over there?" and he answered much too loudly, "I said I'm doing the best I damn well can!" He felt instantly bad about it.

She might have picked up on the fact that he wasn't just struggling because of the cold. She was studying him now. His feet were slipping. He struck out at the water, pushed himself back as he slipped farther toward the dark. Her face furrowed as a cloud passed overhead and covered her in the clarity of its shadow: sober, gray. A wild panic gripped him: he was slipping out into nothing; his big frame crashed backward into the water, flailing as she began to laugh and it was all he heard as a rush of cold water gushed over his chest and poured into his mouth. "Can't you swim, Hanky dear?" she said then, between her laughter. "Didn't you ever learn to swim?" It was friendly laughter, he could hear that. He could even imagine the kind cheerfulness in her face as he coughed out the water, but it was laughter nonetheless. Laughter at his expense. He scrambled back, half-crab-walking, and got a tiny bit of footing, enough to right himself and pitch desperate spouts of water toward her, saying

"What do you know about it?" hoping that somehow a silver line of playfulness might assert itself through the trails of liquid.

But his feet just couldn't get him upright. The water broke all around him as her laughter rose up and twisted everything inside him. The guys on the shore had noticed. They splashed toward him now. They'd throw him in. Finish the job.

"Stay away," he yelled. "Stay away!" He flung water at them, staggered, twisted, fell forward.

"We're just here to help man; we're just here to help," their voices said. "We got you man, we got you."

"Back the fuck off; back the fuck off," Hank said.

"Take it easy," the old man said as Hank swung at him. "Take it easy," he said again, like he was coaching him.

"I can't," Hank said, and swung a desperate look at Suzanne, caught the confused and concerned look on her face as it suddenly, for just a moment, shifted into complete understanding, as if she had seen everything as his eyes reached out for her. Then two hands gripped his armpits from behind and without thinking his elbows came down and met the big soft resistance of a stomach. He scrambled, turned, hit out at Tim's face and got enough that he felt what must have been his knuckle breaking on the side of the old man's cheekbone.

And then he ran. He ran up the slope and past the voices buzzing all across the deck and then he was in his truck and he was gone.

Barreling down the roads he was repeating to himself, "I can't swim, I can't swim, I can't swim, I can't swim." He had the windows open and the radio on and the wind rushing in so he couldn't hear anything, not anything. He was crouched as low over the steering wheel as he could go so he didn't have to see barely any of the road, so he could just drive, keep driving, keep turning, keep muttering "I can't swim, I can't swim." It was a relief to say it, like he was saying it to the air coming in his windows and to the trees he was passing and to the mountains that rose up all along the road. He was telling it to them and telling it to them until they filled with it and the sky heard it too, that presence up there, and it became smaller and came in closer and closer and closer until the valley was all in tight around him and he was hurtling down through it and his stomach didn't feel quite as empty, didn't feel quite as exhilarated as that one look he had had, that one look with her, where she had known everything.

I WANT YOU TO TELL ME

I

IT WAS THE FINAL LECTURE before Spring Break and Sasha's classmates were already packing up with five minutes left in class. Sasha didn't do this. She wanted to listen to what the professor was saying right until the end. Plus, it was rude to make all that noise by thunking your books into your bag and zipping everything up like you were getting out of a tent. Maybe if they weren't so dull, maybe if they had a little more intellectual curiosity, her classmates, they'd still be listening. Even Lindsay was packing up, but of course she didn't need to listen to get A's. She got them anyway. Sasha brushed over a little fissure of jealousy that opened along the desk and tried to focus back on the lecture so that she could draw the class out to the last minute. She wanted to put as much time as possible between herself and the week ahead. She was dreading it. Her boyfriend Paul had gotten her to agree to meet his parents and stay with them for the entire break at their house in the country somewhere in upstate New York.

If it were up to her, there wouldn't be a break at all.

The professor was rounding into his final thoughts. They had gotten on the subject of truth, capital T. His voice was like a book on tape in the way it could lull you into the sway of his words and sentences, a soothing wash. It was one of the many things she liked about him, his calmness, along with the gray hair at his temples, the sweater vest pulled tight over his hard round stomach, how he always turned a pen between the fingers of both hands in front of that hard round stomach like he was unwinding a tiny scroll. How he stood very straight at the board without pacing, the desk between him and his students. "You know," he continued, "Flaubert, that critic of middle-class life, was walking once with a friend when they passed a family outside: husband, wife, the children playing. And he turned to his friend and said, 'They are living the truth!' This middle class family. It was as simple as that. But it is complex too, and maybe we go to literature for it, to find the truth in an author's vision of the world, or even in the shape of their sentences, the specific aesthetic that has allowed them to craft an experience of life that has the truth wrapped up in it. And especially for those of us who do not have religion, increasingly more of us in modern days, right? For those of us who are seekers nonetheless, for those of us who wish to find it, to pull it out of the messy interactions we have with each other, with the institutions we've created. Either way, I challenge you all to find it, to recognize it when you are in its presence. After all, that is what separates the great minds from all the others, the ability to recognize, and that is what you are learning here in this class when it comes to literature, how to recognize. But I also hope that you will come to recognize truth in your own lives outside of literature, to see the truth where others might not, and to dig it out when the opportunity presents itself." He paused, looked down at the pen, gave it a turn as if to see if it had anything else to reveal. He tapped it twice against his fingers, sighed, and then put it in his pocket. "That's all for today. Have a great break."

 Sasha lingered in case a conversation started up at the professor's desk so that she could step into its periphery, let

I Want You to Tell Me

the other students go, and then, at just the right moment, say something no one else had thought of just loud enough that the professor would turn to acknowledge her and say, "That's right. Yes, did you all hear what Sasha said?"

But no one gathered to discuss the idea of truth, which was disappointing; she felt especially equipped for it, as though she was just about to reach out and grab some passing filament of its import as the class emptied out.

Sasha fell in with Lindsay and Caroline as they cleared their row.

"Have a great break!" Lindsay said to the professor, who turned and smiled at the three of them without responding.

"God that didn't eeeeend," Caroline said out in the hallway. She was tall and dark-haired and swayed down the hallway unsteadily on her long legs. She got B's and not much else and it wasn't surprising she felt that way. "It's so annoying when professors try to say like these profound things about life that they think no one else has ever thought of just to keep us hostage before our break. Like, yeah, we get it, artists look for truth, we should too. How exciting. You're so cool and deep."

"Ouch," Lindsay said. Lindsay was short and cute and brown-haired with a little snub nose like a chipmunk. The cuteness of a nemesis.

"I liked it," Sasha said.

"Of course you did," Caroline said.

"You are his little favorite after all," Lindsay said, and raised an eyebrow at Sasha.

"Hey! I am not. I just happen to think he's one of the best teachers at this school. Also, last time I checked you were his favorite, Mrs. A-plus."

"Well, who can blame him?" Lindsay said, and nudged her.

Sasha attempted something like a joking response but couldn't hold down her annoyance. Taking shit from Caroline was expected and didn't matter. Lindsay, though, had somehow managed to achieve an A+ on a paper, which made the A Sasha had gotten feel like it was good, but not exceptional, not unique. Not without peer. She was used to being the most original in class, which this professor had recognized in her the term before when she had been the only person who, in a reading on Freud, recognized that the dream one friend was telling the other was about his wife missing her period. "Because she's pregnant," Sasha had said. The professor smiled, looked around at the class and then said, "You are the first student I've ever had who's been able to guess that."

But Lindsay just did everything so effortlessly and had such calm confidence in her abilities that it was as if she never even thought about whether or not she was good. It just didn't matter. If she knew how much it upset Sasha she would probably just be perplexed by it. She was so self-contained, so without ego, so able to just move from one task to another. At parties it was as if she were completely unaffected by the new context. She simply behaved the way she always did. There was no trying to impress anybody, no acting out, no dressing up, just plain old perfect Lindsay. It was like there was nothing wrong in her life. Didn't she ever just *feel* too much? Didn't things bother her?

At the entrance to the T she left her friends and couldn't help yelling, "Don't forget to search for truth!" as they went down the stairs. They waved, Caroline a little wildly, as if she was trying to shoo her away, and Lindsay with her cheerful polite little hand up in the air.

Still, Sasha was happy with herself.

I Want You to Tell Me

On her walk home, she stopped for an iced coffee at a shop in the basement of an old brownstone. She sipped it as she thought about the class, about what the professor had said, about the truth. The sun was slanting down in long bright staves of light over the edges of buildings as cars rushing from light to light passed her. She let the class filter through her thoughts and let it run out over her life, which suddenly seemed small and predictable. She was just a college student with a boyfriend and a major going back to a small apartment just as any professor might predict. She was no one to take seriously, just a sophomore handing in her little papers for marks and as so often happened on these walks home, her life started to dissolve around her, as if it were paint oozing down the walls revealing a nothingness behind them.

She was a black silhouette proceeding through a world of white outlines.

She tried to bring the world back: she was walking outside in the city and she loved to walk outside in the city. She was drinking her coffee, cold and sharp and sweet. The ice sloshed around in the clear plastic cup, the condensation was cold on her fingers. The world rose. She had a solid boyfriend, she was taking classes. It fell again, dissolved.

She was surrounded by a buzzing kind of white static.

She tried to gather it in, form it into some kind of manageable mass in her hands, peel it off the buildings around her, the brownstones and the large gray office buildings behind them. When a bike messenger whizzed by she scooped a snowball from the static and threw it at him. She expected his bike to veer off and crash. She expected that the static would zap him, infiltrate his immune system like a virus. But he just kept going like there was nothing wrong. How did he keep pedaling, keep delivering his pointless envelopes? How did anyone? She thought she saw him wobble, saw her doubt spread to him. It would start peeling everything back and his world would dissolve to pointless static emptiness.

Her legs got weak and heavy and numb. She stopped, leaned up against a wall, breathed for a moment, squeezed her eyes shut, and then kept going.

She was back in the world.

The static had fallen away and was small enough for her to grab it like a piece of paper, crumple it up into a ball, and bat it away. There. That was better.

Once she got upstairs to her studio apartment she put her school bag down, squashed the flat light brown squiggly bugs that had started showing up on her white kitchen tiles, and settled at her small table by the window before she threw herself down onto the bed and looked up at the ceiling. She was supposed to be packing. Paul would pick her up the next morning to go to stupid upstate New York. As a siren howled far away and someone emptied cans into a dumpster in the back alley, the ball of static floated back into view through a water stain in the ceiling. She looked at it for a long moment, floating up there, and decided that she would observe it, would study the emptiness that irradiated the space around it. She would analyze it to get at the truth, something clear and strong and sharp enough to pop it with. Something all her own. As it floated down toward her she batted it back up, like a beach ball at a party.

II

Sasha rose to the balls of her feet on the front stoop of her apartment building and willed Paul's silver Accord to appear at the tree-lined top of her street. She didn't like not being able to decide when they would leave. Instead of Paul's car, she noticed an old woman dressed in a long sleeping bag-turned-jacket drag her little grocery cart over the rough terrain of the brick sidewalk. The woman looked straight ahead as if she had seen Sasha and was observing her. She immediately got off the balls of her feet, adjusted her hair, and made her face empty so that the woman did not see her impatience. Instead, she stared into a blank distance ahead of her and filled her face with the misery she was sure she was about to experience and the bravery inside of her that would surely rise to meet it. She was a sad young woman with long dark hair and a slender frame pulled tight into an elegant peacoat about to be taken up by the plot of a story she had not asked for, and yet, there she was, as if standing on the precipice of . . .

Oh, what did it matter? Who was this old woman anyway? The silkiness of her fantasy threaded through her fingers and blew away up the street. It was stupid and childish performing for someone whose eyes she couldn't even be sure were on her, creating a story and a self she wished were real. Sasha dropped her handbag on the duffel next to her and looked across the street at the row of brownstones where a man was pushing gravel into a gutter with his hose. The water made a frothy line that pushed against the crud. Cars on other blocks sounded like the rush of a distant river and their honks were like birds over the water. She floated up over the street like a bird herself and saw the line of foam turn the bricks clean behind it and saw herself on the stoop with the old woman advancing toward her like old age. Isolated in the small pocket of her youth it was as if a dusting of mortality had permeated her skin, polluted her bloodstream, crumbled her bones. She swayed, regained her body, then drifted back out again, as if her head were wide open at the top. It tilted and pulled then righted and tethered her back into her body before tilting again. She felt faint. Had she eaten? The old woman, worried, quickened her pace toward the pale girl on the front steps who was faltering. Her trolley bounced and tugged urgently behind her, wrenched her wrist. The girl tipped, a car whipped onto the block, honked, and the dull sound of bass drums beat like an increasingly distant pulse. It entered her cranium. The stone steps were hard-edged and burned in a white threatening granite glare. Her head was a robin's egg drawn down toward the hard stone, the delicate blue vein in her temple pulsed once before the inevitable crack.

Music spurted out of Paul's window as he rolled it down. "Hey, you comin'?" he asked, leaning over the passenger seat to look up at her with his practical green eyes.

The completely normal solid block of Paul's face dropped directly into her sensation of tipping, of being tragically weak, and she stared back at it as if it had just interrupted, just ruined, a highly delicate operation.

"Only if you help me with my bags," she said, blinking back into reality. He sighed, flipped the car into neutral, and pulled up the emergency break. As he was getting out, she lifted her duffel, descended the steps, and cut right in front of the old woman whose cart fumbled and tipped sideways against her leg and fell over.

She didn't stop to help her.

I Want You to Tell Me

Paul came around the back to reach for her duffel. "Never mind, I got it," she said. The trunk was bouncing open, waiting for someone to lift it all the way open or slam it back down.

"You sure?" he said, his voice defensive and concerned at the same time.

"I'm sure. Sorry I made you get up."

"I don't mind. Seriously. Here." He tried to take the bag. His curly hair made him look too boyish the way it hung in his eyes. He had let it grow long and she didn't like this affected stab at a more artsy look.

"It's fine, I'm a big girl. I'm just being difficult. Sorry."

"You're not being difficult."

"I'm being a little difficult."

He stood back and gave her a helpless look and she laughed at him in spite of herself and said, "Shut up, okay."

She flung her duffel in and let him slam the trunk shut.

They drove by the old woman, who was once again dragging her cart down the walk, and Sasha hid her face so the woman wouldn't see her going off with some normal boring boy.

Paul's parents lived a few hours west of Boston over the border in New York. She had never met them before and wasn't expecting very much. From Paul's stories, she imagined large derelict sheds and a big round dirt driveway, dirty tractors and men in thick green coats with mortar splattered on their sleeves. She imagined them looking up at her sideways as they bent to pick up a heavy bag, a dull menace in their eyes. Maybe they'd dig something around in a hole. Her image of the place was in direct conflict with what the truth probably was: that they would be normal and straightforward, practical and clean, just like Paul. They wouldn't be dirty and hostile all the time. But the image had set itself up in her mind and even when she had addressed it and tried to wipe it away, it would catch her sleeve like a bramble and she'd have to stop and carefully disentangle herself so she wouldn't get bitter.

Paul's father was a landscaper and his mother kept the house running and helped with the business when she had time. Her specialty was with the plantings. She would come to design the gardens for his projects while he created the layout, the stone paths and walls and patios. Paul himself had worked in his father's firm and his older brother Jerry had done the same. Jerry had since started his own company, which specialized in building stone houses and chimneys. Some part of her believed that when Paul was finished with college, he would go back and end up working there too. It would be like a T.V. show or movie, where the college-educated son returns to the country to run the business properly, with all the modern methods. This idea briefly excited her: Paul as the main character, the romantic lead. On the other hand, it also depressed her: Paul in some yet undefined future, diminishing all the possibilities of his life and taking her with him. What a small existence she would have then.

Sasha's parents were both professors, and though she didn't look down on Paul for his parents' occupations, she also didn't get that same excited feeling she usually did when meeting new people. For example, the kinds of people that often stayed at her house when her parents invited them to give lectures at their school. Of course, some of them turned out to be boring, and she would, in the privacy of her father's study, mimic their slow pedantic speech to his appreciative laughter. But there had also been some very exciting guests, like one woman, a painter, who made quick color pencil portraits of each family member in the styles of different artistic periods. Sasha's portrait was in the cubist mode, and she hung it next to the mirror where she did her makeup. It made her unbearably happy, seeing herself as a pile of geometric shapes fallen into haphazard place in a garish mix of colors. She could look from this to her image in the mirror, her physical self, the reality of her soft skin, its rosy smoothness, the dark strand of hair along the side of her face, which became just one in a series of ways to see herself, instead of just the original, the baseline. There were so many ways to see the self and the expansive possibility of these selves opened out like endless rooms, all for her choosing. All for her invention.

And there had been the poet. He was from Croatia and barely fit under the doorways in their colonial-era house. He wore long light blue shorts that didn't even reach his knees. His broad face held the constant possibility of a joke, a smile at someone else's expense, delivered with cosmic knowing. He sat out on the back patio and smoked cigarettes all afternoon and drank his light beer from a tall glass her mother set out for him. He told her how when he was her age, or no, maybe a little older, he had gone to the beach where he saw people selling art on the boardwalk and thought to himself, "Why not? I'll try it." He gave her that smile again; it was a trick he had played on those people. He painted just what was there: the ocean, a few people lying on their towels under their sun umbrellas. People always handed over cash for stuff like that. It was so easy.

"I was in art school then," he told her. "I wasn't so bad."

That was before the war, when he was twenty-two. Then, when the war started, he ran away, left everyone, and lived in Germany. Every two months he had to go to this building downtown. It was a nice building, one of those old European buildings. "Staatlich," he said. "Stately." And those people inside, they told him whether or not he could continue to stay in Germany. "Each two months I had to register again. It was a stressful period. The week before, already I started to say goodbye to everything in my life." He took a long swig of beer from the tall glass. "Maybe it was because I was sad that I started to write poetry. Maybe because I missed the ocean. Maybe I stopped painting because I didn't want to only just see the world anymore, to only paint it. Everyone like me, all the refugees who went into that building in Germany, I am writing poems for those people. Not for what we see of them, but for what we do not see. Cannot see."

When he handed her the glass of beer and let her drink from it she felt that she was in on the joke with him, and that she too, was now more than ever only interested in what one couldn't see of people. Then, when her mother wasn't there, he slid the pack to her across the table as though it were assumed that she would smoke with him, two adults, equals. And so, when the silence in the house was right, when she knew no one would come out to the patio for a long while, she reached for the pack after having shaken her head no, and saw him nod and smile to himself as she lit the cigarette, and knew that she too, would one day write poems about the heavy lives of people displaced by the larger machinations of nations, the cruelty in the world. She was giddy and weak as she drew on the cigarette, her blood pinpricking the skin along her forearm and fingertips. She was lightheaded and thought she might faint into the brightness of the afternoon like a poem absorbing into the cosmos. She grabbed the beer and took a long cold drink and the bubbles tickled and scratched their way down into her stomach like an important truth.

I Want You to Tell Me

And so that was what she wanted from people. And Paul's parents. Could they give her that? They couldn't. They wouldn't be able to light up the future possibilities of herself. There was no chance that they would really be able to recognize her special talents, her ability to pick up on intellectual and artistic things that were usually assumed to be far beyond people of her age, which led some of her parents' friends to comment that she would likely, herself, "Make a mark on the world someday." It made her wonder what some landscapers could offer her after all. What could they know, anyhow, about the Truth her professor had asked them all to keep an eye out for? Surely she wouldn't be getting it from them the way she did from the Croatian poet.

Nonetheless, there was still a vague anxiety about how she would be received because she wanted them to like her. Her anxiety about this was more like a distant noise, like someone using a jackhammer on a nearby block, loud, but muffled. When they finally reached Paul's house she would have to confront that noise and what was worse, it might erase her completely, since they wouldn't see any of what made her great. She knew nothing about gardens or stone walkways, and honestly, she didn't really want to know. In truth, it was evident to her, on an intuitive level, that it was Paul who was lucky to have her, that it was he who should have anxieties, that it was he who should be working to impress her. She was the jackhammer.

III

Sasha was in charge of the music as they got on the Mass Pike. She didn't like Paul's music much, even though he had told her romanticized stories about listening to Nirvana and Pearl Jam on the mortar-flecked work radio during the summers with his father's company. She flicked through the radio channels as she looked through his CD binder. "Can you just stay on something? This is giving me ADD," Paul said.

"I don't want to listen to bad music and the radio is terrible."

He didn't answer. She switched it again to 106.7 and "I Believe I can Fly" came on. She decided to let it play and watched his head flick toward her to see if she was serious before staring out the windshield.

"I didn't realize you liked this kind of music."

When he turned to look at her again she was smiling.

"Ahh, you're punishing me. Well, if that gets you to smile, I'll take it."

"Should I switch it?"

"Do whatever you want."

She didn't switch it and continued flipping through the CD binder while he shook his head and laughed. "Didn't he like pee on a girl?"

"Oh God, I don't know. Did he? Who even is this?!"

"Wow, the mighty Sasha doesn't know someone. I'm shocked."

"Not the kind of person who pees on girls, that's for sure."

Still, she wanted to know, but now that he had this on her she didn't want to ask. She thought it might be R. Kelly.

I Want You to Tell Me

Wasn't there a story about him that had just come out? Didn't he do something terrible?

"Okay," he said. There was a long silence in which he was clearly waiting to see if she would ask who it was. She kept scanning through his CDs and pretended to ignore him. "It's R. Kelly, just in case you were too embarrassed to ask."

"I knew it was him!"

"Mm hmm."

"Stop it," she said.

She switched the station again. A country song came on. Paul "tolerated" country, which meant he secretly liked it, so she let it play.

She was a little ruffled but kept looking through the binder. She didn't like the idea that someone who had done something like that was still being played on the radio. Maybe they hadn't had time to investigate, but shouldn't there be some kind of punishment? A sense of wrongness pervaded the car. Frustrated, she flipped the heavy plastic sheets bloated with his crappy mixed CDs.

"I should have brought my binder," she said. She could feel him tense a little but he said nothing. She remembered that she had given him some music and flipped to the back and put in *The Firebird Suite*. Paul shifted but didn't say anything again. *Coward*, she thought. She would force him to listen to it the whole way through as punishment; he might even learn something.

She liked music to be educational. She felt that listening to music was about understanding culture better. It was less about enjoying it and more about learning to appreciate difficult music and gathering the knowledge to be able to speak about composers from a multitude of eras. It was a waste of time to just listen to something stupid and poppy on the radio because you liked it or because the artist had done something terrible to someone else and so you listened out of morbid fascination. But she already knew *The Firebird Suite* so well that she pulled out her copy of *To the Lighthouse* and started reading. She figured Paul could continue the education she was giving him without her, though she was tempted to tell him about the wizard who had enchanted the princess and trapped her in the lands that surrounded his castle and gave her savior impossible tasks to complete that only the magic of the firebird could handle. If only that girl who got peed on had had a firebird, she thought. But she decided he probably didn't want the lecture, and another part of her feelings for him blackened and began to rot off for his lack of intellectual curiosity. She turned to the dinner scene, which she knew she was supposed to love, but which in truth dragged a little, but she wanted to be someone who had read it, and had understood it, and knew to love it. Ah, the dinner scene, she could say. So good.

Paul had won her over mainly because he wasn't trying to be some kind of personality. He never talked himself up, never gave long lectures in conversations or during class mentioning Duchamp or Foucault, and never pretended to be more than he was. He was studying business and management, enjoyed the lit and art classes he took for fun, which was where he had met Sasha, but didn't make a big deal out of them. He was calm, kind, and gentle, and more than anything, solid. Very solid. In his presence Sasha was a minnow, happily flitting around him. She sensed that he liked this about her, and so she let it become a part of her personality that she enlarged upon. She was flighty and conversational, engaged people at parties, talked wildly and sometimes even sang. In many ways Paul allowed her to become what she always wanted to be: a person who was entertaining at dinners, capable of grand gestures, who could speak fluently and at length on important subjects, and who could grapple with big and difficult ideas in public settings. At the end of the night, as a party ended, it was always surrounded by Paul's big arm that she made their way home to her apartment in the South End. And it was always in Paul's arm that she was most comfortable, most sure of the truth of this image of herself. The role she was playing, though admittedly pumped up, was an accurate representation of her intelligence, passion, and uniqueness. She had been too young before she met Paul to really take it on, but now she was growing into it perfectly. Her true self.

The one problem Paul presented was that he was not very exciting, at least intellectually, which was really the only excitement that actually mattered to her (the other kind was fun, and they had good sex, and all that, but even doing something like running recklessly into the Charles at night and getting all soaked was not something Paul thought especially fun). When they would sit at a café to eat a sandwich, have an iced coffee, and talk about a lecture, Paul would smile, agree, and maybe add a small piece of his own judgment to the discussion of jealousy in *Othello*. Or, if they went to a dive bar, which Paul liked for the greasy food, cheap beer, and easy access to arcade games with large plastic guns, he would get distracted too quickly by other things, like those guns, and wander off. "Is this really the place for talking about Iago's psychology?" he would ask. But to her it was exactly the place. No one would expect it. Not in a dive bar. *Look at us,* she would think, *no one looking over at this table would think that we're having this kind of conversation,* and the idea of a divine viewer entered her mind, someone like God, or like a person with a television camera who was filming her amongst the crowd. No one would know that she was special, not until the camera zoomed in, not until the viewer got close enough and actually heard what she was saying. Only then would the viewer recognize her special talents and be delighted by them, just as someone might peel away from that group at the bar, walk toward the bathrooms, overhear them talking, and reveal himself to also be someone special, a famous critic who was so delighted to hear bright young people, people like her, talking in this way at a place like this.

But this anonymous person at the bar or this divine viewer would have nothing to distinguish her by if they weren't talking about anything. It took the whole fun out of going to a dive bar.

So, yes, Paul gave her many things, but he didn't add much to a conversation, to the way in which she wanted to live out her self-perception. She wanted him to sweep her away with his ideas so that they could be united, intellectually united, and carried off far above the other petty things that people usually cared about. Who Paul had slept with before would not matter, or what she had done that time when she was drunk her freshman year would not matter. Even though now, annoyingly, it did. Paul was bringing them both down into this predictable small-mindedness, and it made her irritated with herself that she cared about small things. And yet, jealousy was a passion worth knowing about. She could use it, anyhow, the way Shakespeare had: for his art. But it shackled her. She didn't want to think about these things, that battery-sharp shock when Paul would bring up his ex and the things they had done. Paul should lift her above that. He should get her not to care. Instead, he was shooting deer with a big plastic rifle and turning around to grin at her. She never played, except the once, when she had held the big gun and laughed, aware of the eyes of the other men at the high tops leaning on their elbows to see the girl feign perfect marksmanship, one eye squeezed shut. She asked him to photograph her and pretended to shoot at the screen. The delicate English major in her little white blouse. The idea of playing was enough for her, and she'd given him that, the image of her to tack up on a wall, to show his friends.

Her reverie lagged as she watched the Mass Pike run by in a blur. The trees were cusping as though some pointillist had come along and dotted each branch with green. The farther from Boston they got, the more the green dimmed, the more the fallow dead brownness of the landscape established itself. She began to think of emptiness again, and let her eyes lose focus until the trees and the grass along the shoulder all turned into a nothingness. She returned to the subject as though reentering a dream after losing it for a moment, or like a child coming back to her play. This common preoccupation. The world filtered out and there it was, the nothingness, as if she had conjured it. She stared at it for a long time, felt her insides warming, dissolving, until she regressed into something like an original state, childlike, an amoeba, and she floated back out into the dark infinity of space before her own conception. It was wonderful to float so freely, so undefined, but she saw that she had created this wonder for herself, this sense of free floating, and was snapped back into the austerity of the white world around her, leeched of color. And with this, a kind of terror overtook her. The car disappeared even as it was speeding into the nothingness and a claustrophobic sensation overtook her, as if she was being erased and couldn't find any way out of this lack of definition. There was no clear path, nothing demarcated, and herself wiped away.

Paul flicked his blinker and pulled into the fast lane and proceeded to pass a tractor trailer. Its immense weight and the large block of text advertising a super enhanced cheeseburger rolled through the emptiness like something both real and absurd and she was pulled back through the nothingness by the drag of the truck's velocity and the sound of its engine lit up in her ears as the starkness of its reality asserted itself.

Paul, yet again, had been unable to save her. But of course, she hadn't asked him to, and he hadn't noticed her distress, didn't know how to carry her out and above and away from the emptiness. It had been pure coincidence that he had changed lanes just then. He never was able to carry her out and above anything.

She had only ever once really had this feeling of floating over the emptiness, the pettiness, the smallness of the world with another person. It was at a café in Harvard square. Her friend Spencer from high school had come up to her in the hallway their senior year and said, "Hey, I'm trying to get someone to go have lunch with me. Will it be you?"

"It will," she said, and laughed. Had he always been this charming? It was like out of a book. They signed out and found a little café in the city that had a large terrace under a bunch of maples where metal chairs were set up that people kept trying to claim without ordering anything from the café. The waiter kept having to ask people to leave and when they sat down and were asked if they would be eating she immediately felt superior when Spencer had said, "Yes, menus would be nice."

They were pretty much all done with school and only had a week left before graduation. "What do you think you'll do next?" Spencer asked. "Do you have a college all picked out?"

She nodded and told him that she was undecided on a major, but would probably go for literature, "or something impractical like that."

"Impracticalities are what life's all about," he said, and smiled in a way that reminded her of the Croatian poet, as if they were at war with the practical world. After that they started to have fun. Spencer had blond, straight, thin hair and was party-avoidant. He had long slender fingers and played the piano passionately at school recitals. He was dedicated to art, not triviality, and his tall lanky body had a frenetic energy that was barely contained by his intelligence. His amused eyes were always on people, situations, and then, with the least opening, a whole gush of words and ideas and gestures would come out of him. This happened when she brought up their "current events" class, and all of a sudden he was off on the Patriot Act. She had gone to school with Spencer her whole life, but they had never been close. It was only now, when everything was ending, that it seemed normal to go out to a café with him, as if their maturities had only now properly aligned. Being out didn't have any commitment attached, and there was the genuine desire on both sides to get to know the other person before they both went off into their separate lives.

Sasha knew that Spencer was smart, but it was only through actually talking, and looking back, that she realized, sitting there at the café, that he was just as smart as she was, or could keep up anyway, intellectually. She thought he might be more of a philosopher than an artist, which was how she saw herself, an artist. He was analytical, incisive, whereas she was symbolic, passionate. He had created a basic personality profile of all their teachers, dissected their strengths and weaknesses, and said, sadly, almost compassionately, that Mr. Bernard was probably one of their most promising teachers but it was his own fear of taking a stand on anything that held him back. "He could probably be, if he wanted, some major intellectual, but I think he's so afraid that his ideas aren't original that he never puts anything out."

A pang of fear barbed in her chest considering that maybe one day she too would have nothing original to contribute and she pictured Mr. Bernard in his pants that were pulled up just a little bit too high and shoes that were so clearly from a discount store and belonged on the feet of someone much older than himself, that she saw in him the picture of what her own failure could look like. But a rush of energy burned up from inside her like a countermeasure that convinced her that she was far beyond him, that her upbringing and education had built inside of her a constitution of ideas that was so natural to her that all she would have to do would be to transcribe them for the world. Her only obstacle was to find the right medium.

"If I ever become him I'll die," she said.

"People become him every day," Spencer said, and then he smiled at her grimly, and they both scanned the tables, their eyes pecking at the people spread in their chairs, victims of their gaze: the man who stared into his open newspaper, the bicyclist pausing to rest against a lamppost, the man in a suit hurrying by. When their eyes returned to each other a knowledge passed between them that revealed the clarity of understanding that they had witnessed the failures of others and would not, ever, become failures themselves. They smiled knowingly, and looked back out at the square. As they continued to talk, the warmth of the sun cycled down into her body so that her blood became all lit up and golden, giddy. She became acutely aware of the geometry of the café, the round tables and long rectangular

I Want You to Tell Me

menus, the high-backed chairs and ornate metal legs that scraped across the cobblestones, the people slouched in them like sunken organic matter while the delicate glasses were round-edged and soaked in condensation. Her and Spencer, they could take these shapes, this moment, and make art and ideas with them, with it. They could hand it back to the people around them as if they had never seen it before, as if they were seeing it all for the first time, the miracle of a new vision lighting up their existence and awakening them to it.

It was like the photograph of Sartre and De Beauvoir at that Paris café. Both of them, these two intellectuals, her and Spencer, seated there amidst the tea cups, plates, the quotidian napkins, while the aura of their future immortality was soaked into it like sepia. And no one knew it now but them. The waiter with his dark hair slicked and parted to the side was just as much an apparition as he was a supporting player in the act of her life. He looked just the way a waiter was supposed to look, a part of the scene, but also a potential audience member. The waiter, the patrons, the pedestrians, each was a type ready to be cracked open by her vision, revealed by her understanding as though she could open the whole world up: the old woman with her large black purse like a saddlebag slung to her side, the bald man with the sun glinting off his head, the sounds of the café from the dark shadow of its interior, and the flapping table cloths held down by metal clamps; the clinking of the ice cubes in their glasses. All of it would be constituted in her art. The waiter might be the one to ask for a picture.

To someone walking by in the street, she and Spencer were just two teenagers out on lunch break. They could never know who the two of them really were. It was a secret that thrilled her and she couldn't wait to have it revealed, for the whole world to see this special thing she had to show them. How far above the world they swam. How far below her everything seemed, as if the world were just made of toys, and she was there to play with them, to understand the game, to explain it to other people who could never reach it on their own.

And then there was Paul. Poor bland Paul. She hadn't ever felt anything near this kind of excitement about him, much as she tried, and even though she didn't talk to Spencer anymore, hadn't seen him again except briefly at graduation, that afternoon remained with her as the example of what life with another person could be at its very highest, it's most exciting. She knew that she was trying to recreate it, at parties, in classes, and even yes, with Paul. She had written a poem once, and shown it to him at her apartment, and he had read it dutifully and then placed it down and said, "I like it. The image with the bear is really great," and she had said, "That's it? That's all?" He had nodded, then looked guilty, a little embarrassed, and lifted the paper again to look for something else and had finally said, "There's a cool violence in it, you know. Like, the tone is violent." And she had waited, because it was right, but wanted him to go on, to say what it meant, how it affected him. "Is that not what I was supposed to say?" he asked.

She got annoyed. "No, it's fine, it's perfect."

There was no "supposed." Couldn't he see that? Didn't he understand that she didn't have this scripted, that she didn't want to know what he was going to say. He was the one that was "supposed" to enlarge her understanding of the work, to find something unique to say about it, some new angle. But of course he couldn't. She waved the conversation away and walked off. But then she couldn't help herself and came back. "I just wish, God, I don't know, why can't we like, really talk about it?"

"What do you mean really talk about it? Look, we're talking about it!"

But she was already soured by his response and looked off through the window at the buildings turning purple in the twilight. He didn't get it. Their conversations always ended this way, up against some blockage where his interest stopped, or his ability. Why was there nothing else? Why couldn't he get caught up in a rush of excitement the way she did? The way Spencer had? Didn't his mind ever just burst open? She was disappointed, sad. She had tried to hide this from herself but knew it was there like the voices of people arguing in the apartment next door. She hadn't fully given into it until she admitted it to herself once as she sat on the toilet with her elbows on her knees. What could she do? She sighed and sank her chin down into her hands and decided to leave it, to see if something would change, if it would get better.

Some nagging sense inside her told her that it would be hard to replace him and that maybe she was with him to learn something about what it was like to be contented but not happy. That this was what, most likely, so many people lived. Maybe she had to live it too.

Once they got off the highway she put the book away and turned the music off. Her attention was gathering and she admitted to herself that she was nervous. It was not an overwhelming nervousness, but it was there nonetheless, weakening her legs. A windy pressurized tightness built in her stomach. How were his parents going to react to her? She was in Paul's territory now, and the long strip of highway had eroded, piece by piece, her connection to her own power. On top of that, she might find out things about Paul that she wouldn't like. Things about his past. The slope of the Mass Pike appeared in her mind again and she wished to be reversed back up the mountain to the highest point of elevation and slowly returned along the incline to her home in Boston. As in-control as she usually was, she also didn't want to learn anything about his exes or anything like that. She liked to imagine that there was no one else who had been able to make Paul powerless, and it would diminish her to think that Paul had been under someone else's control. A vague image of a blond girl in cut-off jean shorts by a pond floated into view. The girl's pretty face would have used its flirty look on Paul, the eyes crinkled, a grinning smile, and she could just see that helpless dumbstruck expression he got when he was blind with stupidity and lust. God, she hated him sometimes.

Plus, now that they were on their way to his home, he might change. Or her view of him might change, since in Boston he was always a little out of place. It was what, initially, had made him interesting to her. She remembered seeing him at a party in an apartment after only having seen him in class, and he was standing against a wall in the living room in a gray t-shirt and big work boots (the kind that had actually seen work) holding a blue can of Bud Light. He looked perfectly natural while everyone else around him looked like they thought about what they wore. Paul hadn't thought about it at all. If anything, he *was* his clothes. He had an expectant excitement in his face, and a nervousness too, like this was his first party and he was trying to figure out the rules of the game, laughing too easily, too quickly. At the same time, it was also clear that none of this, absolutely none, would touch him or change him at all. He would just watch it, partake in it, and come out the other side as is. Or that's what it looked like, anyway, which to her meant that he was authentic, even if his face was a little bashful, a little boyish, a little sweet, even.

"Having fun, country-boy?" she had asked him.

"It's a little different than back home. We mostly partied in fields or someone's garage. A few people had pools or ponds. I like this though." She squeezed in next to him to watch a group of girls take Jell-O shots in the kitchen and tried to see the scene through his eyes, the crush of bodies in the tight space of a second-floor apartment. From that vantage point she spent the rest of the party going everywhere with him, straight through the crush, their arms lifted up, drinks in hand, to squeeze through the tight hallway, bumping up against knees in the kitchen where people sat on the counter, and pressing their drinks tight against their chests as they talked in a crowd. They opened a room where two friends were crushing up pills on a dresser, another where a group sat in a circle surrounding a three-foot bong, and went out to the porch where the smokers were talking about Nietzsche. She could tell that he caught on quick that she was both showing him the scene and looking at it through his eyes, like a voyeur in his mind, and when he finally looked at her with a face as close to beaming as she had ever seen a boy's face, she reached up and kissed it, and then kissed him everywhere, his nose, his mouth, his forehead, his temple—everywhere, a mess of kisses until he took her face in both his big hands, held it still, looked at her full in the eyes, and then kissed her deeply on the mouth till she went weak.

His appeal had been his difference and now that they were heading to his home there was a good chance that he would just become another part of the common scenery and if that happened, what would they have left?

"Look, over there," Paul said. "The Catskills." A shouldered line of smoky blue mountains appeared as they crested a ridge. "They're beautiful," she said, and watched his face, which was quiet, alert, and confident in his homecoming, as if he were sure of the things he would show her. His eyes landed on a bridge, his head just barely inclining toward a driveway where he must have known someone once, a girl maybe, a place he used to turn into. They passed a silver diner with a row of long windows. "We used to go there all the time before away games. I always got the same thing: sausage, egg, and cheese on an English muffin."

"You've always had adventurous taste," she told him, and his face looked happy as she said it, as if he was watching himself still, sitting at a corner booth with his teammates, and didn't care that she was chiding him, or worse, that he believed the idea that she liked him just like that, as someone who always ordered the same thing. Still, in each road or house they passed lay the possibility of some past experience, something about him she might not like. As habitual as he might be, there was a good chance she would actually learn new things about him, and a troubling anxiety instilled itself. She wasn't used to him having power, and as she looked at his familiar freckled arms as they held the steering wheel, that tight column of muscle coming out of his short sleeve t-shirt, she remembered their first few months together and the hunger and need of his large muscular body. It was so boyish, and yet so big, and a little frightening with everything it wanted. She had been proud when she had taken it over and found him tired and vanquished and happy beneath her.

As Paul pointed out a spot where he had gone fly-fishing with his father she realized that Paul was beginning to enjoy being in charge, that he liked bringing her into unknown territory.

I Want You to Tell Me

"It's still another half hour," he said, "so you can relax."

"I *am* relaxed," she said, annoyed that Paul was able to read her so easily.

Her eyes skirted the river where sunlight glanced off a rushing current and into the shadowy underbrush along a narrow road lined by trees. She began again to consider the emptiness as it registered in the tangled growths at the side of the road, the static that was visible in its shadows like snow. She was separated from it by the passenger-side window, which insulated her in the quiet interior of the car whose speed rushed her by all that brown bushy tangle growing through the static in the ditch.

Then the emptiness jumped inside the car, played along the gray line of the seat belt strapped over her chest, crawled along the mass-produced dashboard with the radio and climate controls and tuned into the slow hum of the world coming at them through the windshield, until a floating sensation entered her chest, as though it were inflating her, lifting her off until she sat high above the road in her seat, all cushioned for comfort and safety, and something like a sob wracked her body as she reached for the road below in a plea of return—for the trees that lined it, for the fields now visible on either side. To be dropped. To be let out. To be scratched by brambles, irritated by long grass on her calves, to fall rolling down along a slope and to hurt herself as she slammed into a fallen tree at the bottom.

She knocked at the door with her knuckles by reflex.

"Whoa, you okay?" Paul asked.

She blinked, shook her head. "Yeah, of course, of course, I'm okay. I think I just fell asleep for a minute."

"You're supposed to be paying attention to all the special landmarks of my childhood."

"Right. Right, I'm sorry."

"I'm kidding . . . a little."

"I'm back. I'm paying attention. Don't worry. I'll be the best girlfriend ever."

"That's really all I ask," he said, and nudged her before he lay one big hand along her thigh and squeezed it. The hand held her in place, kept her from floating off.

The car slowed and they pulled into what looked like a long dirt driveway. A knowing smile was playing on Paul's lips and she poked him.

"Excited?" she asked.

"Yeah," he said, and turned to her to allow the moment to pass between them, a happiness glancing back and forth. "It's been a couple months since I've seen my parents, and of course I'm curious to see what they'll think about you. They'll probably wonder how I pulled it off."

"I doubt that," she said, but let the compliment play in her mind. Attending to Paul's happiness had made her a bit less nervous. This might be a strategy. She could become the attentive girlfriend, the wonder-filled guest who marveled at everything. They would love her for the excitement she showed toward their house, the property, all the wonderful nature. They would be so impressed that Paul had found someone with so much appreciation for the world.

The driveway was long with a wooded slope on one side that leveled out to fields on the other. She saw goats and donkeys grazing.

"Are those donkeys!?"

"They are."

"Are they yours?!"

"No, they're our neighbors'. Rich city people. I think they keep them for fun."

She turned to him. "Later can we go and pet them? I love donkeys. They're so cute with their big ears."

"Of course."

"A neighbor of ours had donkeys once too. Did I ever tell you that?"

"What, out where you lived?"

"Yeah. I'll tell you the story sometime."

"What's to tell?"

"Enough," she said. He looked at her questioningly but she waved him away.

"It's really beautiful here isn't it?" she said. The trees had just the tiniest hint of green in them still, to the point that it was difficult to tell if it was even there, but there it was, shimmering.

IV

When they pulled into the large circular drive, a long low barn on her right with flaking faded red paint that was a deeper red beneath slouched along the road. Sagging sliding wooden doors were partially open to shadow beyond. There was a much newer large brown two-story house on the left with green shutters. Just visible past the house on the left was a large pond with an island and a dock where a small boat was moored. Though everything was still muddy and brown she could tell that in the summer the series of small stone paths and little walls, the various trees and flower beds, made this a beautiful place. She was impressed, excited even. It was like in *To the Lighthouse*, a summer place where people came, where Paul and her would come (she imagined him as the boy cutting the long grass with the scythe), and where literary things could happen. Her heart ticked up lightly.

A blond woman with a utilitarian haircut parted in the middle and cropped close around her neck, who must have been Paul's mother, came from the shadow in the barn followed by a tall man, a bit bent, that must have been Paul's father. Paul jumped out of the car and made for them. "Paul!" she hissed after him, but he had already abandoned her. "Shit," she said, and held onto her seat belt. She watched him jog up to his mother, whose face brightened in a way that even Sasha could tell was rare. They hugged as Paul's father stood behind them, smiling and nodding, and it was as if she didn't exist at all outside of their small triangulation. She got out of the car slowly as Paul was hugging his father and saying, "Hey Pop!" and slapping him on the shoulders.

Paul's mother's glance caught her as she slowly leaned the door to, as if a memory was registering in her face, and she began to walk toward her with a serious expression that was devoid of all pretension. She was wearing earth-toned pants that were brown around the knees where she must have been kneeling in a bed earlier that day. The pants didn't seem to mind any dirt. Sasha was overdressed in her slacks, her blue blouse, and the blazer she had unbuttoned as she got out of the car.

Paul's mother took Sasha's hand in a rough though somewhat limp shake, and said "Welcome."

"Hello, thank you," she said

After that she didn't know what to say. The image of herself as a bright flash of cheerful energy in the muddy atmosphere of Paul's home was draining out of her. Paul and his father, who were of no help, still stood talking farther away. She was trapped and got a spiraling feeling as if she

I Want You to Tell Me

were twisting up to the sky like a bird suddenly looking down at herself. She could barely move.

"It's so nice here," she finally squeezed out. Then, with too much enthusiasm, she said, "Really wonderful. Did you do all the gardens?"

"Oh, I do a little here and there," Paul's mother said, as though talking about her accomplishments were indecent.

Paul's father had turned and noticed her then and he and Paul looked across at her with something like playfulness or pride.

"And you must be Sasha," Paul's father said, lumbering toward her and reaching one long arm out. It was bent at the elbow, as if it had been broken there.

"Delighted," she said stupidly, shaking his large rough hand.

If it had been a stupid thing to say, nothing showed in his face. He was all warmth and humor and a little shyness, where Paul's mother was self-possessed aloofness. Sasha was immediately comfortable with him, and felt that she could say anything stupid in his presence, or anything brilliant, and they would each be accepted. He was still looking at her as though through his son's eyes, though his large arms were now swinging at his side, a little cheerfully, a little nervously. He had similar features to Paul but they had been softened and sanded over by time. His blond hair was dusted with gray and his cheeks had a burnt ruddiness, but his light blue eyes sparkled humorously down at her.

"It's really nice to meet you both, Mr. and Mrs. Cleary. Really wonderful."

"Oh, just Dale and Gloria. We're not all that formal around here," Dale said.

Paul was watching her and a self-conscious inkling grew in her that she was not quite behaving how Paul had hoped, and that he wasn't surprised either that she would be a little off. She wondered whether he might actually be the tiniest bit embarrassed by her. The idea shocked her. She had been too formal, too stupidly British or something. But he had abandoned her! A quick stroke of hatred speared through her.

Paul's father took her bag from the trunk and wouldn't hear of not carrying it. She followed his loping step up the rough stone walk to the house and wanted to slip in next to him, to fall into easy conversation, to have him chide her the way a father might a daughter, so that she could achieve an image that appeared in her imagination where she became his especial favorite for her easy ability to draw him into banter, to reach him in ways others couldn't, so that anyone watching might say, "Those two are close, huh?" And Paul, or whoever was listening, would answer, "They just took to each other right away. Don't know what it is. He's usually so quiet around other people. Especially women."

She didn't have the same urge with Paul's mother, who she knew had immediately noticed that she was upset with Paul for abandoning her at the car. It was clear that she was the type of woman who kept her opinions to herself, and probably only rarely let them out, and that when she did, they would be severe and irreversible. She knew that in these moments, Paul's father would likely smile at her, demur, and walk off. Some part of her was a little disappointed in him by this.

From inside the front door she heard dogs barking and scratching and whining.

"I hope you don't mind dogs," Dale said.

Sasha had instinctively moved closer to Paul but said that no, no she didn't. "I love them, in fact."

When he opened the door, the dogs rushed out, a black lab and a brown lab, Ginger and Basil. She tried to move out of the way but the blond one, Ginger, tucked around Paul's leg, followed her, and was about to jump when Dale whistled and said, "Down!"

The dog whined and strained, before it leaned back on its haunches, completely under Dale's control.

"Well, that was a happy reunion," Gloria said, looking down at Paul who was wrestling Basil on the ground.

Sasha squatted and Ginger came toward her. "Eaaasy now," she heard Dale say, and the dog approached carefully, and then excitedly let her scratch her behind the ears, butting her hands up with her nose.

"Looks like you've made friends," Dale said.

"I hope so," she said.

"Well, now that you've met the dogs, why don't you give her a tour, Pauly? Show her around. We'll get started on lunch."

"Won't you come?" Sasha asked him from her crouched position, suddenly bereft. Needy.

He studied her as if something unexpected had tripped him up before saying, "Oh, I'll help Gloria in the kitchen. I might be out in a bit when you go around the property."

He handed her bag to Paul, who brought her inside and began to take her through the house, which Dale had built himself. Paul had helped on an addition they built when he was twelve and which was where they would be sleeping. It was a little guest wing, with a bathroom and two bedrooms, one of which was being used as an office that Dale and Gloria shared. Their bedroom looked out on a small garden and had a somewhat obstructed view of the pond, though she was happy to note that, lying in bed, she would be able to wake up and see a small curve of the glassy green water.

She had an itching need to change. Her blouse and blazer were all wrong and now they were trapping her with their soft tight delicate cuts. She was happy that she had brought some jeans and a sweatshirt along. "For roughing it," she had told Paul over the phone and giggled. He had sighed, and she could imagine him shaking his head and trying to decide whether or not to be insulted.

"I really love your parents, Paul," she said, opening her bag.

"How can you tell? I mean, isn't it a little early for love?" He had opened his bag too, but didn't take anything out of it.

"No, I don't know. You get a sense for people right? I think I really love them; they're great."

"It feels weird being in this room. I'm like a guest in my own house."

"Do you want to sleep in your old room? I wouldn't mind."

"That would be weird too. I don't think either will really feel right. Anyway, it's not really my room anymore. They use it for my brother's kids."

"Can you pull the curtain? I want to put different pants on."

"Costume change? No one's gonna see you." But he walked toward the glass doors anyway.

"It's wonderful to see where you grew up and to meet your family. I think it's all just really grand."

"Grand?" He turned to her with skeptical bemusement. "Who says 'grand?'"

"I do," she said brightly.

"You're not like in some novel in your head right now, are you?"

"I'm not in a novel! Stop it, silly."

"Do I even want to know the plot?"

"There's no plot!" God, how did he always know?

"Fancy girl goes to see boyfriend's country roots."

"Screw you," she said, and laughed, still trying to hold on to this image of herself as the bright and cheerful (ebullient?!) girlfriend, though she hated him for being able to tell.

She kissed him anyway (and also because she had to respect him for seeing through her) and went to the door. "I'm going outside into the garden to wait for you." She had seen a little bench outside their window where she wanted to sit and read a book of Louise Gluck's new poems from *Wild Iris*. She liked to think of Gloria seeing her sitting out there reading poetry in defiance of her sober practicality and of Dale being quietly delighted by having the kind of girl who loved poetry in the house, someone completely unlike Gloria. Someone special.

"I mean, I'm ready now."

"Just for ten minutes."

"Sure," he said. "Whatever you need."

V

Sasha couldn't tell if anyone had observed her as she sat very upright on the little bench reading her book, but she did notice Gloria's eyes flicking across her clothing change when they came into the kitchen to continue their tour.

The house was built in an open concept timber frame style with large exposed beams that slid into each other, tenons into mortises held together by wooden pegs. From the kitchen Sasha could look out across the space to a massive bank of windows that revealed the smoky Catskills beyond. The dining room adjoined the kitchen and two long wooden steps led into the living room where they passed the massive stone fireplace and a bookshelf with Dale's histories and Gloria's mysteries and up a wooden staircase along which was a gallery of family pictures. Sasha wasn't sure, but she thought she saw a picture of Paul with his arm around a blond girl. She avoided looking at it, at the whole wall, as a low orange flame of jealousy lit in her abdomen. It must have been her, Kate.

She saw the room that Paul had grown up in, which was small and had a loft where he had slept under a skylight. It was now outfitted with a rocking horse, a crib, and a baby jumper in the doorway.

"Is this where you had your first kiss?" she asked, trailing a finger along the railing of the crib.

"No, but . . ." and a bashful smile told her all she needed to know. This admission reverberated in the hollow of her stomach. As she looked up at the loft a tingling sensation pin-pricked its way up her arms. A blond girl's face laughed down at Paul from up there. Then it hid playfully in the covers. She could see Paul monkeying up the wooden ladder to dive under the covers to find her, to find what he wanted, what she wanted to give him.

"I guess I'm glad we're staying in the guest bedroom then," she said, and pressed her lips into a tight line.

She turned to leave before Paul could tell her anything else about what had happened in that room. Dale appeared in the doorway and casually put a hand on the rope of the baby jumper; her way out was blocked.

"Did you tell her about that time with all my cardboard boxes?" Dale asked Paul.

Paul's face looked trapped, pleading to her not to be difficult while trying to tell the story of how him and his brother had hauled all of Dale's old material delivery boxes up there and had made this crazy fort out of them, cutting tunnels through one box to the next and taping them together to the point that his parents couldn't get in. Lunch and dinner had to be passed into the box closest to the door, and they'd clamber out just far enough to drag their spoils to the inner sanctuary. "No one could reach them in there," Dale said, and chuckled.

"Sounds like you've had a lot of fun in this room," Sasha said.

Paul gave her a look that said, *What the hell?*

"Yeah, they were good boys," Dale said, letting his arm fall against his thigh. "They kept us busy, that's for sure." He turned and Sasha followed him out into the hall from where she could look down at the living room below. The image of the girl, of Kate, appeared to her, lounging on the couch, walking barefoot up the steps and into the kitchen, casually popping a grape into her mouth as though the place was hers. She was like a noxious presence that spread like invisible gas through the whole house. It was hers, not Sasha's. She had established her right to it long before. She owned this part of Paul's past and there was no going back to yank it out of her hands. No matter what Sasha did, ever, she couldn't get it back, even if Paul wanted her too. It was unreachable and made her hate Paul for ever having let Kate into his house, for ever wanting her, for falling for it. His stupid attraction. Why did he do that? Why was he such a horndog of a boy?

She followed Dale along the upper hall and imagined that Paul was still in his room, sulking. Let him crawl into the crib, she thought.

When they came to a balcony overlooking the yard, Kate appeared, running down the slope of the lawn toward the pond where Paul had watched her slip out of her shorts and dive into the water in only her underwear.

"Lost in thought?" Dale asked her.

"Who? Oh, no, no, I just—" But she didn't have an answer except for the shame that now clotted inside of her as she stood next to Dale's tall and unassuming body. She wondered then what Dale had thought of Kate, whether he secretly wished Paul had stayed with her, hadn't gone to Boston. Whether he was comparing Sasha to Kate in each thing she did.

"I guess I was just thinking, trying to imagine Paul here when he was younger, his life, his friends," she said.

"Yes, a lot to imagine, I'm sure," he said. "Paul lived his whole life here. Going out to Boston has been the first time he ever really left. I sometimes wonder whether I shouldn't have taken the boys away more, but they had a good life here."

"We did," Paul said, as he stepped out on the balcony. "You shouldn't feel bad about anything."

"I agree," Sasha said. "It's a really wonderful place. I think Paul has been very lucky." Paul gave her another look but she ignored it and forced her hand into his closed fist. She tried to be the girlfriend Dale might be proud to have around, even as she felt stupidly betrayed that Dale hadn't stopped the whole thing between Paul and Kate from happening. She knew it was completely unrealistic, but she wished Dale had advised Paul that someone better might come along, someone that he could really be proud of and wouldn't want to disappoint, someone that might expect him to be better. That he should consider this future person's feelings, that he couldn't just let girls come over here and get naked with him like he was some kind of little player. But of course it was insane to expect that of Dale. She couldn't hate him for that. She couldn't. Though at the same time she disliked the feeling that he had probably been just this nice and welcoming to the other girls that had come here, to Kate, that he had opened his doors to them, and by extension to his son, given them access just as he was doing for her now. It wouldn't be any different. She was just coming in as another girl that Paul would take to his room in a gray sequence of sheets and naked bodies and sex. It made her want to smear Paul right off the edge of the balcony in a blue streak with her thumb.

VI

As they toured the grounds she had the distinct sense of Kate's presence walking with them, unasked. Kate had probably taken this tour before and it was as if she were whispering, "This has all already been mine." Sasha locked her out as Dale pointed to a dark tangle of branches and said, "These will be light pink, soon enough," and a large bush that Dale explained was a lilac tree that would explode into clutches of purple blossom. "Such a nice smell too, the lilacs." It was surrounded by a low stone wall with a bench built into it. Kate's presence was there as if she were the weather and again she appeared to pull Paul down to sit on that bench so that she could wrap her arms around him and lay her cheek on his shoulder.

Paul looked at Sasha as if checking to see if she was still mad. She shot him a glance.

She wished he could just say that he didn't care about what had happened, what he'd done, that it was his past. Then, she could take it or leave it. But he didn't. He always looked abashed, and so she had to handle it on her own, hold it, as though it were this big thing she had to carry. He was forcing her to be alone with her jealousy. It wasn't fair.

But she had her ex too, Ryan. Paul could think about him a whole lot too, if he wanted. Though of course he didn't. He was too big for that. Still, she wasn't really sure that Ryan actually counted. He was so pale and skinny, and she had been so surprised when she lifted his shirt off and saw his angular collapsed chest. His face though, was so intense, handsome, the shock of dark hair. But then the clamminess of his hands, his long feminine fingers. His face, his personality, was in contradiction with his own body, and when they were in bed together she couldn't help thinking his body belonged to someone else. A weaker, less spirited person. It repulsed her. But still she had tried, but there was always something off. She knew that it was Spencer that Ryan reminded her of, and the fact of this disappointment made it even worse, since he was stealing the memory of Spencer from her as well. Maybe that's why Paul didn't think about it. He wasn't threatened by Ryan and didn't care. She hated him for being so calm about it all, as if there was something wrong with her, that she was the jealous one. Shouldn't he care more? Shouldn't he be upset that someone had gotten to her first? He should want all of her, even her past self.

And if she was going to be a big artist, was Paul really content to have shared her with someone else? For her entire career people would be asking who she had been with first, her first kiss, her first love, her first passion. Didn't Paul hate that he would not be that person, that again and again, he would be erased in those questions, that there would be this fog of otherness cast on her life, oozing into everything, rotting it, this sense that he was there as a second, a replacement, someone who couldn't, who wouldn't ever, really, have her to himself? And then the embarrassment for her too, that this husband of hers, that Paul, in some future version of their life, had fallen for someone else. Didn't it cheapen her that he had reduced her to being on the same level with someone like Kate, who she knew worked behind a bar, which Paul admitted he knew since they were still in touch sometimes through a stupid new social media site called Facebook. It seemed to her like a place where people went behind each other's backs, where he could still have his cake and eat it too. She didn't want to be placed alongside Kate for her entire life. She didn't even know her! Why did she have to think about her all the time now? But of course this was stupid. So many great artists were promiscuous lovers. No one would care. She could just say that she lived wild and passionately and looked for this in her lovers as well, in her strong passionate Paul, though of course it would be a lie, wouldn't it?

As they circled around the front of the house where the big bank of windows looked into the living room, Kate appeared again, reflected in the glass.

Sasha could see that this would ruin the trip. Kate would be everywhere. It wouldn't be fun at all.

She decided not to think about Kate. It was over. Sasha was far beyond her, and though Paul couldn't lift her up above this the way Spencer would have been able to by showing her how small Kate was compared to them, she could still squash her down, deflate this stupid ex by pushing the air out of her with the weight of the present over the past, until she was totally flattened. With a little kick Sasha launched her off into the grass where she lay like discarded trash.

Sasha could focus on the garden, on Dale as he bent down and drew her toward where phlox would break out in light pinks and blues in the spring, where lavender would pipe up in its purple stalks, where crocuses and daffodils would burst out with purple and yellow. She began to see the barren ground light up with pops of color as if they were already there. Dale must always see the gardens this way, a world of color in each dormant thing buried along the wheel of its cycle. She wondered, did he see her too as the possibility of some great flowering? She turned to look over the valley and imagined it turning green, imagined the power of encountering each person not as they presented, but as they might, at some distant point on their cycle, bloom into life, and a conviction of deep excitement took root in her, of being the artist to see that in everyone. She felt herself lighting, taking off. "The milkweed here," Dale said, and she swung around to hear more, to learn what else he might tell her, "is for the monarch butterflies. They just love it, and you'll see them on their migration stop here to eat it. It's amazing to think, we can connect them all the way to Mexico," he said. "That's where they start out." She followed the fluttering orange line of their migration across a small map in her mind, dangling on it, clinging to the link Dale had created in the possibility of envisioning such a shimmering route of beauty.

She was realizing that she liked Paul more because of Dale. Being in Paul's life meant that she could also be in Dale's life. As they passed by the pond a distinctly literary sensation spread through her. That of inspiration, which she traced to the vision she had just had and the way in which she had played as a girl, when the smell of the grass and the rough bark of a tree was pressed against the skin of her knees shimmying up its trunk, when she imagined the fairy who lived among the shaking leaves in the dappled light, when she saw how the imagination filled with the extent to which the imagined thing was real, trees sprouting up in the mind, mud rushing down a slope, the perfect distillation of a clear idea on the page of a book. This garden felt to her literary because it sat perfectly in the intersection between the real and the imaginary, and she decided she might sneak out that night, take the small boat and lie in its bottom to stare at the stars, no matter how cold. To be alone and illuminated under the many eyes of the person who had created this all. Of God. Because she did believe, after all, in creativity, and was there anyone who had ever created anything more perfectly and with more complexity than God?

They passed the vegetable garden, surrounded by a tall fence. "That's mostly Gloria's domain there, and I'd better let her tell you all about it." Sasha nodded and tried to imagine herself walking alongside Gloria in the garden and the silence that would build between them until it would be clear how little they liked one another. The notion filled her with dread, but she tried not to think of it, to plod happily along behind Paul and Dale and to avoid imagining the way in which Gloria's presence would blacken out whole swaths of herself, one galaxy after another blinking out.

A gazebo sat against a line of trees behind the garden that blackberry brambles had started to claim by snaking into the railing, like the forest was trying to eat it. "We used to go there all the time," Paul said, "to get away from my parents."

He nudged his father in nostalgic conspiracy.

"Lord knows what went on in there," Dale said, and they both chuckled. The hot rush of jealousy returned but Sasha pushed it off so it went right through her and kept going. Continuing to do this would be difficult, she saw. She would have to try hard to be a person she wasn't used to being. She would have to be steady, to hold tight to this bar of equanimity in her hands.

As they came back around to the patio adjoining the kitchen a little rush of spirit broke out in her as she remembered the bright persona she had meant to become.

"You've just made everything so pretty here!" she said. "I'm so impressed. My parents pay some people to come and they sort of do the bare minimum, but there's nothing nice about it, no character, no personality. It's so much better here! You've just clearly thought about everything, and it just, it just, feels like real people live here. Like there's, I don't know, *character!*"

"Yes, yes," Dale said, as if he barely noticed her outburst and just took it at face value. "It's turned out pretty nicely, even though there isn't much to see this time of year. But wait a few weeks and it'll all break into blossom. Takes a lot of upkeep though. I sometimes wonder why I take the time. Now it just needs more and more. Each time you build something you end up having to tend to it. It gets to be a rotten lot of work."

"But you can't have clients coming over and the whole place looking like a mess," Paul said.

"True," Dale said. "And I do love how it all looks, and the stone holds up pretty nice so long as you prep it all in the right way. You see patios heave all the time when they haven't been prepped right."

"Well, and it must be great to know it's all here now, and will stay here," Sasha said, hopefully.

Dale massaged his chin with a big freckled hand that had gone pink in some spots, like the skin had peeled off after a burn and never come back. He looked at a fixed spot of patio stone as if he was waiting for it to say something. "Yes, but it all moves and changes." He started smiling, but it was a weary smile, with regret in it. "That's the thing, nothing you do ever really lasts, except some of the stone, but that will move too. I mean, Michelangelo and people like that, people we still read about—their things will always be there. But all of this, it just goes away."

I Want You to Tell Me

Even though he was smiling, there was darkness in the words, like he was being robbed, or that he had somehow gone wrong somewhere, made a poor choice, spent his life on things that wouldn't matter, in the end. A feeling of smug victory kindled in her that she had chosen right, that her works would last much longer than a flower bed or a stone path heaved out of whack and covered by moss and grass and finally dirt.

"Lunch!" they heard Gloria call from a door that slid open.

"Well, I guess that's our cue," Dale said. He wiped his hands across his thighs as if he was brushing the subject away.

He walked up the path to give her and Paul a little moment of quiet together.

Sasha's small flame of glee left her and she worried about Dale, about what he had said.

"Is your dad okay?" she asked Paul.

"Why, what do you mean?"

She fumbled with the zipper of her sweatshirt, annoyed that Paul needed everything explained all the time. Couldn't he put things together from context? Wasn't he listening?

"I don't know. About the paths. About landscaping and patios. About things not lasting."

"I don't know. Maybe. Hard to tell. He might just be going through something."

"Like what?"

"I don't know. He's always been working and he's always been the strongest and best at everything but now he just sits in that office of his and does paperwork and I don't know, maybe he has too much time to think or he doesn't get to build and finish stuff enough. Who knows."

"So, does that mean he's just depressed about getting older, about not having more?"

"More what?" he said, defensive. Paul's hand hovered over a bare bush that had been pruned into a flat table of pointy sticks.

"I don't *know*. That's what I'm asking." She could tell that she had to be careful not to insult his father's occupation. "More certainty, maybe. I don't know. The idea that none of this will last. It seems like it's bothering him."

Paul was looking at her but she could see how she was turning invisible in front of him. He went into a distant daze and the defensiveness in him dropped, as if he had shrugged his shoulders and it had fallen to the flagstones. His hand started running over the sticks, bending them back and releasing them.

"I guess it's probably just hard getting older," he said vaguely, and all of a sudden, she had no idea where Paul was, where he had gone. Some watery room of thought whose walls held back the gray spring air. *What did men even think about?*

She moved toward him, unexpectedly hungry, like a bird who wanted to reach her talons into that room and rip through the thin film of those walls and claw him back out to her so she could devour him for herself, just like the promise of all of those buds shimmering just beyond visibility in some world beyond the static.

She dug her fingers into his side through the thick fabric of his blue sweatshirt, pushed up close against his stomach and said, "Kiss me; kiss me hard."

"All right, all right," he said.

And he did.

VII

Lunch was simple. They worked their way down the counter assembling sandwiches from plates with little wooden tongs next to them: tomatoes, dewy lettuce, smoked turkey, and sliced red onions placed on long wobbly slices of sourdough bread dusted with flour on their sharp crusts and spread with mayonnaise. They paused, reached, asked for mustard. They ate inside, looking out through the glass at the terrace and the pond below.

"Dale was telling us earlier, on the tour, that one of the sad things about landscaping is that nothing ever really lasts," Sasha told Gloria, though she was addressing it to the room generally.

Dale shifted in his chair and uncrossed one of his legs. He was wearing dark leather slippers over his white socks. He cleared his throat, placed his plate on his knee and took another bite.

Sasha thought he might say something but in the presence of Gloria he had gone quiet.

"Oh sure," Gloria said. "You can just see it in those rose bushes there at the edge of the terrace. Got them last year and already one of them is dead. Didn't make it through the winter."

Sasha knew she should probably just leave it, but she wanted to hear more about what Dale thought. Plus, she thought of herself as being especially skilled at getting people to talk about things they didn't want to talk about. At getting into the truth of things. The trick was just to put them out in the open, to throw them out there the way that most people were too uncomfortable to do. It was part of her role as a truth teller and it was easy because people never thought ill of her and so she was the perfect messenger for it. Life shouldn't be all clogged up by secret struggles that people were too afraid to bring up. She could just do it for them.

So she forged ahead. "But he was saying how Michelangelo, the Sistine chapel, that those are the things that really last."

"Oh well, of course, my little row of rose bushes can't compete with Michelangelo!" Gloria laughed and wiped her mouth with a napkin. "Nope! They're just plain old roses."

She didn't seem in the least bit bothered by this. Sasha couldn't fathom how there wasn't in her at least some desire to try, to at least attempt, something worthy of history. Or maybe she had given up on all that long ago or never even thought to try?

Dale put both hands on his plate and stared blankly into a distance somewhere past the pond, or through it.

The room had started to shift so there was pressure in the air near her neck. Still, she needed to continue. She would give her solution.

"Well, I think that roses are wonderful. And what I think actually really matters is the experience people have of a place," she said, leaning over to look at Dale, who kept staring into the pond, into its dark watery hole. "There's this park near my house and there are these rhododendron bushes and this stone path goes in a little curve around them, and then it comes to a stone archway, and when you go through it, suddenly you see this lake below, right? And there's something in that design that's just so perfect, like a little threshold to revelation. And I mean, imagine how many people take that path every day. And when the rhododendrons are blooming! Oh, it's just so perfect. And I mean, that's what you do, right? You create that for people.

You give them that experience. So, I think it's not so different from Michelangelo."

"Hmm mm," Gloria said.

Dale nodded, as if to agree, but whether it was with her, she couldn't tell. He picked up and dropped his napkin on the plate. He pressed his lips together and looked at her, as though he had nothing else to add.

She was betrayed.

"So tell us about your classes Pauly," Gloria said.

He did, and as they finished eating she resolved not to say anything else, nothing else at all. Clearly, they didn't want what she had to offer.

When they had finished eating she got up and asked if she could take their plates. They thanked her and when she brought them to the sink Gloria came in behind her and said, "I'll do those darling. Don't you worry," as if she couldn't even be trusted to do the dishes properly.

As she walked back to their room with Paul she said, "Well, I guess your parents hate me now, huh?"

"It was a nice little lecture," he said, like she should have known she was doing it, like he wished she hadn't talked at all.

"Oh, okay, so you agree with them?"

"You don't think you were being just a little condescending?"

"What?! How? I was trying to tell them that their work mattered."

"You don't see how that's condescending?"

"No, I don't. Please, explain it to me."

"Oh God, don't get mad. My parents don't need you to like, approve of them."

"That's not, that's not what I was doing."

"Okay well, look, they're, I don't know. They're not in college anymore. They don't sit around and talk about what art means, or ideas or like why a path or an archway is like a symbol for something. They do their jobs. They try to do them well."

"And that's what I was saying, that they are doing important work. And also, I don't think you can live life without thinking, or without like, really trying to, um."

"Trying to what?"

"Never mind."

"No just tell me."

"I don't know Paul. Find meaning in things? It doesn't matter. All I know is that your dad was thinking about this stuff. He told us on the terrace, and then he got embarrassed at lunch and didn't want to talk about it in front of your mom and so he just let me drown."

"Wow."

"You think I'm wrong?"

"Yeah, I think you're being super unfair to my dad."

"Fine. I'm sorry."

She walked off to their room and stood by the window with her arms crossed and looked down at the pond. Paul came in and stood behind her waiting but she didn't turn around. A little while later he sat on the bed. Then she heard him taking something out of his bag. It was his book; he was reading. He wasn't even trying to reconcile.

She saw Dale walk across the yard to the far edge of the lawn where a pile of stones was lying at the border of the forest. He placed them into a cart with easy fluid motions as if they didn't have any weight at all.

When the cart was full, he pulled it toward a sapling and dumped the stones out in front it. They looked like a pile of blue corn chips and must have been leftovers or scraps. He started pulling them from the pile and placing them around the tree in a circle. He didn't pause to think about where to place them, he just laid them out in an easy circle, shifted them, adjusted them, exchanged one for another, knocked off corners with a hammer and used the chips for shims. Then he lay down the second layer, then a third, and within minutes a little wall had been built around the tree, as if it were growing out of a well. The whole process looked to her exactly like play. Pure child-like creation. It was exactly how she wrote a paper. Her thoughts just ran out in front of her and she could reach out and put each one down as it appeared, right in its perfect place.

She didn't care then what had happened at lunch. Dale had seen the emptiness just the way that she had. He had just built that wall like a blockade against it because it was always there, buzzing in the gray static light through the dead bushes behind him like the sound of summer cicadas.

VIII

In the afternoon, Paul pulled the four-wheeler out of the barn in a semi-circle that kicked up stones and dust. He rocked it to a stop and held a black helmet out to her. It was huge and heavy. "Make sure it's tight."

There were trails all through the woods, she had been told. She pulled the helmet on, reached in through the eye-slit to move her hair out of her eyes and then tightened a little strap that went under her chin. "Aren't you wearing one?" she asked him.

"I usually don't," he said.

"So I'll live and you won't?"

"No one's going to die."

"Just put one on."

He sighed, got up, and went into the barn.

The argument from earlier had settled between them like an unresolved gray silt that washed one way or another with their mood, weighting everything. When he sat down she locked her fingers around his stomach and pulled him close, the intimacy of the act grating against that silt between them. He jumped the four-wheeler into gear and then with a bounce they were off.

"Not too fast!" she screamed, but he barely slowed. They went down the driveway and she saw the pond and then up ahead, the other house where the donkeys were. Before they got there, he nosed the four-wheeler down and across a ditch and up a little path into the woods. Soon they were climbing a steep incline. The fat tires bounced over roots and stones and kicked up mud that splattered her when Paul made a tight turn. She was tiny in the big protective clothing of Dale's work pants and fleece-lined sweatshirt as the engine strained over stones and dipped, bounced, and then revved up the slope, rocked and jumped forward. They mounted a small ridge and came out of the tree line to a long field that sloped down toward another pond thick with reeds where he stopped.

"Having fun?" he yelled.

"I think so!"

His stomach laughed in her arms. After a minute of looking down at the water, he lowered his visor and they tore off over the field. The wind cut cold through the sweatshirt along her sides. She was happy for the heavy helmet, which made her head oversized and warm. The speed was thrilling and with so much field ahead of them she leaned into his neck and yelled, "Gun it!"

He did.

He manipulated something on the handlebars, the machine lurched, and then kicked into a higher gear and they flew off. A giddy expansion tingled through her stomach. It was just like when her horse reached gallop and the smooth exhilaration of speed took over from the bounce of the canter. Only this was much louder. She was gritting her teeth. They were tearing at the earth, not floating over it. It was wonderfully and thrillingly aggressive.

After the field they entered the forest again, climbed up another steep path, circled around, paused by a waterfall that gushed down a wall of shale and then continued up until they finally reached a ridge with a lookout. It was a shelter made out of rough-hewn logs that Paul called an "Adirondack Structure." He turned off the engine, threw his leg over the handlebars, helped her off, and they sat on the bench and looked out at the Catskills in the distance.

"Is this where you come for manly reflection?"

"Yeah, I sit here in steely-jawed contemplation."

She grinned at him, and then brought his face toward hers, her mouth suddenly gentle, her eyes closed, and kissed him very carefully.

"I love you," she said, in an effort to wash away their argument from earlier.

"I love you too," he said.

She looked at him seriously. "I mean, I really do."

"Good," he said. "Me too." He was grinning at her, a little as if it were a joke.

She wavered between being angry and believing him. Then she took his hand and they looked back out at the mountains, which were a pale line of blue shoulders leaning against one another.

She was reminded of swaying in the arms of two of her girlfriends on a rooftop, wine bottles clenched in their hands, stumbling as they pointed out over the purple night of the city and said, "There, that, that right there, right there, that, that's what I'm talking about, right there." They whooped and pointed out at it, laughed and fell against each other, and none of them had to explain it to the others. What it was. They knew, they just knew.

Now she lay against Paul and let the sun shine across her body till it filled with warmth. The light pushed into her eyelids. Though the common emptiness was there like a static veil hanging over everything, she had somehow stuck her head through it and could look down over it as if it were mist in the valleys. It wasn't gone, but she was above it for a moment, on her small peak. This week might all be like that, bright and open, before they drove back to the city and dipped under the clouds again. She began to dread the return.

IX

When they got back to the house, Paul stripped her clothes off and very efficiently and purposefully made love to her. She straddled his waste until she lay back on the covers and he came on her stomach.

He wiped it off with his gray shirt and chucked it in the hamper. "Your mom better not find that," she said.

He looked back at it thoughtfully, then rolled it up more carefully and stuck it into his bag.

She sighed and lay back on the pillows, then swung herself up for a shower. Paul tried to follow.

"Not in your parent's house."

"But we just . . ."

She gave him a look.

He didn't argue. He had already gotten what he wanted, after all.

When she came back out he was asleep. She got in next to him.

She felt clean lying between the sheets and closed her eyes. She slept for only moments. It was a watery kind of sleep, tidal, like she was floating up and down and in and out of perception. The gray afternoon light through the linen curtains dimmed and brightened as she sunk in and out of it. She could still feel the engine of the four-wheeler, the bumps of the rocks and roots vibrating against her body, the feeling of speed.

Soon she rose out of the gray mist of her sleep and stared at the ceiling.

With her thoughts clear she reached into her bag for the canvas journal and slipped the pen from its small elastic loop along the side. She opened to the first blank page toward the back of the book and looked for a long time out of the window. Her journal was essentially a diary of noticing, a sketchbook. She began by making quick sketches of the landscape, the trees, bare and spiny, like coral swaying in the gray sky. She was pleased with that image and added the faded muddy grass interlaced by the arteries of runoff. Then she thought of Dale when he had walked across the lawn in his large boots to stack the rocks around the tree. She forgot who had said it (she was embarrassed to admit this to herself), a poet maybe, but the poet said that all poets' work was just an argument with God and she thought of Dale's hands stubbornly working on the small ring of creation. She lay the journal down on her stomach, looking for a long time at the swaying trees, and decided that she was there to hear Dale's side of the argument. She picked up the journal and wrote that she meant to compare his truth to her own.

She put the pen down again, ashamed for having given the impression in her journal that she already knew the truth, her side of the argument, and had pretended to compare it to someone else's. Future readers would be misled, and she wavered over crossing it out and replacing it with something more truthful. But she didn't. She was certain that she almost had it. It was just there, just close enough that she was about to grab it, to figure it out. All she needed was for Dale to reveal his own so that she could erect a structure from it just as she had done with the Croatian poet. It would be a step closer. Another piece of scaffolding to press against the outside of the great truth she was constructing, this edifice against the emptiness rising into the white misty light of everything above her, the great unknown austere sublime.

X

She got up and left Paul sleeping. Dishes clinked and water ran in the kitchen and she thought she could make herself useful with dinner. She didn't need Paul there all the time. She could be independent and talk to his parents without him. If he came to find her she might be casually leaning on the counter, popping a cherry tomato into her mouth and talking to his father on a stool. She wouldn't have lectured, not even once.

As she approached the kitchen, she heard dog tags clinking and the scritch of claws on the tile and was greeted by Ginger, who butted her hand with her snout. She knelt and said, "Hello," and touched her gently behind the ears so that when she came into the kitchen she was accompanied.

Dale was sitting at the counter, just as she had imagined, and Gloria had her back against the sink. They were both

I Want You to Tell Me

holding large mugs and Dale said, "I see you've attracted a loyal follower."

"I inspire loyalty in all my subjects," she said, and scratched Ginger behind the ears.

Though Dale's eyes crinkled in the corners, Gloria's face didn't change at the joke at all, as if it were blank, as if something inside her just didn't have the capacity to register silliness.

Sasha knew from Paul that Gloria had been the oldest of six children, had worked hard to raise her siblings, and hadn't gotten much of a break between raising them and raising her own children. She had only been twenty when she married Dale. She wanted to ask now how they met, but those kinds of questions didn't seem appropriate to ask Gloria. There was something like a nun about her, a mother superior in training. She walked with the posture of someone shielding a candle, devout and focused. Sasha considered Gloria's life a kind of tragedy before having even met her, and now, seeing how fully unbothered by her life Gloria seemed, the tragedy deepened. Paul told her how she had attended each school play and Christmas concert, and how now, even with her children grown, she still attended. "Oh, she must love going down to the city to see shows on Broadway then. We could get her tickets!" she had said. Paul got uncomfortable and said his mother probably wouldn't want to, or never did things like that anyway. It dawned on Sasha that Gloria wouldn't have even considered getting in the car and traveling a few hours south for something as world class as the ballet at Lincoln Center or the opera at the Met. Those things just weren't for people like her. It would have been frivolous. A school play would do just as well. She didn't need all that, didn't seek out excitement, she just took what was offered. She had probably lost her virginity to

Dale, or some other straight-laced farm boy, which she probably still regretted. And though Gloria would likely judge people wanting to do things like going out to parties or bars or clubs to meet people, to have fun, it was really actually that she didn't even conceive of them as options that made what came across as strictness just actually a failure to comprehend the many other things available to her that other people might actually want. What terrified her about Gloria was not that Gloria wouldn't like her, it was that Gloria wouldn't even be able to comprehend her, even if she tried, and that being herself around Gloria would be something close to an affront. It stifled her.

And what could Dale love in her, in Gloria? She was practical, true, but there was no sex in her anywhere, seemingly no imagination. It was like a studied absence of personality. However, she could picture her at a high school musical with both hands in her lap, laughing in spite of herself at something on stage. The faintest glimmer of pity entered her then, even as Gloria's reserve in all other things frightened her.

"There's coffee in the pot, if you'd like some," Gloria said.

"Might help wake you up after your nap," Dale said, and she wondered if they had heard, or suspected, what had just happened in the bedroom.

She decided to brush right over that.

"Oh, God yes," she said, "that would be wooonderful." It seemed appropriate that a college girl like herself would be starved for things like coffee. She chose a cup that looked like an old airstream camping trailer.

"Dale just loves tacky cups."

"I find them at the tag sales," he said, and lifted his cup toward her, which had a giraffe growing from the handle. She giggled as he slid a small blue bowl of sugar toward her.

I Want You to Tell Me

She asked about their days off, the weather, and couldn't help getting back to the topic of their work. She asked Dale how he had gotten started in landscaping.

"How did you know you loved it?" she asked.

Something crossed his eyes, as if there was yet another thing she had missed. She gripped at her coffee mug.

"Well, I s'pose it had to do with my father. We came over from Ireland when I was still very young, and it was my father worked in stone, and sometimes he'd have me out with him, working on little things, patios or brick work." She hadn't noticed it, but the tiniest twinge of an Irish accent had entered his speech, like remembering his father had brought it back. "We were outside of Boston then. Lots of brick work there, all those old brownstones, and I s'pose it was because that's what was there. I just fell into it."

His work had nothing to do with love, she realized. It was because he didn't have a choice. She had been naïve again, privileged.

"Did you ever want to do anything else?" The question came out of her so quickly that she only saw how it could be insulting once it was gone.

"Oh, I don't know. Maybe long ago I had some notions."

"Notions?" Gloria said.

"Of artistic grandeur," Sasha said, playfully.

"Oh no, not grandeur. Not for me. They were always vague. I saw myself at university though, like you two, you and Pauly. What I'd do there who knows. History maybe."

"So you never went?"

He shook his head. "Pauly's the first of us to give it a go."

She nodded, and as if he saw some disappointment in her face he added, "I did like it though, stone. And being with dad. We did quick work then."

"Is it like play sometimes, losing yourself in the work, when it's really flowing?"

"Play?" he asked. A strange look dragged itself across his face as Gloria made a noise that sounded somewhere between a laugh and a scoff.

"Ah no, sometimes maybe, I see what you mean about the flow, when you forget the day and time just flies by." He paused, and she kept thinking of him building that small stone circle, how easy it had been, how perfectly he had created its small beauty. It had been play, whether he thought so or not. She knew that she would always think of him bent over and hacking small pieces off a corner of stone with his hammer.

"But no," he continued, "it has always felt more like work to me, specially now that I'm older, you know, with these old bones."

"You don't seem at all old to me," she said.

He waved her off and Gloria walked into the pantry, as though this too had been inappropriate to say.

"But you lose yourself in it, don't you, the work? It happens to me at school. Suddenly I look up and it's night time."

"Oh yes, yes, you do lose yourself, you do," Dale said.

She thought of her father then, how she had never seen him lose himself, immerse himself in his work. At the computer he always sat very straight, the chair a little pushed back from the desk, his sleeves rolled up and arms hovering above the keys as if he was trying to avoid infection. His head always seemed slightly turned to the side, one eye in a squint, as if whatever was on the screen might infect him. He tapped away like that, his pointer fingers like little beaks pecking at the keys, and though he was brilliant in all of these ways, it was as if he could only approach the great ideas from a distance, as though he were observing them from afar, cataloging them without ever really letting them course through his body, his hands, and out through the keyboard where they could be projected onto the screen. They weren't his at all.

This thought made her sad. She slumped back against the counter and looked out the window where a mass of gray clouds hovered over the barn roof.

"It will be you and Pauly though, you young ones, who go on to do the great things," Dale said quietly. His eyes caught hers for a moment, and she knew it then: he saw the world just as she did, the emptiness they were both pushing against.

XI

She eased the door open and looked in on Paul. He had wadded up the blanket and was straddling it, an arm thrown over both pillows which he had jammed under his head. Late afternoon light fell across the room in an architecture of geometric slabs. His hair was hanging over his eyes, like a boy's. He was probably dreaming of riding on four-wheelers, chain-sawing something, dragging it out of the woods. His arms looked big and muscular over the pillows, the blanket scrunched up in his crotch like he was defiling it. His sexual urge was so strong that she wondered sometimes if it even had anything to do with her or whether she could just be any girl. Something naked for him to empty himself into. That's what he was probably dreaming about: Girls. Or Kate. He must still sometimes dream about Kate so that the blankets would squirm alive until he was helpless to them, taken over.

She pulled the pillows out from under his head.

"Oh! What the hell!"

"Wake up sleepy butt!" she said, and jumped on him. She straddled his body and pinned his arms down.

"Did you have a nice dream?"

"Well, I was having one." His speech was slurred and muddy.

"I bet you were."

"Yeah, until you came along."

"I just ruin everything, don't I?"

"Yes," he said, in a dreamy voice, and pulled her down toward him, closing his eyes and nuzzling her.

"This isn't one of your dreams. I'm not just some girl you can straddle like a blanket and empty your juices into."

"Jesus. I wasn't even doing that."

"I know; I'm crazy."

"You're not crazy. God. Just, let me wake up like a normal person."

"Sorry, no time. Dinner's soon. I'm supposed to come and wake you up. Your mom's been slaving away in the kitchen."

"No one's slaving."

"Except for your mom."

"Right, except for her."

She was quiet a moment, a thought occurring to her as she ran her fingers through Paul's curly hair, which made his head fall back, his eyes close.

"It doesn't bother you that she does all the cooking?

"What? No, she likes to cook."

"Are you sure?"

"I don't know. Yeah, I think so. She's always done it."

"Yeah, but that's what I mean. It seems pretty old fashioned, doesn't it?"

"Old fashioned?" His eyes were open again.

"Yeah, a woman cooking and cleaning."

"Oh stop."

"Stop? Why, you think I'm wrong?" She pushed herself back against the headboard.

"Why are you always picking fights?"

"I'm not. We're just having a discussion."

"No, I just, listen, you don't have to come here and start criticizing my family."

"I wasn't! I was just asking if you thought she liked it."

"Clearly you don't. Clearly you think she's trapped in some warped old gender dynamic, right?"

"I mean."

"Just stop."

He pushed himself away from her and rolled out of bed.

"Hey!" she said.

"Hey what? I'm just getting up."

"Yeah, and pushing me out of the way."

"I didn't. Ah God. Whatever."

"Well, don't expect me to be like that, okay, cooking and cleaning up after you all your life."

"What!? I didn't expect that. When did I ever say that?"

"I'm just saying."

"You know, fuck you. My mom works super hard too. It's just how they divided things up."

"And it just so conveniently happened that it broke down perfectly along gender lines?"

She realized as she said this that she had totally and completely exonerated Dale in her thinking, as if Gloria, in her old fashioned stoicism, had taken on the role and expected him to do the same. That she had created this and would think less of her husband if he didn't go out and work.

"You know, I wonder if your dad would have been happier if it hadn't been that way. I mean, he was saying earlier that he wished he had gone to school. To university!"

"What!?"

"Yeah."

"Listen," he said, holding a white t-shirt in front of him and taking a long deep breath. "I appreciate that you're thinking about relationship dynamics and that you're curious about my parents' relationship and all that, it just, right now, it just seems like you're dissecting my whole family life and upbringing and judging it all pretty hard, in the span of, oh, I don't know, an afternoon. I mean, I could do the same for your parents, by the way."

"Ha, oh yeah?"

"Was that sarcastic?"

She realized she didn't know. Behind Paul, through the window, she saw the hillside suddenly burst into orange light, four telephone poles shining, the wires spanned between them like bright orange liquid. It was as if the sun had chosen, for just this moment, to shine all of its light on this one spot instead of all the others.

"Well, I don't want it to be that way," she said, her voice distracted, distant.

"Okay me neither, but you know, there are more delicate ways to bring these things up."

"Delicate never got anything done," she said, and folded her hands decisively in her lap.

"Yeah, it just pissed off the people that love you."

She looked up at him as if he had slid aside the curtain of the argument. He widened his eyes as if to say "Come on, you're attacking the wrong person." They regarded each other for a long time, their eyes flicking back and forth in the silence like a decision was waiting to be made.

Finally she swung her legs off the bed, went over and put her arms around his waist.

"Come here, Mr. Patriarchy."

"Oh, fuck you."

XIII

Dinner was rich: carrots; peas; squash; rice and chicken; white rolls thick with butter. They ate with the last of the sun disappearing behind the smoke-blue mountains. The heavy food pushed them from the house into the cool of the night air. Sasha was wearing one of Gloria's coats. "None of what you have is thick enough," she had said.

Sasha asked to see the donkeys so she could say hello before it got fully dark. They walked as a group down the driveway, scuffing the gravel as the dogs ran out ahead of them. She told them that the house she had lived in for the first twelve years of her life, in the suburbs outside of Boston, was next to a couple who owned donkeys. "They used to keep them in their garage. I used to go over there and open the little back door to let them out into the yard, which was all fenced in."

"Sad to live in the suburbs with farm animals," Dale said. The group was walking slowly, and Gloria added that it was nice that she had some access to animals though.

"Yes," Sasha said. "I used to go there as much as I could after school. I was obsessed!" She smiled and shook her head at this younger version of herself, could see herself running up the sloped driveway, clinking the side gate shut, opening the back door to the warm thick smell. "The donkeys were so sweet. And they were a nice couple too. Once they trusted me, they left me alone with the donkeys and I even fed them and everything. They had a whole bunch of children. I think some of them were theirs and others were adopted. I was just another little body, running around in their back yard, shrieking and playing with the donkeys. Anyway, I think it was really donkeys that led me to horses. I just fell in love with them and their round dark snouts. And they had such big ears! I used to hold them and whisper stuff about school into them the way I had seen in a children's book and then I would stare right into the donkey's big eye to make sure he had understood. I always thought that he had. This was the gray one. There was one that was gray, and one that was brown, and the gray one, he was my listener."

"That all sounds very Catholic," Dale said, and chuckled.

"More than you know," she said. The story she had never told occurred to her then. She could tell it, now.

"Oh?" Dale said. He slowed, and Gloria and Paul, who had begun to move ahead, turned to look back at her. She had an audience, and for the first time that day it seemed like they all wanted to listen. She decided to tell them with a little zip of nervous energy bouncing up through her.

"Once," she said, "the couple took in a man. I think he was some kind of vagrant. I'm not sure. He was dirty and down on his luck. He had a big beard and they showered him and he wore the man's clothes. Anyhow, I liked brushing the donkeys. It was something I did way more than I needed to. Donkeys don't need all that much brushing, but I loved standing next to them and doing something nice for them and imagining the gray one carrying me to Jerusalem just as if I were Mary. I liked the idea of that, of carrying this incredible, this special thing to a place where it could be born, Joseph silent and strong next to me. Anyway, this vagrant, as I've come to think of him, would come in and talk to me. For whatever reason it was me more than any of the other children that he talked to. He had this long hair and was missing a tooth. I was fascinated by the black gap in his mouth, this shadow keyhole that he often ran his tongue through. He'd sit in this lawn chair while I brushed. It was one of those kinds made out of aluminum, you know, with the little plastic straps?"

They nodded, and the group started to move again. She had them now.

"Well, he'd ask me to come sit on his lap as if I was just another child, sitting up on his knee. All the others out in the yard, running around and playing their games. And I did, and he would talk to me quietly as the silence curled in around us, keeping everyone out and his hand would go up my skirt. Just like that, right up. Foop!" And she repeated the quick motion with her hand.

"Jesus, Sash," Paul said as he turned right around. "You never told me that."

"Oh, yeah, I don't know. It wasn't anything so big." She was flushed over having such a story to tell. A shocking revelation. This terrible thing. Her eyes sparkled across at Paul. She had won something from him. Her past had supplanted his. She wasn't just some stupid girl who hadn't known things. Bad things had happened to her. Trauma. Though it had never felt serious enough for that. She was strangely removed from it. And there was a smooth beauty in being able to tell it so lightly, as though it were so long ago, a straight translucent highway back to that afternoon, and the few after, which she had kept to herself.

"Sounds big," Paul said. His eyes were hard, intense, hurt.

She shrugged, her face still held in easy nonchalance. "It was all so long ago," she said, and felt very adult as she said that. Gloria must not think of her as some stupid girl now.

"Long ago or not," Paul said. "It's still just." He stopped and squinted up at the hills.

"He never did anything more than that. I always wriggled off him, or he'd give me a quick nudge if any of the children were about to stomp in."

"Do you know what happened to him? I mean, could you turn the guy in now?" Paul asked.

"I don't know. I don't remember his name and I don't even remember the couple's names either. I think he moved out a little while later because the marriage fell apart, only the woman lived there after that, and a while later, they came and took the donkeys. It was probably too much for her, what with all the children.

"Fuckin people," Paul said, shaking his head.

"Language Pauly," his mother said.

"Well Jesus mom, did you hear what she said?"

"I know, I know," though it seemed to Sasha that Gloria had thought this an inappropriate thing to bring up.

Sasha just continued to make a face that said, "Well, that's what happened," her lips pressed together, and every time Paul looked at her, he'd shake his head. "That makes me so fricken mad."

She took his arm and remembered how the donkeys had walked up a narrow metal plank into the trailer after the man moved out and how the people who came to get the donkeys were strangers. The woman had most likely sold them. Her gray donkey, the one with the big ears, her first listener, first audience, and the shadow of the vagrant behind him, always in that chair, slouching.

Even though Paul had been the one to get angry, and had given her the reaction she wanted, she realized that it had been for Dale's benefit that she had told the story. He had been silent, had said nothing at all, and she was curious about what was in his silence.

Darkness began to pool in the bushes along the side of the road, the forsythia with their long pointy branches that would burst into allergic dandelion yellow in the weeks ahead. She kept pace with Dale's very slow long walk, the big steps he took, and soon disentangled herself from Paul and let him wander on with his mother until there was a fine distance between them. How easily mother and son were in conversation, how they looked like a painting, the son returned from the world in which he had made something of himself and the mother still able to give advice, she who had raised him, and wandered along with him now into the chalky twilight.

Sasha was the woman he had brought back with him, who was now walking slowly along with the father, in a tender, slightly nervous, shy silence. They were still trailing along with them the story she had told, as though it were the gathering darkness following them. His silence was an invitation to speak, and so she thought that she would ask him the question that had been waiting and growing inside her all day. From the start, Dale had a look of knowing, of cheerful kindness. They could see each other clearly, she thought, and the silences and misunderstandings of the day were just like two magnets whose reversed poles pushed at each other. All that was needed was for one magnet to flip and they'd click together.

Paul and his mother had made it to the fence and leaned against it as they looked down the empty field and across the valley. Again, she got the sense of the landscape as a painting, the feeling of being myth before the myth was created. It was as if she were looking at the image as a much older person who had the benefit of placing it in its correct sequence of events, of knowing what it would come to mean.

"Looks like the donkeys aren't there," she said with trailing disappointment.

"Sometimes they head back at dark."

She nodded. "I guess I won't have anyone to whisper my secrets too," and laughed.

"It looks that way."

"I probably shouldn't have told that story."

He looked off down the road and didn't say anything, as if it wasn't for him to decide.

"It made Paul upset."

Dale nodded, but he still did not look at her.

"What's the truth, Dale," she said, turning and touching his arm at the elbow. "You have it, don't you? I know you do. You've thought about so many things. I knew today, in the garden, when you were talking about things not lasting, that you have it. What is it for you, the truth?"

His surprised face stared back at her and he lifted his arm a little, as if trying to wriggle a worm off it.

"Oh, I'm sorry. Paul tells me I always come on too strong and scare people off with my personal questions." She released his arm.

"Oh, no, that's all right," he said, and brushed at his sleeve as if he were getting some dirt off it.

"Do you know what I mean, though? Do you know what I'm asking?"

"Well, I'm not sure I do, no."

There was a long silence. She had thought that he would just understand her, that he'd be able to read it in the air and then slowly, after having thought about how best to say it, that he would tell her gently as they approached Paul and Gloria, so that they would carry it between them as they stepped into the painting along the rails of the fence, the beginning of the myth.

Now she wasn't sure what to say, how to describe it. "It's, you know, my professor says all the great artists have it, and, and, well, I was watching you building that wall around that little tree today and I could tell that you have it too. That you understand beauty, how to create it. It was so easy for you. So natural. Like you knew just what you were doing, building this little structure against all that emptiness, that meaninglessness, right?"

"Oh, I don't know. It just needed doing is all."

She looked helplessly at Dale and then stared back toward Paul and his mother, who were draped in the twilight romance of their posture. Tears came into her eyes.

"But it was how you did it that mattered. My father, he never does anything like it really matters. He's successful, but he doesn't live into anything he does." She was quiet, torn between bitterness and hope. "Maybe I'm all wrong," she said.

"Oh no, I don't think so. None of us are all wrong, are we? We just muddle through." He looked at her so warmly then.

"Then what is it Dale? What's the truth?" And she reached for his arm again.

"The truth?" he said. He looked off down the road, uncomfortable, and he reminded her of Paul in that moment when she expected things from him that he couldn't give to her. But no, Dale had much more to give than Paul, didn't he?

"I was just hoping," she said, "I wanted to know what it was for you, what your truth is," she said. "For some dumb reason I thought you had it. The big truth. All of it. That you had understood. Am I making sense?"

His eyes skirted over her, and his face fell into a tangle. He bit his lower lip.

"Oh, I'm not sure of any truth," he said, as if he were shaking the conversation away.

She looked at him pleadingly.

He pressed his lips into a tight smile as if he hadn't understood her at all.

She stopped then. It was shame that knifed in then.

As if saying goodbye, he squeezed her wrist and lifted her hand from his arm and walked off to join Gloria and Paul. His big boots scuffed the gravel as the distance between them spanned.

She was alone, stung. Her body paralyzed so that she couldn't move. Instead, she watched Dale as her circulation rushed and pricked through her. The farther he got the more he turned into a dark, featureless form, a silhouette. When he reached Paul and Gloria he stood next to them like a sentinel, tall and straight, guarding them against her. It wasn't a painting anymore. It seemed ludicrous, her fantasy about them, as the whole painterly wash fell from the scene. What was left was just a remote farm field on a dead-end dirt road where they stood leaning against a weather-beaten fence set firmly in the smallness of reality. And there she was, staring at them from up the road after she had told this story about herself and for what? It didn't bring them any closer. It didn't advance the truth. It was just wasted, wasted on them, wasted on Paul's anger, on Gloria's judgment, on Dale's incomprehension. The small, dark, hardened kernel of the sadness inside her that she now recognized as some essential self had been betrayed. She had tried to shine a light on it, to open a chink in the dark wall that held it in. She had wished to reach through illusion toward some essential truth in another person. Was that so dumb to wish for, to try for? Or was that also just another dumb thing to think was possible? Was it all just stupid fantasies? The darkening sky, the gravel road, and the field that shifted in and out of reality, the horror of the three shadows who turned from her along the fence.

She began to back away from them in a slow cautious panic as a kind of buzzing static filled the air, lowered through it, an emptiness that began to cloud them out. She backed into the cover of the stand of trees that arched over the road, the darkness that sifted through the branches, the inkiness that took her back into itself, pin-pricked her skin with apprehension until she couldn't see them at all anymore through the blaring dark emptiness. They had disappeared and all that was left was the distant barking of dogs.

She turned then, and ran, as fast as she could, the whole world transforming into a bright white terror.

WATCH ME

IT'S HIGH TIDE and the water has turned the beach into a narrow strip of colorful stalled traffic where towels and beach umbrellas and coolers are arranged along the base of the sand-dune cliffs. Abby lies on her stomach with her face on her hands playing adult as her three young new foster siblings build a sand fort out of buckets and driftwood under her supposed supervision. She follows the progress of a boy and a girl as they pick through the crowd toward them, scanning for a place to settle. They're older than her, in college maybe, and they're together. A couple. They're not here with their parents. She tries to imagine it. "There?" she hears the girl ask as they come alongside her family's spot. "Yeah," the guy says, and gives Abby a friendly look, like he's about to scoot next to her on the bleacher at a baseball game. He slides the two beach chairs and an umbrella from his shoulder and blocks the sun to become a silhouette. The light haloes behind him. Her eyes catch on the angle of his body, on the way he lets the bags hover for just a second inches above the sand before his fingers release the straps. When they fall his eyes strike up and catch her looking as the sun blasts free across his shoulder and something like a tight shock of surprise registers in her chest and flares outward.

From then on, a bright tension shines on her from the spot where the guy is arranging their site in his red swim shorts. She wonders if he really is that much older than her before she decides to ignore him, to pretend he isn't there at all.

Abby shakes the sand out of her discarded book and begins to focus on the words, tries to follow their logic down the row of one sentence and then another, but a hitch in her concentration makes her peer over the top of her page at their new neighbor who is flicking off his flip flops. He's definitely older than her, she decides. College or maybe even after. The ages above her disappear into a vast openness of undefined bass-heavy music and cars with tinted windows and college dorms and parties she can't quite imagine. Maybe he's the same age as the volleyball guys who cranked their radio, popped beers open out of floppy green cooler bags, walked to the water in long uneven lines, tackled each other so they careened into the waves like logs. How they whooped and shouted and made enough noise for everyone to notice.

But he isn't loud, her new neighbor.

And he isn't like that one tall pale skinny guy from the day before who peered at her from under his white visor, as if his eyes were touching her, curling into her towel. All day she kept her beach dress on over her suit, and when she went to swim, she ran into the ocean as quickly as possible to hide in the waves.

As she fought her way up out of the pebbly surf, he had stopped her, wavering in and out of definition with the sun behind him.

"Hey, we're playing volleyball down the beach, if you want to come."

She shook her head, ran for her towel, and fell into its crumpled rectangle of safety.

"What did he say to you?" her mother asked.

"He asked if I wanted to play volleyball."

"And what did you tell him?"

"No, of course."

"Good. You don't need to talk to those older boys."

"I know." She had done the right thing and now they were still on her about it.

"They shouldn't be asking you to begin with."

Her father coughed in agreement from his chair, where he was reading a nautical history.

"Why not?" she shot out.

"You know why dear."

"Actually, I don't, please explain it to me."

Her mother gave her a look that meant she was being needlessly difficult.

"I don't think I have to explain to you why it's inappropriate for an older young man to ask a young lady like yourself, a fourteen-year-old, to go and play volleyball."

"I'm not a 'young lady,' ugh," she said. "Plus, it's only volleyball."

"It's never only volleyball," her father said.

The air above the dunes turned glassy.

"No, then what is it?"

His book lowered just an inch.

"Don't start."

"Walter," her mother said, but she looked at Abby with something like concern, pity, and loyalty to her father. Her eyebrows furrowed, a bit perplexed, as if Abby was supposed to know what they meant without ever having to explain it.

Why couldn't they just say it?

But they never would. Instead, it was a danger flaring around them, caught up in the glare of the sun over the far part of the beach where the volleyball players shouted and laughed.

***

No, the guy next to them is playful. He lifts his shirt over his head and throws it over the girl's face and she giggles and says, "Hey!" Abby stifles a laugh, as if he has thrown it on her. She bites her lip and looks away. She wants to go back to reading, to recapture a warm feeling the book has given her.

But she can't concentrate. Instead, she decides to let herself observe him, to give herself full permission, even with her mother sitting right next to her. Something like a bubble of excitement rises up in her chest.

He is shoving the white spiked pole of the umbrella into the sand. He rocks his butt back and forth to get it farther in while his forearms hold it tight. The girl is laughing at him again, so he shakes his butt at her. He keeps working the base of the umbrella, his forearms muscled and tan.

A few feet away her father sinks down into his chair and his thin hairy white arm lifts a sweating can of Diet Coke out of its cupholder and her mother's legs are hugged tight by denim shorts clamped over the arterial patterns of varicose veins bruised on her thighs.

The girl unpacks a blanket and flaps it open in the breeze and lets it fall to the sand, so delicately. Then she tucks the edges of it in to keep the wind from blowing it into a sail. She wears her hair down in a neatly brushed side part. His hair is all in a mess, like it still has salt in it from the day before. The girl must like to be with a messy boy, a boy who doesn't care about hair or neat clothes. The idea of this difference sends nervous sparks down her legs connected somehow to the static bristle of his hair, as if it has come too close to her.

Her mother sighs, scans the beach, and asks why Abby doesn't go on a little walk, now that the children have stopped paying attention to her for one second. "I used to love taking long walks on the beach all by myself when I was a young woman," she adds. Abby had already imagined herself doing this later in the day, of turning into a small lonely silhouette in the distance for everyone to wonder about. But now, since her mother has suggested it, the idea is ruined. It's not hers anymore. She'd just be doing what her mom wanted, a young woman who goes on long thoughtful walks. "Or just lie around on your towel all day," her mother says, even though they've only been at the beach for maybe an hour. "Fine, I will!" Abby mutters, afraid he'll hear her mother suggesting things to her as if she's a little girl and not a young woman.

She lingers on the towel, torn between staying in protest and walking off as if she were forced to. "Ugh," she says, stands, kicks the towel loose, and circles up behind the couple and forces herself not to look at him.

Soon the towels and beach umbrellas thin out, the lifeguard stand blends into the air behind her and the squeals of people getting splashed by waves grow dim. The beach stretches into openness. On her right, the dunes are a long wall of cool shadow that run the length of the beach. She comes across a wrecked lobster cage, a black trash bag tossed over the side of the dune, and a plastic blue tampon applicator. On her left the ocean has been poured into the basin between continents and she squats to place her palms over its foamy outer rim, the farthest, thinnest extension of its reaching. The bubbles brush through her outstretched fingers, then suck back, sluicing past her ankles. She jumps up, is zapped by the delight of her sudden companionship with a presence so massive, so full of noise and movement and endless ineffable silence, this life force that does not speak but seems to notice her nonetheless, that she runs through the splashy shallows as the sandpipers whir their mechanized legs to avoid her and a gull swoops down in a low angle across her path and squawks. The sea spray is lit up as she dashes into its golden haze hoping to be subsumed, to turn into a golden sparkle under the eyes of God.

As she comes back she passes beach walkers with their dogs, a couple far off alone on a blanket, and soon, the small encampments that multiply until she sees her parents, her father like a slumped Roman field general in his chair under the shadow of its canopy, her siblings scattered around the fort in front of their towels, and the couple parked in their spot. This time she'll walk in front of them, she decides, as the tension rises along the swell of the high tide behind her.

"Abby! Abby!" her siblings shout as they take off toward her, kicking up sand as they go. She lifts the oldest, Marquis, into a wide arc, and swings him around her. Laquisha and DeShawn crowd around saying, "Do me, do me! Lift me!" And she does, aware that she is now part of the show.

"Where'd you go, Abby, why'd you leave us?"

"To go for a walk. To be by the ocean," she says, quieter now, as if he is listening, as if he'll know how she ran when no one could see her, ran as hard and as fast as she possibly could until every pent-up squeeze of muscle was all worn out and she collapsed into the shallow waters and let the ocean come up and touch the outline of her body and seep away underneath her, as if it was trying to suck her back into the sea.

"And what did *you* rapscallions do while *I* was gone?" she asks, itching to get off this stage she has walked onto, in full display. The children break out in a chatter over her as she skips to her towel, shakes her hair out, pats herself dry.

They tell her all about the fort they built until DeShawn loses interest and yells like a soldier diving for cover on a small bank of sand right next to the couple, immediately checking to make sure they've noticed him.

"Whoa!" the guy says.

DeShawn laughs gleefully as his siblings sit down in a silent pair to watch him do it again.

"Look at our little performer," Abby's mother says.

Abby smiles in shared recognition as DeShawn gets set, runs up, and does sit again, this time making a sound as if he has exploded.

"Always looking for attention, that one," her mother says.

"He just likes people," Abby decides to say.

"Oh, I know," her mother says, then looks at her with both appreciation and appraisal. "What would they do without you, their little protector?"

"I am not."

"Well, I'm very proud of how well you've adapted, how much you've taken on being a sister to them, a sister and a kind of a mother too."

Abby lifts a handful of sand and lets it run through her fingers and says, "It's what God would want," but feels immediately stupid for saying exactly what her mother would want to hear because it has nothing to do with God. The love was immediate. Plus, selfishly, she likes the role she is playing with them. Quite often, she thinks, her ideas are better than her mother's.

"Yes, he would be quite happy with you," her mother says as a long dark strand of hair is caught in the corner of her mouth, the wind lifting and dropping it, her eyes squinting in the light as if she were looking out at the open water where God was watching the family, the destiny of this small encampment on the beach, the lives of these three young children, and Abby, thrown together in a sudden configuration of potent meaning.

Again, DeShawn flies through the air and hits the sand bank, making even bigger exploding noises, this little human grenade. Abby smiles at her little brother and, without thinking, takes her mother's hand where it hangs from the end of the chair and lays her cheek on it.

"I hope we can keep them," Abby says.

"Me too. So much," her mother says.

"You're not getting hurt?" the neighbor girl asks him in a high sweet voice, as if she's the friendly new babysitter.

"No!"

"Okay, well, be careful though," she says in a voice that Abby thinks sounds too sweet, too over-nurturing, too fake, the way she used to talk to them when they first joined the family.

"I'll make sure nothing goes wrong," Abby says to her mother, lifting her towel to be closer to the children. She says it loud enough so that the guy can hear her, so he'll know that she's moving closer only to keep a watch on the children, nothing else.

"Booom!" DeShawn says, crashing into the sand again.

"Wow, that was a big explosion," the guy says.

They probably want to be left alone. It's too much, having these kids blowing up all around them. She can protect their quiet, Abby thinks.

But the air goes all loud and clangy when she considers how to start. She jumps up, says, "A race. Who wants to go for a race?" tugging the words out of her throat as if they are made of bent up metal.

She begins to run half-heartedly, but the children do not move and now she is standing directly in front of him with her legs caught in mid-stride and the words hanging stupidly in the air behind her.

"Come on," she says, "leave these poor people alone!"

Then she dashes off and the children book it after her so they're not abandoned, flinging sand from their feet as they cut for the waves. His eyes pursue her straight into the water—she's sure of it, even if she's just a stupid little girl playing mother.

***

"Bee." He calls her "Bee," and sometimes he says, "My bumble." Abby wonders what the name could stand for: Beatrice? They are playing catch with a small red football that looks like a kidney bean. When she misses, he calls her, "Stumble bee."

Abby studies the girl, though she has wanted to ignore her. She is blond, wears a light pink flowery bathing suit, almost paisley. She's pretty, has small features and a large forehead that makes her face seem smaller and cuter. An acute shot of envy tightens Abby's eyes, though she considers that her own face is easily just as pretty. She is not allowed to think this, as it is immodest, but she thinks it must be true. Others have told her.

But it's his name Abby is waiting for. When Bee throws the football, it kinks and wobbles far to the left, and she says, "Come on, Fuzz, you gotta catch that. Show me those moves, Fuzzy Bear."

Fuzz. She whispers it: "Fuzz."

He must have a formal name too, though she can't guess it.

He dives into the sand and the ball hits his shoulder, his head. She bends over laughing.

"What?" he keeps saying obliviously. "What? Is that not how you're supposed to catch footballs?"

Watch Me

He's skinny, except for a little lip of pudge on his lower belly, like a man's. But that's what he is, after all, isn't he? A man? The thought sends cold water runnelling down the inside of her stomach.

The children have gathered in a line to watch them play and make up a ridiculous score-keeping system, shouting out numbers every time one of them throws the ball: "70 points, 10 points, 50 points, 85 points, 90 points."

"That throw wasn't worth 50?" Fuzz says. "The last one I threw was 90 and it was terrible!"

"Fine! 65!" DeShawn shouts.

"70!" Fuzz says.

DeShawn is suddenly shy. As if he doesn't know what to do with all the joking and attention.

"Only give me the high numbers," Bee says, with a kidding laugh.

"Do you see what she's doing here? You can't just let her win," Fuzz says.

The children aren't sure what to do. But in a second they start yelling scores again. Abby comes up from behind them and wraps her arms around Laquisha, her little part-sister. She squeezes her and tightens a pink ribbon in her hair. Laquisha is a small shield in front of Abby. She is giving her permission to sit and watch. To be part of the audience. Abby can take Laquisha's braid out and do it over again slowly, or she can hold her little hands.

Fuzz walks over to DeShawn and shows him how to throw the football, right next to her. He smells like sunscreen and sweat and warmth and campfire smoke. He tells him where to put his fingers. There is uneven stubble on his cheeks, patchy. His arms are much darker than his body. They must have only been at the beach for a day or two. Maybe she will see them again tomorrow. A swell of hope runs through her.

No one has been introduced. The children have just come over and lined up to watch. She wonders if Fuzz will extend his hand down to her. "I'm Fuzz," he'll say, and she'll take his hand. But he doesn't, even though she is the big sister and should deserve to get an introduction. Instead she watches, like one of the children.

Bee has stopped playing and takes her red-and-white-striped beach dress off to go swimming. Did they ruin the game by coming over to watch? She wishes it wouldn't stop, that they would be drawn into it and soon they'd all be playing together.

Fuzz gives the ball to DeShawn, telling him to throw it to Marquis. "Or you can throw it to your big sister," he says, and looks right at her. It takes her a second to realize that he's talking about her. The sun lights up his hair all golden from behind, his focus fully on her, a smile on his mouth, his hands on the football. She slackens. She knows then that he saw her right from the start, that he was just waiting to come talk to her.

All she can do is stare upward as if she's gone empty, her eyes brown and bottomless—spread into nothing. She forgets that she could say something. Instead, she just twists her mouth and looks back up at him from a small X of silence made by her crossed legs.

An unsure smile gets caught on his face and he hands the ball to DeShawn.

Then he's gone. He leads Bee by the hand and they stand together in the waves. She is sick with failure; she doesn't understand what has just happened. It went too quickly. She wants to run back, say something to him, pull him back out of the water so she can try again. The invitation in his voice

Watch Me

was right there. She could have responded, gotten up from the small spot on the sand. Now she is craned, twisted to watch him, suddenly anonymous in the shallows.

***

Now, each time she looks, he is there. Back in his chair. His face turns, slow as a lighthouse beam, and the nervous current bunches up in her stomach. His sight lands right where she is sitting so she freezes, stares back desperately. Feels knotted, thorny, dark, complicated. Intense.

The beam passes on. Is she a ruined thing? As her eyes follow it, the belief that she isn't washes over her silent twisted lip, unknots the intensity, reveals her beneath. She is hopeful as his eye casts over the beach with the silence of a beam of light. She is taken along with it, stretched out to the entire length of the beach, spun along the shoreline, her nervousness dancing and sweeping and crashing along the white furl of surf.

He holds a notebook, stares at the water, draws something on it. His hands take shapes from where the sun has lit them and plants them in his book. When he slides the notebook into his bag she thinks she sees drawings of umbrellas, towels, a body lounging on the beach. Has he taken her?

She lies on her towel and faces away from him. She reads her book. The black words are stamped onto the white glare of the page, they separate, float free, move through her and are lost to the concentrated glow of his presence. It draws her toward him, constantly.

She gets up from her towel and does the only thing that occurs to her: she tips her head forward and lets her long, curly dark hair fall down in front of her and then gathers it back up. His face is close in profile, looking out to the water, inclining toward her as though his eyes are one with the sun, present in every particle of light and air over the beach. His watching is spread over everything.

When she rights herself, she pretends just to be squinting out to where a tiny tanker moves in centimeters across the horizon, just as he pretends not to see her. She lets her hands run back up through her curls to reach and bundle it all at the top of her head where she holds the posture, like a sculpture on her plinth of sand.

She drops her hair again, gathers it up, drops and gathers as all the noise of the beach recedes into silence and the waves break on a shore of felt in wooly linings of foam. In this silence, still as water, tense as waiting, a jumble of darting bugs shoot across the interior of her stomach and leave electric ripples everywhere.

"Don't you think you've untangled your hair by now, dear?" her mother asks, and Abby lets it fall, startled, exposed, as she stares at the water for a long terrified moment.

"I guess I forgot what I was doing," she mumbles, before she gathers it up into a quick ponytail, scoops her book and her towel from the sand, and goes to hide in the shadow of the dune with the look on her mother's face following her: that same concerned, perplexed expression.

***

From her spot under the dune, she has a view of his back, a view that allows her to observe how once, just once, he turns all the way around, as if to check if she is still there, back there behind him under the dune in the small tent of the towel she has draped over her head while she reads.

Soon she will return, and he will pretend not to notice. Only a slight incline of his head will give him away.

Watch Me

***

The couple has gotten up to hit a little rubber ball back and forth with wooden paddles. It sounds like a clock: tick, tock, tick, tock, tick. Before she can think, Abby jumps up and starts kicking a soccer ball toward them. She circles around and then alongside the game, the children trying to get it from her, screaming, "I want to kick it! I want to try!" and she keeps dodging them, keeping it deftly behind her body so they have to follow her until she is behind the Bee, right in Fuzz's view.

Marquis tackles Abby and the other children pile on. Soon they are lying in the sand and she is talking quietly to them and they are looking up at wisps of clouds. DeShawn's hand is in hers and she opens his palm toward her, traces the line where it turns from pink to dark brown. She stares into Laquisha's eyes, who is too shy to hold her gaze. Her sweetness makes her eyes drop, then rise, then drop, then rise again into a full bright smile. Abby melts with rising love, squeezes her to keep from dissolving. She lifts a handful of sand, each grain falling slowly from her palm, so distinct that she sees each speck flowing back into the numberless stream. The tick-tocking of the orange ball behind her becomes physically palpable, each hit making dents into the plane of sound behind her.

She jumps up, kicks the soccer ball, and runs right between the couple's game. His racket goes "tock" and something hits her shoulder.

The little purple ball falls into the sand at her feet.

"Sorry," she says, stunned at what she has done. Caught, she scoops the ball up, throws it to the girl, who studies her in perplexed surprise.

Abby doesn't dare to look at Fuzz. Instead, she kicks the soccer ball back down the beach, as far as she can, into the ocean, so the children follow, screaming.

The point where the rubber ball has hit her shoulder throbs, like a bruise, like a touch.

***

The couple have eaten the sandwiches and chips from their green bag. He has squeezed the aluminum foil wrappers into little balls, rolled up the bag of chips, and stowed it all away. He has wiped his hands off on his shorts.

Bee has gotten up, walked toward the water, stopped, and looked out at the horizon.

Abby is still hot with shame, wavering and flickering, sick with it. She is waiting for his eyes to find her, to ease what has happened with a look. She needs their eyes to catch each other, for him to understand, so she can try to fire herself back across at him to erase the transgression.

Or has he not seen her at all?

It is only Bee in his eyesight who spreads her arms out over a wave and screams as it splashes her stomach. Laughing, she looks back up at him, her small teeth a neat childish row of white.

He gets up, walks into the water, and his hands reach through the waves for her. Now they are swimming out and his head is inclined toward her as she talks. She envies their quiet conversation. Its naturalness. They float in the swelling waves as though they are lying on recliners. Bee rises and dives under, resurfaces, smooths her hair. He drifts into the swell behind the breakers as she swims back to shore. He has left her behind and is now only there for her, for Abby, to observe, as if he is giving her permission.

He is like a seal floating out there, a black silhouette, looking at the sky. She lies back on her towel to see what he sees, a few wisps of clouds like whispers in an emptiness that reaches no one. Beyond the wisps the blue is smearing in and out of itself the longer she looks at it, the color not a surface, but a distance. Endless, so that it makes her tip into vertigo.

She gets up and goes toward the water, toward him.

He rights himself. She dives into a wave as it breaks. She comes up, locates him, decides to swim in his direction. When he see her, he flips over and swims into shore, cuts right past her so that their paths cannot intersect.

Is it intentional? Has he avoided her?

***

Hurt, she decides to swim on, to pretend that he hasn't ignored her.

With self-conscious focus she readies herself and her body folds between the waves. Coming up, she turns to the beach, and from this distance does not care if he sees that she is searching for him. She must make sure that he is watching. She stares directly up at his motionless form, which is now in its chair, both hands on the armrests. As though he needed this distance. From there, his eyes are burning at her. This two-way fuse. A flare of orange flame, black ash in the salt air.

Held again by his attention, she dips into the water and squeezes the sun out of her eyes. Bright yellow bouncing orbs. Underwater, she kicks deeper, extends her legs as far as they will go, reaches her arms out so they stretch her body into complete extension. She comes up, turns on her side, scissor kicks and pumps her thighs. When another wave approaches, she flips forward into it. She starts to forget him, begins to feel good in the strength of her body, frog-pumping and strong as she pushes out past the waves into the open where she floats into the push and pull of the current. She goes out past his gaze, past anyone's gaze, is freed in the sensation of being alone. She tucks her body, dives all the way down into the blackness of this large mass, this presence of ocean, then flips and comes back up, closes her eyes and hears only her ragged breathing. On her back, the sky is an endless smearing of blue that she brushes over herself with her messy blue hands, as if she is painting over God's vision. Slowly, she takes her hair tie out and lets her hair spread like an ink spill haloing her head, tendrils pulled from her cool scalp at rest on the surface. She is like a mermaid. From underneath, the sun's rays spear down around her body, her hair a mass of electric tentacles. She remembers him, senses how his hands might reach up from the cool sifting shadows below, hesitating for just a moment as if asking permission, before taking her, before pulling her under.

***

With a gasp she opens her eyes into a shock of sun radiance, air the color of a photo negative. She slicks her hair back, wipes the water from her face. She has floated far down the shore and is lost. She digs into the current and swims back up, orients herself, locates her family's umbrellas, and strikes toward the pebbly surf, comes up at a diagonal toward her family and avoids the bright glare of his watching. She works the hair tie back in with the spotlight of the sun dazzling her and settles down on her towel, onto its warmth, its safe parameter. She wraps its rough sun-dried material around her shoulders and runs her hands down her smooth legs, which she has started shaving that summer. It feels as if she is still sliding through the water, her skin like a dolphin's, slick and muscled, the sensation of motion like a second skin settling, stilling, pinpricking through her blood. When she lies back on her rolled-up shirt, his looking is so close to her own sensation of being released from the water that she is like a mermaid in a bubble, curled in flight, floating over her towel.

***

The day has melted away as imperceptibly as water from a block of ice, pooling in the shadows of the slanted sun and the dented craters of footfalls in the sand.

A stitch of worry threads through her. They will pack up soon and leave and the beach will empty and be meaningless.

Up the beach the children have begun to build a sand sculpture of a mermaid as the sun starts to slant golden over them in the west, Laquisha holding long dripping strips of seaweed for the hair as her mother gets up to supervise. The cold drips down Abby's back as the beach slowly clears of people as if they have all floated up the dune and away into the clouds. She shivers.

Fuzz goes off alone for a walk down the beach just as she had done that morning. Will he think of her? Will he look for her there, in the golden haze of light, as though she will materialize from its radiance?

When she sees him return, she puts her book down, leans up on her hand, and readies for him to notice her. He does not see yet that Bee has left her spot, that she's gone. Abby will need to help him find her.

A nervous jangle rings inside her head. They will actually speak.

Just as she had guessed, the realization that Bee is gone registers in his face. He checks the water, scans the beach, finds nothing. Then he finds her.

The pressure in the air rises and knocks against her insides, knocks like a pulse. She holds his look until he knows that she has the answer, that she will get up and give it to him.

She knows now that it has been real. Everything. Everything between them, palpable across the beach chairs, the sand, the towels, the distant radios. It has smoothed the sand clear so that she can walk directly across to him, doesn't have to be afraid of coming too close.

His eyes expectant, tipping directly into her, as if they can see all the way in, but this time she isn't erased, made blank. Instead, she lifts the answer up toward him, raises her arm, and, because she can, touches his shoulder, warm through his shirt, and turns him, directs his vision. Her hand is gentle, as if she is ministering to his confusion through his ruffled linen shirt.

"She is in the dunes," she says. His focus is still strong on her, his mouth parted, as if he has to concentrate for the answer, lean in close to hear, to listen, not just for the answer, but for her.

His glance breaks and he looks away, scans. She takes a step closer to him, points. They both shield their eyes. Together they find her, Bee's blond hair at the top of the dune where wiry grasses and bramble bushes are a rough ribbon along the top.

"She's not supposed to be up there," he says.

"I know," Abby says, and when he looks at her again, she can feel this agreement settling between them as if they both know that one shouldn't disturb what is beautiful and wild, that Bee has transgressed against this, that they are worried, that they are scanning the far rise like protectors, together in a pair, two columns holding up what is right. That they would never do what she has done. That they are the same.

"It's bad for the erosion," he says, as if to say what they both already know, and she nods to make it real. She can be silent this time.

The blocks of time between them have slipped free and aligned, synced up properly so that no obstacles remain, no accidents of family or age. They have known each other forever and are suddenly reunited in this foreign circumstance, the blocks rolled apart to reveal this beach where they have found each other again, for just a moment among the umbrellas and coolers. She wants to grab him, take him with her, pull him into the wide-open floor of time where they can escape together.

But Fuzz, his expression warmer now, his eyes bright, says, "Thanks," touches her arm lightly, as if to say goodbye, and then stalks toward the dune and waves up at it, and shouts, "Bee!"

Bee waves back, but doesn't move.

Abby takes a step forward with the rush of excitement and disappointment beginning to course through her. She is losing him. The blocks of time have started to shift again, their outlines falling out of sync.

He keeps waving and this time Bee starts running full tilt down the dune, a river of sand collapsing behind her.

Fuzz turns to Abby as if all the erosion is collapsing over them and she presses her lips together, takes another step toward him. He holds his hands out as if to say, "What can you do?" and in that last moment of understanding he smiles at her, a big wide smile that envelops all of her, as if he is holding her in it, just as he is saying goodbye.

Then he takes off to catch Bee as she reaches the bottom, her legs beating hard against the sand as it flattens out. With all her momentum she swings around Fuzz's body and he twirls her in the air like a carnival ride.

Abby watches as if a sober evening light has come in. Everything is visible to her in clear relief. Fuzz holding Bee, admonishing her and grinning while she punches him in the stomach as he puts her in a headlock.

***

The poor mermaid has been destroyed, partially, by DeShawn's catapulting, and the children have turned to collecting sea shells and stones. They bring these over to show the couple, who say "Wow," and "Good finds," as DeShawn holds up an iridescent purple stone and asks who he will give it to. Fuzz doesn't take it, but instead motions toward his sister, toward Abbey, who plucks it from the boy's hand and gives Fuzz a last look into which she presses all of her warmth and pushes it down toward him. He holds her gaze just long enough for the prickling dancing warmth to pass between them. A happy flushed beating circulates through her body, a beating that will stay with her that night in her tent, that she will be able to think over that whole week, that will be like a smooth talisman in her hand, glowing purple.

The next time she sees Fuzz she is far out in the waves with the children and has turned back to find him. It is low tide and he is a small silhouette lifting his chair from the sand and collapsing it. When she looks again their site is all packed up and they are trudging toward the parking lot. A quick emptiness knifes through her, an emptiness she already knew would come—his absence in the air like a purple mist, like dust settling over her as she drops backward into the waves and kicks hard into the cycle of their motion.

TORNADO WARNING

THE KRAMERS had one of those old flat black plastic weather radios on their kitchen counter that screeched to life as Catherine and Eric headed for the door. They were house-sitting for the Dean of Eric's graduate school, who lived just over the border in the Berkshires. The wailing radio siren stopped them before it dropped to the repeated screech screech screech of the static preceding the announcement of the weather report spoken by a man in the windy cluttered signal of an AM radio: ". . . warning, tornado warning issued for Western Massachusetts. . ." The couple wavered in the door, stuck between listening to the report and heading out to the car so they could run into town to get some new sneakers for Eric's marathon training.

"Let's just go," Eric said, his arm braced over her head in the doorframe.

"Wait," she said, "this is a tornado we're talking about." Eric had a tendency to gloss over things that were inconvenient.

"We never get tornadoes here, or barely ever," he said.

"Exactly," she said.

He sighed.

The National Weather Service listed the affected counties and advised its listeners to "take cover; take cover."

"Look babe," he said, pointing upward. "There's nothing. Not a cloud in the sky."

They stepped into the yard to get a better look and he was right, not even a scrap.

"We'll just do a quick run into town and come right back. No harm, no foul."

"Fine," she said, though it seemed to him like she didn't really mean it.

On the way to town there was a perfect blue sky with no sign of trouble. They drove along the country roads, smooth and easy. It reminded her of the first days of their relationship, free and open, when he'd pick her up after work and they'd grab takeout, go for a hike, or head into town for a bite to eat. How sometimes they'd drive just to be together.

Soon enough they arrived outside the outfitter's on main street. As he held the door for her, Eric checked the sky one last time. Above the row of scalloped stone façades, a cloudy tuft of black wool appeared, all teased out by the wind, as if it was reaching for them.

Take cover, the warning had said, and he skipped inside, smiled broadly at Catherine as if he hadn't seen anything at all, and followed her down the stairs to the basement. The silver racks of clothing hung in dim silence against the audience of sneakers on their floating shelves along the wall. If there really would be a storm, he'd get away from it just in time, he thought. He'd get lucky. He always did.

A clerk who was probably in his early twenties, roughly their own age, and whose glistening dark gelled hair was slicked forward into a spiky swoop, emerged from a gray doorway in the back. His teeth were bleached white, his eyebrows threaded to cartoonish perfection, and his skin so smooth that it could only be makeup. He wore dark-rimmed glasses that were likely fake. It was as if he had ordered a face-kit and assembled it all into this mask of a person. Catherine wondered if anyone fell for this highly manicured superficiality.

They realized that they had all met each other at a party before. Eric was test-running his sneakers up and down the aisle and said, "Oh man, I remember you now, I must have been too drunk when we were hanging out to place you." The clerk snickered knowingly, and Catherine scoffed. Eric never drank more than two beers, hadn't ever been drunk in the three years she'd known him, and now here he was pretending to be some party animal for the sake of this fake mannequin of a person. Why was he aligning himself with this tool? Maybe they were more alike than she wanted to admit, Eric with his blond hair in a side part, his salmon shorts, the blue polo with the little anchors on it, the aviators tucked into his open collar, his boat shoes neatly placed next to an open box. She'd been so proud to support him in his studies, and now, with his graduation not far off, she wondered what he'd do with the new earning power he'd likely get. Would he just become one of these rich New England WASP types? He was already wearing the costume.

Eric, on the other hand, smirked self-satisfactorily, knowing that Catherine would have picked up on his lie. She would have seen how he was trying to be polite to the clerk, since both of them had clearly not recognized him. Eric had fixed this bit of rudeness and was happy that they had a relationship strong enough to communicate in these secret ways, making fun of the clerk who probably "partied super hard." He thought of the couple times in their relationship when he had said, "I love you," and actually meant it: that time on her front porch when they were first getting together and it had felt like an admission; and that time at a restaurant a year later, for their anniversary, when she studied the menu with such a lack of self-consciousness that the self-evident nature of their togetherness dawned inside him like a kind of miracle—the fact that, in all of these small ways, she had chosen him and didn't seem to have any second thoughts about it at all—so that when the words came out of his mouth, almost as if he had thought them aloud, she raised her face, flushed, surprised, and bent forward to kiss him across their place settings.

As Eric was getting out of his third pair of shoes, the overhead lights flickered, went out, left them momentarily in darkness, and then blinked back on. Catherine and Eric tried to read the level of seriousness in each other's faces, just as the store's manager rushed down the stairs with her permed hair bouncing with each step and said, "You guys gotta come up here and see this. It's that tornado they were talking about on the radio. I've never seen anything like it; the whole sky's black." Eric cast a quick look at Catherine again, but it was as if she'd gone blank, as if someone had turned the power off inside her and she'd shut down. A perfect animatronic doll, with her short black hair in a pixie cut, her white blouse, her tight jeans cut to just above the ankle, the black canvas slippers she was staring past with her glass eyes. All perfect, he thought, except that tattoo of a bird on the top of her left foot, trying to flutter out of her slipper

He had no idea what she could possibly be thinking, though he often felt that way.

Probably she was blaming him for coming into town.

It was dark out, the whole sky blackened over with only a green seaweed-like stream running through it. The air below was in a static freeze above the white pop of the blooming pear trees along Main Street. The gathered crowd had come out to stare up in common wonder at this total eclipse of the light, as if it wasn't a sign of approaching calamity, as if a sudden wind wouldn't descend to lift the rooftops off the buildings and pull the glass from the storefronts and send all these spectators up into the sky. It was incredibly stupid of them just to stand there, Eric thought, and he got the urge to grab Catherine, tuck her under his arm, and run off with her to safety.

"They say it's coming in from Lee," Colleen, the manager, said. "If you two get out of here now and head in the opposite direction, you should be able to outrun it."

This was good advice, Eric thought, and he got ready to move out, though Catherine was stuck in some kind of reverie, which, again, he couldn't read.

She was thinking back to the first big tornado that had blown through some years before. It had torn along the outer edge of town, taken out the fairgrounds, and crashed into the mountainside where it left a massive stony gash that was still visible. Somehow, all of this reminded her of Oliver, who had cheated on her at the end, who had been able to do just that to her: tear through her life, lift everything up she had known and place it down somewhere new. All reconfigured. She had had to scramble to figure out exactly who she was and what she wanted afterward, which had given her enough clarity to wind up with someone solid like Eric. Though now she was beginning to question all the reasons she had ended up with him to begin with: he was too predictable, like an old boring machine charging ahead with his ingrained coordinates that he never bothered to question. She had the urge to upend the machine, drag it under ground, smash through to its core, and rewire it into a complex living organism.

Once they got moving, Eric felt immediately better, even with the uncomfortable sensation of being exposed to the storm out there on the public sidewalk. There was no way to take cover, as the radio had insisted, and Colleen hadn't invited them back into the store to ride it out in the basement. Just ahead, in a crowd that had gathered outside a pub, he recognized this kid Derek.

"Come on, let's go around," Eric said, and they made a wide arc. He made the mistake of checking to see if he'd been spotted, and Derek's eyes had landed on him and he was sure the face had broken into recognition. Eric ignored it, pretended this kid he'd gotten drunk with by accident one night wouldn't remember him at all. The thing is, he never got drunk, but after playing tennis with a buddy, he'd been introduced, and Derek, who everyone in town seemed to know and love, had just hung out, listened to everything Eric had said with this appreciative smiling nod. Eric's enthusiasm to keep talking, to keep sharing, ran off with him, and soon they moved from a café to that exact pub, just the two of them, and he was buying Derek round after round, and it wasn't until near midnight that they left, Eric with a hollow, raw, embarrassed and thrilled vulnerability opened inside him. He had told this kid everything, everything about his life, from his dull insurance salesman father, to his uptight mother, to Catherine, who rode horses on her father's farm, a place they'd bought when land was cheap and horses needed rescuing.

"She's too good for me, man," he'd said. "Too fucking moral. And too fucking wild, to be honest."

Luckily, Catherine was still all tranced out, hadn't noticed, and let him steer her to their car.

"Imagine if the storm just blew through here and lifted the whole place up and they'd have to start from scratch? Do you think they'd build it all the same, or would they try to make it all new and better?" Catherine asked.

She always had these hypotheticals.

"Probably won't happen," he said as he got his keys out.

"Yeah, but if," she said.

"I'd rather just think about getting us out of here," he said.

As they got to the car, they shut their doors, strapped themselves in, backed out, took a left, a right, another right, and got out onto Main Street where people were still gathered outside the store fronts with their faces tilted toward the dark. Soon they were making good progress, just tapping the brakes a little as they maneuvered through a blinking yellow light. It was just like during races when Eric started to blow by people and an inner sensation of superiority established itself: he had trained harder, eaten better, made smarter decisions, and, if he were being honest, was just blessed with better genes than them which, again, supported his belief that he was, in some fundamental way, better than most people, especially those suckers who were standing outside waiting to get blown away by a tornado.

Catherine leaned over him to peer out his window and said, "It really does look bad, doesn't it?" It seemed like she was out of her trance and they began to discuss whether they were actually going in the right direction. It was impossible to tell, really, it just looked so bad everywhere and the storm was masked in all that black sky so who could tell?

"I really can't, Eric said.
"Me neither," Catherine said.

Since they were headed west anyway, they decided to head back to the Kramers'. As they left town they passed the big stone structure of St. James Church, where Eric remembered once having gone to perform in a Christmas concert when he was in high school. A girl from his choir had taken his hand, run with him through the hallways, pushed open a door, and taken him to the freezing darkness outside. They had found a niche in a corner where the stone buttress met the main building, hidden from the road and hidden from the parking lot. Here she pressed him against the masonry and told him to kiss her. She had brushed her dark hair from her forehead like a shadow, and her mouth had been warm and her cheeks cold. The knowledge of everyone inside rehearsing was like a faraway lantern whose outer edge of light just barely reached them, as if they were pressed up against the whole cold stone structure of religion, this ecstatic moment like a flame burning at the wall of its rules.

The memory skirted across his consciousness, registered for a moment in his chest, and then relinquished itself.

Catherine would have liked a moment like that, he thought.

"I kissed a girl outside that church once," he said.

"What? You?! I never thought you'd blaspheme like that."

"I'm very blasphemous."

"Maybe you're more of a bad boy than I thought, though I've already dated a bad boy once and I don't know that I could go through that again."

Eric got that emptied-out feeling whenever she brought up a past lover, like everything good in him drained out and left him empty and shaky. Why ruin their banter? He didn't like that there was some guy out there, some "bad boy," who had somehow been too much for Catherine to handle. And now, he, Eric, was just some tame boring guy who was easy to get under control. No bad boy, this one. Plus, this bad boy, Oliver or whatever his name had been, hadn't cared about her enough to treat her right, so he had just dropped her. Cheated on her. Did whatever he wanted and now he, Eric, the good guy, was supposed to come along and make everything better even though the other guy had fucked it all up. And, even though he was helping her through her insecurities, there was also probably some part of her that didn't thrill to Eric the way she did to Oliver, that probably thought he was a little vanilla, a little basic, just a good old boring person who wouldn't do anything wild or rash or exciting. That was his reward for not being a dick. She'd probably like him more if he was one. The irony. Clearly he was being played for some kind of a sucker. Fuck.

Then again, he had brought up an ex too, and she had been mature about it, even joked about it, which actually also hurt a little.

She was either more evolved than him, or he couldn't make her jealous.

Either way, he wasn't going to let her know how easily she could make him feel small. That she had this power over him.

A massive rain drop smacked the windshield as if someone had flung it at them out of the clouds.

"Jesus," Eric said.

Another hit, then another, and another after that, followed by a full sequence that cracked against the windshield like fireworks. And then the full rain came on hard. Eric turned the wiper blades up as high as they could go. The windshield fogged along the dash and spread up the glass. Catherine adjusted the blowers and held her hands over them to test the air.

"Nothing like driving blind in a rainstorm," Eric said.

"A true delight," she said.

The houses became less and less frequent the farther they got from town until only intermittent driveways were visible at the edge of the woods.

Catherine turned on the radio as if there was nothing else of significance to say, and a country song came on, followed by a commercial for auto insurance, a restaurant with great wings, and then "Hotel California."

"God, can you change it, I don't want that stuck in my head for the next twenty years."

"Yeah, I'm just trying to find out more about the storm."

"Sure," he said

The NPR station played music, went to a break, and then informed them that a tornado warning had been issued for the following counties. Their county was once again on the list. They were warned to please use caution and seek shelter if possible.

"I just wish they could tell us exactly where it was," Eric said.

"Yeah," she said.

"When we get to the Kramers', we're going straight into the basement."

"Yes sir," she said, and when his eyes knifed over at her she said, "I'm joking, I'm joking, of course we'll do it. It's the only sane choice."

They drove on in silence, though it did seem like he always got his way, Catherine thought.

After a turn onto a smaller back road, they passed a farm with its yellow signs warning drivers to slow down in case of farm animals crossing the road. The barns were sagging in the mud as if they were miserable in the rain and the white plaster of the farmhouse was splattered with dirt and large cragged arches had peeled off, revealing the encrusted lath beneath. The place made Catherine claustrophobic: the smallness of the life, medieval, tied to the land like that, and the muck, though the hills reminded her of Ireland: shorn clean by the mouths of cows and sheep so that each velvet crease and fold was visible, each boulder heaved to the surface, each flank and swale, just as it had been in the hills banked up against the dark stone mountains of the Burren, naked of trees and beribboned with blooms of purple heather where the flight of a bird was like a hand running over the expanse of the landscape, as though someone had shaped it with the swoop of the wind and the runnel of rain running through a chute in the rock.

She had the urge to run her hands across Eric's body, over each contour of who he was so that he could become visible, known—as if he too had been heaved up from the ground below and revealed to the sky.

But he was hunched over the wheel, all ferocious concentration and probably mild annoyance. She sighed and he cocked his head in her direction but said nothing.

To clear the silence, Eric told her that one of the professors at school said that his wife got caught in that tornado in

Springfield the week before. "She just pulled her car over on the side of the highway and crawled out into the ditch and waited for it to go over."

"Do you think we should do that?"

"What? No," he said. Why did she misunderstand everything and want to jump right to some conclusion? Abandon the plan? "I'm just saying that like, it's pretty crazy, right?"

"Yeah, two tornadoes in a row."

"No, I mean, that she went into the ditch."

He was annoyed at her again, and all she was thinking was that that was exactly what they should do: get in the ditch and lie there and let the muddy rain water run down over their bodies. They could cling to each other while they got pelted and the trees lifted off the ground around them like some wild magic. It would be exciting. It would be just what they needed. The clinging.

Ahead of them on the road, lightning cracked down through the dark, followed immediately by the clash of thunder, whose whoompf shunted the car off to the side.

"God, that was close," Eric said.

"It's right over us," Catherine. "Should we get in the ditch?"

"Yes? No? I don't know, I really don't. Let's just, can we just, let's just hold on for a second and see what happens."

A bucket of water dumped across the windshield and then there was just the silent slinging of the wipers as they waited for the next smash of thunder.

"We never should have come into town today," Eric said.

Catherine nodded, though she wasn't sure she agreed anymore. They would have missed this, and even though they might die, it somehow seemed worth it, being out in all this wild weather. Who knew what could happen.

For a moment the rain eased, like they were in a pocket of calm.

"I was in a tornado once when I was a kid," Eric said into the quiet. "On the West Coast. We were out in the street playing and then I looked up and like, all these branches were just suspended in the air up there. Like, just hanging. I didn't know what it was, and thought I was learning some new rule of physics, you know. That like, sometimes branches would just hang out in the sky, lose gravity. I wondered if at some point it would happen to me too. If I'd float up one day and just hang around in the sky for a while."

"Aww," she said. "I love that."

Her tone was a little too cute and condescending and he couldn't fully tell if she meant it, or if it just meant that he was, once again, a cute safe guy. He regretted telling her, and thought that he should have saved it for someone else, some vague person in his future who could actually understand him.

"Anyhow, we ran inside and told my mom and she just held us tight in a doorway while the storm passed over. Our neighbors had their porch roof caved in and a couple up the street lost their R.V. We went up and looked at it. The thing was flattened. Like some giant had taken this massive club of a tree trunk and just lowered it into the R.V."

"Damn," she said, and this time he could tell she meant it.

Just then, lightning tore through the rain like a searchlight next to the driver side window.

"We need to get out of here," Eric said.

"You don't think we should go to the Kramers'?"

"I do, I just."

He didn't say "just" what. He never said "just" what. That was the problem. He would just go off and do it.

"Let's go to the college," he said. "Their whole weight room, it's underground."

She wanted to ask why, but bit back the question. Maybe because it was across the border? Some invisible dividing line the tornado wouldn't certainly adhere to?

"Sure," she said, even though it didn't make sense to her. Probably, it was the place he felt most safe, in control.

She thought of the gray rectangle of the daycare where she worked for her mother with its red metal roof and its wide parking lot and the way it looked like it had just been lowered into place by a crane one day, just dropped, fwooomp! Right onto the countryside, more or less accidentally. Sometimes, as she approached it, she imagined a tornado winding down out of those hills and just tearing a metallic gash right through the middle of the structure. She'd grab up all the children and hold their small beating hearts close against her and carry them all away from the monotony of this pre-fab life.

Eric maneuvered around a crescent moon puddle that flooded most of the road as their phones buzzed: *Flash flood warning, avoid roadways.*

"How nice of them to tell us," Eric said.

"Ha," Catherine said. Service was terrible in the Berkshires, and she was surprised a message had gotten through at all.

Then, in a more somber tone, she said, "I hope nothing bad happens to anyone today."

"Me too," he said. A shared tenderness settled over the tension in the car like a fine mist.

It was clear how quickly everything could go wrong, like the spring before when the outer edge of hurricane Irene had dragged away the bridge near her house and replaced it with a raging mass of floodwater. The future seemed to teeter afterward, as though it were swaying on a creaky old rusted footing. Anything could go, wash away, and there she'd be on one side of the bridge and Eric on the other, and they'd have to decide: would they jump in and try to make it to each other, or would they look for another way across, or just call the whole thing off?

"Would you save me?" she asked, "if things got like, really bad?"

"Worse than this?"

She nodded.

"I mean, yeah, of course, I'll always save you."

He sounded more annoyed than anything.

She tried to climb back out of her thoughts and into the car where everything was still secure, their togetherness self-evident. She stared down at the gear shift, the center console, the radio with its green digital numbers, but it wasn't enough.

"In Ireland, sometimes, I'd lie naked out in the rain," she said.

"What? Really?"

"Yeah." She was happy, telling this lie.

"Could people see you?"

"The neighbors, probably," she said, casually.

"Huh," he said, and then nothing else. What had emptied out of him earlier was now rushing back in, like a hot tumult.

What the fuck, she just used to lie around naked?

Catherine waited for him to ask something, anything else, but he didn't. There was just this angry flex of his jaw.

"You failed the test," she said finally. "You weren't supposed to ask about other people, you were supposed to ask about me, about what it felt like, lying in the rain."

"Jesus Christ, so you didn't lie naked in the rain?"

"I didn't say that."

"Fuck me."

A wry victorious smile returned to her face and she folded her hands.

Still, it was a disappointment.

Behind them, lightning hit a tree and it exploded, caught fire, tugged at a power line, and fell across the road.

"Holy fuck!" he said. He slammed on the brakes and turned to look at it through the rearview mirror.

"Why are you stopping, dummy?! The power lines could come down on us!"

"Don't call me a dummy!"

"I'm not!"

"You just did!"

She put her hand to her mouth and to his shock, began to crack up laughing.

"What?!"

"Nothing, I just. Fuck. This is really funny. We're going to die while calling each other dummies."

"Who are you?"

Her eyes were glazed with tears and she was still holding her mouth.

"Who do you think?" she said, a little taken aback, suddenly, a little afraid.

"I don't even fucking know, honestly. I really don't. I really don't think I fucking know."

"What do you mean? You know me." She was trying to convince him now, though she hadn't been sure, right before.

"I don't think I do."

Something lurched, snapped, and creaked. The power line leaned outside the car as another tree tipped into the slack rope of its wires.

She reached for his thigh but pulled her hand back. Her eyes welled up with tears. After all, she had wanted him to know her, to love her. She had wanted to be bad and cynical and small and say wild and kind of fucked up things and she had wanted him to know they were more or less all true and untrue at the same time and she had wanted him to love her for it anyway and now he didn't even know who she was.

"Can't you just love me?" she said stupidly.

He sucked his cheeks in as the rain drummed on the roof. "I just, I just really don't think I know who the fuck you are. I just don't. Like, what are you?"

"I'm me," she said, "me." But suddenly it didn't seem like enough for him to understand, like he could never clamber over into her mind to see the open proscenium of her consciousness with all the world projected up on the screen inside her.

"You know, fuck all this," he said. "You're right. We should get out of the fucking car."

He opened the door, which slammed immediately shut as the rain-gusted wind hit it.

"Wait!" she said, and grabbed his arm. "Let's go a little farther. Maybe it will be a little better up there."

He hesitated. Who could really know? Already he was imagining the car lifting up, the windshield tilting skyward until they were hanging upside down in the air. At least then they'd know what was what. At least then, everything would be clear.

"No, fuck that," he said, and ripped the door open.

He was going out into uncertainty. She couldn't believe it.

He was immediately soaked. Just before letting the door go he leaned in with his hair dripping wet and said, "Hey, you coming or what?"

THE SUNFISH

THE MEDICINE CABINET WAS AN ANTIQUE, reclaimed by Lucy's mother and painted white. It was not, to Lucy's eyes, some fancy antique. It was just a crappy mirror that her mother had tried to make nicer, to be, as she said, "A little creative!" Once it was installed she said, "See, isn't that better?" Lucy had just gotten off the bus (which she still had to ride even though it was her senior year because her mother refused to let her drive until she was eighteen because lord knows, the last thing she needed was to find her daughter wrapped around a telephone pole) and stood in the bathroom door and nodded at her mother, who was all excited over her accomplishment. "Plus, I even saved some money. Well, not if I were charging by the hour, haha. This cabinet can't afford me, though it did look like it was injured in a fall before I started on it."

Lucy squeezed in next to her mother and pursed her lips at the mirror. It was smaller than the one it replaced, all metal and rusted, and which had squeaked when it opened, like it was surprised. She ran her fingers through her dark hair.

"I just wished I liked what I saw more," Lucy said.

"What?!? You're beautiful. Stunning. Just look at those eyes of yours. So beautiful and green."

The Sunfish

"Anyone can have nice eyes. They don't matter. Have you ever looked at an eye up close? It's always insanely cool. All those shards. They're like glaciers or splintered prehistoric amber or anything else super cool. It's everything else. My face looks like a cliff that got all messed up. I'm like the face that those stone artists practiced on when they were in their teens before they made Mt. Rushmore. It's like, you can see that there's supposed to be something good there, but it's all jagged and messed up."

"Stop! Stop, stop, stop. I know it's fun to beat yourself up, but that's enough. I made that beautiful face of yours and I won't have you talking about it that way."

"Easy for you to say with your beautiful perfect everything."

"Now you just stop." Her mother looked at her seriously and with a little hurt in the rosy bathroom light, her dark flapper hair curling beautifully around her face, just like one of those old advertisements where the model has arched eyebrows, one just slightly more cocked than the other—sexy, sophisticated, alluring.

"I would if I could, but you don't get it. Just look at how sharp everything is. My cheekbones could, like, cut someone. No wonder people are afraid to get near me."

"Oh, I'm sure no one's afraid to get near you."

Lucy scoffed.

"Plus," her mother continued, "people pay a lot of money for strong cheekbones."

"Yeah, and do they pay for the eyebrows too? It's like someone took nice long eyebrows and then pinched them together into little hideous birdhouse roofs. Plus, my eyelids look all droopy, all melty, like I'm a burn victim or something."

"What!?" Her mother pushed her away, then immediately reached back for her, grabbed her by both arms so that she was standing at attention on the cushiony green mat as her mother searched her face with concerned eyes.

"What are you doing? Where does all this self-hate come from? When did this start?"

"Since forever, when I was born with Quasimodo's face."

"You were not! Stop it!"

"You're right, everyone in school says I look like a horse."

"Oh, darling, sweetie, is that what they're saying, oh my gosh."

Her whole face had bunched up into saccharine concern.

God, get me out of here, Lucy thought.

She squirmed from her mother's arms and ran up the hallway, raw inside from the accidental vulnerability she had let her mother see. Her hand instinctively went up to her chest to try to pull out the long vine of frustration growing inside of it. Get out! She barged into her room and yanked herself down on the bed. Dammit. Now her mother would think she was being bullied. She wasn't being bullied. What they were saying was true. It wasn't even really mean. Just true. It wasn't bullying if she was actually ugly. She could see it too, her horsiness.

Sometimes she did get glimmers of beauty when she would draw in dark pencil along her eyebrows, smooth them a little, elongate them, when she would apply red lipstick and eyeliner, when she would soften her cheekbones with foundation and rouge, like a reverse contour. Her dark hair really glistened then, under the bathroom lights, like there were strands of gold in it.

But forget it. Whatever was happy and pink and glowing inside her would turn to sludge when it passed through the busted sewer grate of her face.

The other day she had walked into the hallway at school as if she had spun all the fresh September sunshiny morning air into bright piles inside her so that when she saw Stephen in a little huddle of people in his big green coat she came up behind him with all that pink sweetness rising in her and tapped him on the shoulder and said, "Hi!" to tangle him all up in it together with her. But when he turned, she saw his expectant face kind of crack or break apart as he recognized her so that he mumbled back, "Oh, hey Luce."

"What're you so happy about?" a girl asked, her hair falling down her shoulders in long beautiful curls as if she'd just had a blowout. Christ. Lucy just turned and walked away and heard another girl say, "Someone's got a crush."

"Shut up," she heard Stephen answer.

Stephen. Stephen who always sat in the far-left corner of the back row near the window, slouched down into the green coat that was much too big for him, the sleeves way too long. He didn't bother rolling them up. He was skinny, and she thought, no, she *knew*, that he liked the coat because he liked hiding in it. She knew this and she thought that none of the other girls knew this. She could help him. She could make him see that he was perfect with his greasy, spiky, dark hair and his intelligent green eyes, which were not so different from hers, not so different at all. They were the same, her and Stephen, weren't they, which she would try to point out by saying, "I have green eyes too," or "This is too crazy, I also love the Ramones." But Stephen would just press his lips together and look off with a "yeah whatever" expression. Maybe he didn't need her help, even though he wore "That dumb jacket," as she heard the other girls call it. They still hung around with him though. "Yeah, because he's smoking hot," she had overhead one of them say. Was he? She couldn't tell. She had known him since he was young; they had even played together. He had been to her house. Like a lot! But that was also when his father was friends with her mother, and then dating her mother, who, over the years, had dated a lot of people. And she guessed that ever since they had broken up, two or three years ago, he hadn't been over again. Maybe that was the problem. Maybe he associated her with her mother. Maybe that's why his face always fell apart that way when he saw her. His good-looking face. It was good-looking, after all, but it wasn't like how people in movies were good-looking where you liked them because of it. It was good-looking as just a part of who he was. It was good-looking because it looked like him, and he was good. She was pretty sure he was anyway. Well, he had to be good. He couldn't not be. He was Stephen. Stephen! He had held her hand once, for a whole hour after she had fallen out of a tree and broken her arm. He had held it the whole ride to the hospital, his body still hot and sweating in his faded gray t-shirt from running around outside and kicking the can. Never had someone done that for her; how he just sat next to her. How he said nothing, just held on to her and didn't move, didn't let her feel afraid. Instead, he let her feel brave.

He was good, and continued to be good, though sometimes she doubted this. It would seem like things were going well, like those moments in class where she would sit next to him and they were melting from boredom and she would pass him a funny drawing she had made in garish red and green marker that showed a dinosaur devouring the teacher, blood spurting everywhere. He had inclined his head, chuckled a little, given her a conspiratorial look, and then gone back to listening to the lecture, so that she could dream of what he would do with the picture: tuck it into the pocket of his notebook maybe, or tack it to the wall above his desk at home to remind him of his hatred of school and of his teachers, and of homework, and maybe even, when he got to her signature at the bottom with the little X's and O's, a little bit of her. When he got up at the end of class he was still holding it with his homework sheet and casually slid it onto the teacher's desk and walked away.

Her hope stalled at the top of its run like a broken rollercoaster. She couldn't understand what he had just done. Had he forgotten it? She jumped up to tell him just as the truth trampled over her from behind. She dashed through the row of desks, knocked over a couple of chairs, and got there just as the teacher was reaching for this curious colorful sheet in the stack so that he was holding one end and she the other. Their eyes met over this tug of war, which she won by yanking it away. A little rip of paper with her signature on it left in his suspicious hands.

And she watched a lot of movies, old ones especially, since that was what her mother had in her collection. They were stacked in a long row on the white shelf in the den over the television under the low eave. They had poisoned her. Made her stupid. It was because of these that she imagined saying these charming things to Stephen, breezing past him with a coy "Oh hello," as though she had just bumped into an Italian column accidentally, adorably, and was trying to pass it off, charming him so much that he would follow her bouncing ponytail all through school as if she were Audrey Hepburn on a *Roman Holiday*. Instead, she'd say, "I like the sleeves on your jacket, keepin' 'em long, huh?" and he'd say "umm, yeah," before he cut by her into the throng of students squeezing out through the door so that she could gently knock her head against the bus window on her ride home, again, and again, and again, and again.

Her birthday party had been a delusion of just this type of thing, stringing up paper lanterns in fall colors on the back porch, putting together to-go bags with mad-libs and handmade candy from the store in town, cleaning everything. Her kitchen, which still had those metal cabinets from the fifties, was perfectly set up with drinks and punch bowls and chips and chocolate chip cookies she'd baked from scratch. It was, she imagined, anything anyone could want to have. She imagined people coming to the door at all hours, streaming in, falling in, bursting in, stumbling, and her in the thick of everything, darting out to answer a bell, holding, well, not a long cigarette, but maybe a drink, and Holly Golightly-ing through the rooms in a slim black dress, and showing them inside.

But when her friends came they showed up all in a big group, knocked on the door but didn't wait for her to open it, walked right past her and said, "Hi Luce, Happy birthday Luce," greeting her like she was the losing team after a soccer game. They grabbed drinks without asking her to pour them, helped themselves to plates, said, "See, we came, we all came Luce," without her being able to do any charming welcoming speeches. "Hi Luce, Happy Birthday Luce." And all the parents were there behind them, as if they'd all ridden over in a big bus or something, and their faces had this severe look, like they had made their kids come whether they liked it or not. She wasn't stupid. She could tell.

Her mother couldn't tell, though. Nope. "Isn't this great?!?" she said. "Look who all came! It's wonderful. I haven't seen Stephen's dad in years. This is so great." Everyone just went into the T.V. room with their snacks instead of finding out what the backyard lawn games were and said, "What, you don't have cable?!" So she chose a movie from the shelf while her mother was in the kitchen, holding a drink up in her delicate, sophisticated, and perfect hand and laughing so loud that it drowned out *My Fair Lady* talking about the rains over the plains in Spain ("This is like a famous old movie, right?"), the adults all crammed in along the kitchen cabinets so that the smell of alcohol leaked all over the house as if they'd all just smashed their bottles on the tile floor. "My birthday party mom, mine!" she screamed at her once everyone had left. "Not yours! You don't always have to be the perfect charming, uggh! Whatever you are. Fuck! Dammit!"

She ran up the narrow wooden stairs as her mother shouted after her that she damn well wasn't cleaning up any of this mess, because, newsflash to her, "It wasn't my damn party! Okay? Not my damn idea to invite over twenty-five teenagers. Nope! Sorry for trying to make it fun. Sorry for trying to gentjlrdhnjtrldhtr;." Lucy had thrown a pillow over her head to block it all out. Gone was her mother and in came her sobs, long wavelike sobs that swelled and wracked and broke all over her, soaked the pillow.

When she went to other kids' birthday parties it was often the only time she had been to their houses. She knew that she was at the birthday parties mainly out of pity, mainly because they went to such a small school that you had to take all the people you could get. But on some occasions, there had almost been a breakthrough with the girls, where she'd get to a party early and it would be just her and the other girl, like the time at Kaylie's right before Easter, basically her last ditch shot at popularity before graduation. She'd helped Kaylie set up, spread stuff on tables, and they'd even started telling each other things about school, about people who liked each other, and she'd even ventured to say that of the guys in their class, not that she was interested, but that Stephen was probably the best looking. Kaylie had just smiled kindly at her. "Everyone knows," she said, "you're pretty obvious." Knows what!? But instead of defending herself or pretending, she had said, "Am I really?" and in Kaylie's friendly nod they had fallen into a kind of synch as they set up, and Lucy was super committed to making sure that everything was awesome. "Thank God you're here," Kaylie said, and Lucy responded by saying, "Of course. I want to *actually* be helpful, not just come over and take advantage of your stuff." Kaylie gave her a little stiff-lipped smile, because it may have sounded like she was accusing all of the other girls of doing that. *Oh well*, she thought, and took over the organization of the back porch even more, so that when a few of the other girls showed up she came into the kitchen and started telling them what to do. "Who made you the boss?" they asked, and she was suddenly rootless. It had been the job that needed doing that had made her the boss. "Kaylie," she peeped. They turned to Kaylie who was red and embarrassed, grasping a packet of straws, and then said, "Oh, I'm sorry, it's just that, I did tell Jessica she could be in charge of party planning with me."

"Well then where the hell has Jessica been for the last two hours?"

"Wow, calm down slut. I was busy getting these from Stephen's older brother," she said, and held up two bottles of liquor. "Stephen was super helpful too. You see, he likes pretty girls, and wants to help them out, unlike other girls I know."

Lucy looked helplessly at Kaylie, who had taken the straws out and was pretending to arrange them one bright color at a time. "Fine, you figure it out then," Lucy said. She grabbed a soda, turned, clomped upstairs and called her mother to pick her up. She was panting. She didn't want to be there later when Stephen showed up, when he drank all that liquor with the other girls, when he drank it and let Jessica grab his face because he was too drunk to say no and kiss him with tongue and everything. She didn't want to think about them playing tonsil hockey or whatever they called it.

"Thank God she's leaving," she heard someone in the other room say as she was getting her shoes on, her mother standing in the open screen door, asking if she was really sure she didn't want to stay. From the kitchen doorway Kaylie said, "You can stay if you want," but Lucy turned and got out of there before she could get convinced to take more punishment.

She did have one friend though, Gloria, or Goria as she called her. "Hey Gore," she'd say, lying on her stomach on her mother's couch, which was covered in a blanket that had all these little balls along the outer seams, which made it annoying to lie on the couch because they'd always dig into her back. "How's the gory life?"

"Full of guts," she'd say. "The guts of my enemies."

"Nice gore, I'm glad you experimented with violence today."

"My parents told me how important it was to experiment. They meant marijuana, but whatever."

Lucy didn't smoke and thought of getting high a little bit like her brain climbing a ladder and entering a low bank of clouds floating above her. What she was afraid of was that her mind would stay like mist forever, or that there would be a residue of mist when it was over, and each time she smoked there would be more of it until she was all clouded out.

She was actually, it was true, kind of afraid of Gloria, because Gloria was unpredictable, a little intense, a little older, and well, Gloria could also just be blunt as hell. But she lived in the same town, and they took the same bus, which picked Gloria up at the public school, and Gloria had slouched into the seat next to hers one day and just started complaining and actually listened when Lucy joined in and so that's why they were friends.

"You want to come over and talk to guys in chat rooms?"

"Wish I could, Lucy in the sky, but I have a killer amount, a just totally crushing amount, of HW."

"I do not believe you."

"Okay, fine, my cousin's in town and I have to go to a lame family outing."

"Nope."

"Okay, the truth is, I'm lying here in my underwear and I don't want to get up to put on pants because life is a miserable hell."

"Bingo."

"Thank you for understanding."

"I always do, girl."

"Sure, 'Girl,' whatever."

"Don't be a mean cunt."

"Don't say cunt."

"Sorry."

"I'm kidding. Jeez. You can say cunt. I am a cunt, I am a cunt, I am a cunt—repeat after me."

Lucy hung up.

Good thing she got out of there. Good thing she was smart. Getting into a "Good small East Coast liberal arts college" as her mother called it and moving a few states over had been no problem. She had been waiting, in some way, to get out her whole life and college was the thing that was going to set her free. But she had wanted to conquer the things that had been tormenting her before she left, and now she felt the shimmer and disappointment of unfinished things haunting her. She wanted to be invited to a small party by the girls because they actually wanted her to be there, to be close with them and to not look like a fool, and for Stephen to treat her differently, to look at her, to remember that they had been friends, to let her help him, to save him, and for them to be together, to hold hands again in the back of a car in an emergency.

But, she had failed and went off to college dragging behind her the messy deflated tangle of her hopes.

The upside of this was that she was wary of any of these hopes when she got to college. She didn't let herself fantasize, didn't think that college was going to be like this great life-changing place where she would have real friends and everything would be awesome and that some boy would meet her and think that she, in exactly every single way, was perfect. No, she had none of those dreams. She didn't think about sitting around for hours talking in small groups with cool new friends, lounging in chairs, watching movies, talking about professors and classes and books and ideas. She didn't fantasize about going to packed frat parties and dancing in green strobe lights with a red Solo cup in her hand while guys grinded up on her or whatever it was called. Plus, she didn't want guys to do that, unless it was Stephen, but Stephen would not grind in his big stupid green jacket, he would just stand there and maybe rock back and forth and if he let her he might hold her and pull her close . . . but wait, no, it didn't matter. Stephen was dead to her and she had to forget him. She was done.

No more fantasies. No more attempts at friendships with girls who didn't like her. In fact, at her hall meeting the first day of orientation, she didn't even look around the circle of metal folding chairs in the basement lounge with the stained red carpet to pick out which one of the girls was going to be her best friend. She didn't even bother remembering what they looked like. Still, she was nervous about being part of the group and wanted people to like her so she could feel comfortable in the dorm, but only comfortable enough to keep being alone and unbothered so that if she walked to the vending machine to get a Mars bar she wouldn't feel weird and could say hi to people as she punched in the letter A and the number 3 and the little metallic coil turned her Mars bar toward her and dropped it right at her feet. Why wasn't life like that? Why wasn't there some great dispenser in the sky that could coil outward and drop your wishes right into a cubby in front of you so all you had to do was reach through the black plastic metal flap and retrieve them? She could punch in the code for Stephen (S, 3) and the code for Friends (F, 4), and she'd be set. She didn't even need a lot of friends. One Mars bar was plenty.

Anyhow, she had become used to her satellite status, so it was fine for her that the only words she spoke to anyone were directed out at the group per the request of the hall monitor. She introduced herself and said her favorite hobby was old movies. And that was it. She made no impression and said nothing strange or wrong. She contemplated this as she sat half-listening to the rest of the meeting. It might be possible for her to go through school completely on this conflict-free half-underground level. This sort of gray wave of calm invisibility. Independent and without incident. The idea of doing nothing wrong? Now *that* thrilled her. She could be blameless and on her own and could live her own life without anyone doing anything to her. Even better, she wouldn't want anything from anybody and so she'd never get

The Sunfish

hurt, never get left out. It would be easy to do, right? She could just go through college all incognito.

And so she hid from one interaction after another during the week of orientation. She went to the café instead of the cafeteria, because at the café you could just order from the counter and get your food to-go instead of carrying a big tray into the dining hall where a well-meaning orientation counselor had seen her sitting alone and asked if she didn't want to join the group at this other table, which she didn't. A whole new orientation group to suffer through? Hers was bad enough, and the icebreakers and all that, it really did feel like being broken, like the shell she was building around herself kept getting cracked by two truths and a lie: "I am super into horses, I have a boyfriend, and Audrey Hepburn is my favorite actress." Somehow they had figured out the lie.

Her friend Gloria told her later on the phone that she was asking for it.

"No I wasn't!"

"You're like a glutton for punishment."

It was true, maybe she was. Maybe she wasn't as good at this underground life as she had thought.

"Look at me. I keep it cool. I just go to my big anonymous state school and avoid everybody and meet people online who I don't have to care about because they never become people. They're all just age, sex, location, and that's it."

"Wow, that sounds even better."

"Right?"

Lucy laughed. She could see Gloria in her underwear on her blue polyester bedspread with her purple hair and some cartoon shirt with the collar cut off. How she always smelled a little acidic.

"I miss you. Why can't you be here?"

"Because not everyone scores a zillion on the SATs."
"It was only half a zillion."
"Well, I got like a 700, so."

Lucy could tell Gloria was about to get gloomy and she had enough of her own gloom so she got off to engage in her new favorite hobby: watching endless hours of T.V.

She discovered that her room had cable television, something she had never had at home, and she decided that this would be her refuge, the outlet for all of her fantasies. She could make a life there, right in the television. Beyond this, she would go to class, she would be a good student, she would get good grades and then, sometime in the future at least, she would have a career, and power, and no one could take that away from her and everyone would, at the very least, have to respect her, take her seriously. But this was only a vague notion, something to which she clung abstractly. It was the television that was more real, the endless situations and scenarios and romances. That was where she was living now.

Late one night a nature show came on about the sea creatures living in the very deep unexplored parts of the ocean. She wanted nature clean and sanitized so she could sit in her pajamas with the blanket bunched up in her lap and take it in without getting wet, without getting dirty, without getting cold, without getting thirsty or hot or sweaty or uncomfortable. She wanted it to feel like she was diving into the colors of the ocean but not into its wetness, that she could be without her scuba gear and without the pressure or the sting of the salt water in her eyes or the coldness rushing in under her wetsuit. It was the same way she watched all that human drama on *7th Heaven* and *Smallville*, without her having to actually be *in* the drama. Free from the hurt it could inflict, the anxiety, the pain, the hope, the love.

The Sunfish

The television cameras took her far, far down into the ocean's deep where there was immense pressure, almost 400 times that of the surface. The submersible was a silvery orb in the vast cavern of dark far below the reach of the sun, sinking farther and farther past the ordinary creatures, until deep in a trench, suddenly lit up by the camera lights, a jellyfish shaped liked a starfruit appeared with blinking neon lights strung along the ridges of its body like a trashy strip club facade. Next, the colonial jelly appeared with its forty meters of tangly stringy electrified tentacles that could zap anything that came near it. In the deep recesses the monsters were revealed, the really ugly ones, like the fangtooth with its mouth of spikes too big to close. Or the angler fish, who looked as though some fisherman had come along once and planted a rod in the muddy mound of its head and hung a glowing lantern on it to attract prey to the poor fish's ugly under-bite of a mouth. The orb hung right in front of her ugly fish's face so she couldn't see any farther than her own small light, her own small hope that someone might see it, might come near. The gulper eel was like the darkness materializing into a shape, opening its endless maw behind unsuspecting fish and swallowing the small light of Lucy's existence in one massive gulp. She felt its power like she felt her own, there but invisible except to the most inquiring of scientists, those daring to take a submersible far into her interior, to the place others had been too afraid, too stupid (she decided), to look.

Wasn't she also like these creatures who hadn't seen light in millennia, ethereal and barely visible except for a small white glow, their beauty made by their residence in the dark? Wasn't she like the sea cucumber, whose body was like a red dress, dyed red because the color was undetectable in the dark, a red only visible when the lights of the biologists caught it, the cucumber lost in the ecstasy of a dance so unselfconscious and beautiful that the cameras froze, that music rose to accompany it, that each face watched with an awed silence as she moved, the fabric of her dress rising, billowing, catching a swell, waving, falling, flowing with each gesture. Evolution had designed, cut, and dressed the most perfect thing it could devise and it had been hidden down there in the dark where no one could find it, no one except those special few well-funded researchers who broadcast what their vision saw out into the light. For a moment Lucy believed that this was her, that it could be her. She knew it like an ache—someone just had to train their lights on her to see how she could dance.

A sickly numbing envy spread through her heavy limbs. Each creature got so much attention in this underwater special, even the spiny ones, the ones who could barely make love because their spines were so long they'd stab each other. The scientists observed them with care and attention and wonder. Even the ugly angler fish was regarded with equal interest as it swam by the windows of the submersible. It wasn't ranked against the sea cucumber based on some skewed metric of worth. It wasn't like they lined up a whole bunch of angler fish and said, "That one's the best looking and that one's just an ugly dump of a skank." No, each was distinct and treated with equal scientific interest. But still, Stephen's face broke apart when he looked at her. Why couldn't he see her like the scientists did, as someone worth knowing and learning more about, as a girl, as a discovery, a miraculous creation?

Instead, she was separated out, labeled "horse-face girl," the girl who sucked at talking to people. Her nerves flattened her out and pushed her down against the mattress. David Attenborough's friendly yet majestic voice declaimed from the dark panels of the ceiling above her, "And here we have the genus girl. A young girl. Just eighteen, by the looks of her, swimming in these dark and uncharted waters, looking, as all girls do, for happiness, for meaning, for society among her fellow kind. But finding this, ah, that's where the genus *Girl* must struggle, must suffer. Only the fittest, the prettiest, the most socially savvy survive in these territories and many are lost each fall as college matriculation commences."

"Shut up David!" she yelled, and threw the remote at the television so that the batteries popped out like shrapnel. It just kept talking. She pushed her covers aside, grabbed the remote from the floor, tried plopping the batteries back in, kept messing up and finally slapped the power button down on top of the television. It zapped off like lightning disappearing into a black hole in the middle of the screen.

She sat back on the floor and wished that her roommate, Anna, hadn't had an anxiety attack after the first week and gone home. "Only the strongest survive, Anna, don't you know that?"

There was a silence in the room, as if Anna's pale and dark-haired ghost, hiding in the upper corner of the ceiling, were still too afraid to speak.

Lucy resolved to go out and sit on a picnic table in the quad the next day. To make herself available. To get out of the dark. To be a red sea cucumber in the light. As protection, maybe she'd bring a book. Or she could buy cigarettes at the little campus store and smoke them. When someone asked, she could give them a cigarette. She could give a cigarette to anyone who wanted one. People always wanted cigarettes. She could be the girl who always had cigarettes and people would know this about her and come to get them from her. My lure, she thought, and made an open gaping mouth, biting at the air with her bottom teeth.

She went to the store the next day, which was really just a small room off the large hall that led to the cafeteria. There she roamed through the few wire shelves looking at bags of chips and candy bars and the little health section with Band-Aids and shampoo, and, to her surprise, condoms. Just sitting right there. Condoms. She looked around. Through the metal-grated windows at the back of the store the quad, the brick classroom buildings, and the white steeple at the top of the administration building stood there like always. Present. Self-evident. Did they know condoms were sold here? They must.

She pictured a severe-faced blond administrator in a dark pantsuit turn her face away from the box of condoms, as though she knew of their existence, but didn't want to acknowledge them, of what they were used for. Nonetheless, this blond woman had condoned their use, and by extension, the thing they were used for. Her justification was that people at college were mostly of-age and they went into each other's rooms and had sex there with each other. People had sex at school and the school knew it. There had been lectures on sex at orientation, and on date rape and sexual assault and it all seemed punitive, like sex were a dangerous neighborhood where in all likelihood you would get mugged of all your happiness and self-worth and yet here they were selling condoms as if they expected (and encouraged?) people to do it anyway. For fun. But how could you with roommates? Did they do it in front of each other? It couldn't be. But did you just tell someone you were going to do it and ask them to leave? That seemed much too obvious. Not romantic, not secret, not personal. Everyone would know. She got shaky and nervous at the thought.

The Sunfish

She studied the labels. How did one choose? Lubricated. Extra thin. Glow in the dark. *Glow in the dark?* She imagined a green glowing nightstick moving toward her through the darkness of a room and giggled. What was one even supposed to do with that? She imagined tugging on it, batting it back and forth. It was like an alien probe. She took her phone out, dialed Gloria. She knelt down and whispered into the phone, "Goria, they sell condoms at my school."

"No shit, dipwit. It's college."

"Glow in the dark ones."

"Yuck."

"Right? Like, anal probe, here we come."

"Anal? Why anal? Geez, you're eager to please."

"What? No, no, no, cause it looks like an alien dick."

"How would you know? Have you been sleeping with some otherworldly dick?"

"No, I mean, imagine it, some glowing green stick coming at you in the dark!"

She was trying to laugh and to spread the hilarity to Gloria.

"I'd rather not."

"You're no fun."

"Neither are you. I'd recommend buying some so you can stop talking about it and actually do it."

"Sure, just as soon as you find me a human dick dispenser."

"I'm not finding you anybody. I am now three states away. You're going to have to grow up and find your own battering ram."

"Why so medieval?"

"Why so sci-fi?"

"Goodbye Gloria, I have purchases to make."

"I bet you chicken out."

"Some friend you are."

She hung up.

Her fingers hovered over the glow in the dark package. It seemed like buying a box of these would make the exchange at the time of purchase more like a joke. The extra thin ones made her nervous that they would rip, and the lubricated ones made her think that everything would get too slippery, messy. "Alien dick it is," she said, and pulled the package down, thinking of the improbable moment when she would actually hand them to a boy and ask him to put one on. They would laugh together. Hopefully that's what would happen. It would be a big joke, and it would be fun, and they would both look down at it, glowing between his legs.

At the counter, a bored student who was probably a senior based on his long wavy hair and beard and the knowing expression, slouched on a metal stool zoning out at a magazine half-open in his lap. Behind him was a wall of contraband: cigarettes and lottery tickets and chew. Again, she couldn't believe that this would all be here, right next to the cafeteria and the student health center, that it was provided to them. By the college! She put the condoms on the counter and asked for a pack of Marlboros, having seen enough of the Marlboro Man to know that this was a brand they must have.

"Lights?"

"No."

"All right then."

"Cool that they sell cigarettes on campus, huh?" she asked, as he was changing her money over.

"Well, not if you consider that there used to be a bar in the student lounge. That's gone. And in the eighties the drinking age was eighteen so this used to be a liquor store too. Everything sucks now. It's like summer camp. We're all coddled little kids to these people."

"Oh, sorry," she said. "I didn't know," like the tragedy was all his own.

He cocked his head at her quizzically. "Don't worry about it," he said, but she was pretty sure there was a shot of irony in his voice.

He dropped the change in her hand and let the bills drift down to her palm and then slid her the paper bag with her score in it as she wondered whether she could ever go back to the store after being so uncool. She might have to start buying cigarettes somewhere else.

Still, her plan to be the cigarette girl was off and running, and who knew, maybe she could be the condom girl too. Ha! For use only on alien dicks. She beamed stupidly as she paraded out of the large glass front doors of the building, quickly averting her face in case a group of students coming toward her would see.

She pushed herself up on a picnic table and fussed with the tight plastic wrapping around the pack, slid it off, then flipped it open and muddled around with the metallic wrapping inside. She remembered that she had to rip it out, pull hard, like you would to release a parachute. This finally exposed the filters, all packed in like little soldiers of death in tight neat rows. It was hard to actually pull the first cigarette out. She got it by using her fingernails to pinch the filter. Not smooth. She lit it, squinted, took a drag, and welcomed the wispy trail of smoke deep inside her body where it made her immediately sick. *How am I going to smoke this whole thing?* she thought. She pulled on it gently, taking tiny drags, and that seemed to work, a comfortable kind of numbness came into her limbs. "This is actually kinda nice," she thought. It was easy to see why people did it.

She was one of a few girls out in the quad: one curled up under a tree to read, two who had brought blankets out to lie on their stomachs to do their homework. As the sun came out, the girls peeled layers of clothing off so they were gleaming. This, actually, probably worked better than any cigarette. Still, mostly the girls were alone, though they seemed to be that way by choice. They could probably just go back inside to their dorm where all their friends were waiting for them and then check their computers for all the comments boys had left on their away messages or on the little white boards outside their rooms. They were just on a little aloneness break, that was all; to work, to read, to nap, not because they couldn't get people to be with them, but because they didn't want to have anyone around just then.

Lucy could just pretend to be one of those girls on an aloneness break too, though this was exactly the opposite of why she was there and in all likelihood everyone in the quad could smell her desperation like skunk spray billowing through the air.

She took a deep drag this time, let it sock her right in the brain so that she got all light-headed and fell back on the table to see oak trees above.

Their leaves were like hands with webbed fingers spread around the spiny palm. The oaks grew along the cement paths and in the corners of the dorms, big towering ones. They covered many windows of the girl's dormitory, so that what happened in those rooms was only seen in blinking glimpses before a curtain was drawn. She wished that the school had placed her there so she could go into a building that was made especially for girls, a dorm that the boys would look at longingly with her as an abstract part of what the building contained, even if, individually, she might not have been desired.

The Sunfish

But she was in a co-ed dorm and though one half of her floor was for girls only, it wasn't really the same. They weren't a group, and when her roommate had left she once again felt all alone. How could that happen? How could she be the only girl on the floor without a roommate? "You're lucky," a tall skinny girl named Tanya had said, her parents' money visible in the perfect cut of her cascading dark hair. "I applied for a single room, but they didn't give it to me. Freshmen never get those. It would have been so much more convenient."

"I don't know," Lucy said. "It's kind of lonely."

"Lonely? I wouldn't be lonely if I had a single. I'd have plenty of company." The two girls sitting at the table behind her snickered. They were in the communal kitchen in her hall, and Tanya was leaning against the back of a chair, waiting as Lucy filled her electric kettle.

"No, forget that," she continued. "It's worth it. Definitely worth it. You don't have to do all that planning with your roommate. There's always a place to go when you're in the mood. I would kill for that."

The mood for what, Lucy wanted to ask. She had filled her kettle and was lingering even though she wanted to leave.

"I guess I should be happy then," Lucy said.

"I'd trade with you," Tanya said.

"And abandon me?! No way," a blond girl with short hair behind her said.

Lucy didn't know what to say, leaning uncertainly in the door frame and holding her heavy kettle.

Tanya didn't answer her, but just studied Lucy with an incomprehensible smile playing on her mouth as if she were putting something together in her head, as if she were reading her.

"We're making her uncomfortable. Just let her go and make her chamomile tea."

Lucy stared back, the derision in the word chamomile lingering in the air. She turned and walked out, the water swishing around inside her kettle.

"I am not fucking uncomfortable," she said as she closed the thick wooden door of her room behind her. "I'm fucking fine. I'm in my own room and I'm fine. My room. My room. I wouldn't trade it or share it with you if you paid me."

She looked around at the dark brick walls, the gray carpet, and the two quiet beds, one stripped, with all of her laundry in neat piles on the bare blue mattress with its rubbery lining.

And anyways, nobody cared if she was in the mood or not. And neither did she.

Lucy began to see that for her plan to work, she would have to actually talk to people. Sell her wares. Well, not sell them. Give them away. She noticed a group forming outside of her dorm. She lit another cigarette and shoved herself off the table and sidled up to the smokers. "I do it for the lung health," she said to a boy who hadn't asked. He turned to watch her as she exhaled slowly, blowing smoke up toward the clouds with her head back, the way she had seen people do it.

"Don't we all," he answered. He wore a green army jacket over jeans and a loose gray shirt. His clothes hung loose over his hunched shoulders, all droopy. His top half was all shrunken and tiny, but his hips were broad, like he had once been very fat. He looked a little like a plastic doll that had gotten too close to a heater, a candle with a long stem all burned down. His meaty mouth curled naturally into a snarl, which made his already slightly crooked face intense and

The Sunfish

judgmental. This as he scanned her from under long light brown bangs so that a zap registered in her chest, like she was lit up by his cameras. Bright and interrogated.

A tall blond boy in a striped polo who looked like the kind of person whose picture would appear over the label *Rich Kid* was bragging to the group about how he had gotten a three-hour taxi ride out of New York after clubbing all night without paying for it. "I totally forgot I didn't have any cash! I spent all that shit." He had just jumped out of the cab in Connecticut and run like crazy. "I heard a gunshot over my head and the cabbie was screaming the whole time, but I just ran into the forest and hid in a bush. He couldn't find me, but it still took him like an hour to leave. I swear to God. It was crazy. I was sooo scared."

The boy in the army jacket turned to her and said, "That guy's kind of a dick huh?"

"Yeah," she said, not really knowing why. "You didn't think it was a funny story?"

"Yeah, if cheating someone out of a couple hundred bucks is funny, then yeah, I guess so."

He *was* intense. He sucked his cigarette hard one last time and threw it away. She got the idea that he might be a moral person, and even though he seemed a little scary, she liked him for that.

Without anything left to say she thought she'd leave before she made any mistakes. She had been standing there with her hands at her sides and without the aid of her cigarette, which she had finished. Her mouth was dry and there was no way she could smoke another one.

He reached into his pocket, took out his pack, and saw that there were only two left. He hesitated.

"Hey, do you have another cigarette? I was saving these for later."

"You're going to smoke another one now?"

"Umm yeah, that's why I'm asking. Who has ever been able to have just one?"

"Right, yeah, of course," she said.

"Shit," he said, he was reading her now, looking at her skeptically from under his bangs. "Don't tell me this is your first cigarette ever."

"Umm no, not technically."

"Technically?"

"I just bought this pack and had one just before but like, I haven't smoked in years."

"Since your time as a chain-smoking toddler?"

He was probably making fun of her.

"I drank beer out of my bottle too," she said.

"Haha," he said, the snarl more like a smile now.

She had saved herself. The line had gotten her some of his respect. She took her pack out.

"Have two if you want." She held it out to him, sliding two out with her thumb. She had seen her mother do this and felt triumphant when they both presented themselves to the boy.

"Fancy," he said.

"That's me." She grinned and thought of her mother, who had inadvertently exposed her to smoking by keeping a pack or two around, "Just for parties," though she never smoked herself. Lucy thought of those parties on the back lawn where everyone showed up with voices that got louder and louder and interspersed with screeches and high-pitched laughter batting back and forth, the cigarette smoke filling with marijuana smoke. It was at one of those parties that she had learned to smoke. She had come down in her pajamas and saw her mother sitting out on the porch with a man in a summer suit who had a perfectly trimmed gray-

The Sunfish

white goatee and looked fancy and sophisticated. Lucy said, "Aren't you going to come say goodnight, or are you too busy getting high?!?"

"My daughter, Lucy," her mother said with a tired roll of the eyes. The man had stood up, taken her hand, asked her to sit with them so that soon she was caught between their conversation and ensconced in his cigarette smoke. When her mother went to get drinks, he had taken out a yellow pack of cigarettes and slid one out with his thumb so that it was pointed directly at her (a trick she practiced for two weeks after). She took it, and he lit it for her, just like in the old movies, and then he had shown her how to smoke it "Like a lady." She learned how to hold it delicately between her fingers and how to inhale lightly, so that she didn't cough. She had sat on the wicker couch in a position that made it suddenly feel glamorous and she had blown the smoke out into the night while the man's strong hand rested on her thigh, encouraging her, getting higher and higher along her leg until it was near the hip. She did not look down but kept inhaling and blowing out, looking at the garden as though she couldn't look down and aware that, though she felt like running, and was trapped by his hand, which had become a steel clamp, she was also aware of the close and intense male desire on the bench next to her, which she was completely unused to. She sat almost coyly, coquettishly, on the edge of the wicker couch, as if to say that she could handle it, even as the pressure of his fingers made her feel like the air was turning to glass, hardening and closing around her, tightening her body, so that any unnatural movement would shatter its brittle shell. She pulled and puffed like a mechanical toy in the semi-darkness of the colorful electrical lanterns as the edge of the man's hand reached the end of her leg, just as her mother's laugh and ranging stumbling step came out through the kitchen door. The man's hand released her and stubbed out her cigarette, and he said, "She was just looking to say goodnight." Lucy obeyed, and as she walked away she turned back to hear him say, "Such a sweet girl."

As the boy in the army jacket took her cigarettes they were joined by a girl with long black hair that hung like a messy cape down her back who introduced herself as Stephanie. She had a short friend with her named Bella, who was visiting from home.

"Can I have one too," Stephanie asked, and Lucy did the trick with the cigarettes again, sliding them out toward the heavyset Stephanie who seemed intense in a similar way to the boy. "I'm a bum, but Nicholas is the worst bum," she said, taking out a lighter. "I bet he asked you for a whole bunch."

"Just two," he said, squinting as he pulled on the cigarette. "And technically she offered."

"I was glad to share them with Nick," Lucy said, trying his name out.

"Nicholas, it's Nicholas," he said.

"Oh, sorry."

"I hate Nick. It's my dad's name."

"They used to call him Little Nicky in high school," Stephanie said, crossing one leg in front of the other and swaying. Her pants were a black swishy material, and long straps dangled off them from a whole bunch of different cargo pockets. When Lucy offered one to Bella, she just shook her head and looked away. She barely spoke the whole time they were smoking, and Lucy thought that Bella might be even worse than her, even quieter, standing there with her fists in her coat pockets like two big fat deposits.

They asked Lucy to come to the cafeteria with them and later, after dinner, Nicholas produced a flask that he drank from as they sat on a bench under one of the trees that blocked the harsh light of a lamppost. He did not offer it to anybody and it was quickly gone. They slowly went back to Nicholas' room and because they never explicitly invited her she decided to go back to her room.

"Big day tomorrow?" Nicholas asked.

"Yeah, I guess," Lucy said. He smiled at her with that snarl of his.

It was hard to tell if he was making fun of her or not, and she figured that even if he were, it was okay because that just seemed to be how he related to people. He talked the same way to Stephanie, and to Bella, whose face, she saw, had several large red blemishes, but worst of all, was covered in very noticeable peach fuzz. She almost had a little goatee on her chin.

Back in her room Lucy was so emotionally exhausted that she threw herself on the bed. Had she made a mistake going in so early? Who knows what could have happened. Dinner had been mostly them standing in line with their trays, filling them up high with cheap food and looking over their plastic glasses at each other as they ate all that greasy crap, as Nicholas had called it. Were they her friends now? It didn't really feel like it, and maybe if she had stayed with them it would have been easier to figure out if she was or not. Or, they could at least have built their friendship. Anyway, if she did see them again she could say hi.

She wondered what they thought of her, and looked down at her arm, pinching, then lifting, her freckled skin, which returned her to a frequent obsession. Within the past two years, strong black hairs had grown in on her forearms. When she had noticed the first one she had said, "Oh no, oh no, please don't. Please don't start growing." But they had. The first one was followed by two more and soon, as if they had all gotten the call, they grew in. She felt immensely betrayed by her body. Next, she noticed them sprouting in a circle along the outer edge of her areolas. Dark coarse hairs. Was this normal?

She had noticed, by looking at the other girls, that most of them had perfectly smooth arms, arms with almost no hair, honey-colored and soft. They probably didn't have hair growing on their breasts. There were some with generous growths of peach fuzz on their arms, but none with dark hairs like hers, except for the French teacher, an overweight woman that everyone called "The Ogre." Would she be the next ogre, or would they start calling her the ogre's child or something horrible? She was thin at least, so she had that. Butterface, they had sometimes called her. "But. Her. Face. Everything but her face," Gloria explained.

"God, that's so mean."

"People are dicks. At least you have the 'Everything' part," Gloria said, pulling at the long doughy lip of her stomach.

But Lucy wasn't so sure she did if it was covered in hair.

She had decided to wear long sleeves. Even on hot days. "Aren't you hot Luce? What are you wearing those for?" they had asked, the questions becoming increasingly interrogatory on a hot class trip they had taken in the school van. But she didn't stop, it was too late. She had committed. If she rolled her sleeves up at that point, everyone would have noticed. A spotlight of shame on her arms.

Sometimes her fingers would toy with the hemline at her waist, and the urge to lift the shirt up over her head and pull her arms free was strong enough that she began the motion without thinking. But a dark line of hair had also grown down from her belly button to her crotch, and it would be exposed to everyone's condemning eyes. It all felt like a big

The Sunfish

reveal, but instead of some beautiful thing at an art museum hidden under its white sheet up on the stage, there would be the hairy runway of the ogre underneath.

"Why don't you just shave it off?" her mother suggested.

"Shave? Are you crazy?"

"Sure, I have friends who do that."

"Really? No you don't."

"Sure I do. Plenty of friends. Women shave all parts of themselves."

"I know that."

"But not just legs and armpits and bikini lines. I mean mustaches, arms, whatever. Being a woman is a constant battle with the body. Everyone has their things. Just shave."

But she couldn't do it. It was too fake, and then, what if she were caught, what if they were on some class trip and stubble grew in? And what if shaving made it worse, gave her obvious razor burn? She couldn't risk it. She would just be her own hairy self.

"Fuck it," she said. The next day she wore a tank top to school, and she knew people looked, but no one said anything to her. Was she safe? She kept listening for words and phrases: "Ogre," "Man arms." But the silence remained, unnerving her. In it she thought she detected the words "Tarantula arms," but no one ever said them around her, or even seemed to look her way. Maybe she had spoken the words into the silence herself.

About breasts she wasn't so sure. She didn't know because she hadn't ever seen any others except her mothers and Gloria's and her cousins', who sometimes, on trips to a lake or river, would sunbathe without their tops on. But she couldn't exactly stare in those situations, and she was always too shy to take her own top off around the other girls, so looking would have been even worse. And she had certainly never seen the breasts of the girls in her class even though she had wanted to and knew that they all showed each other. She had heard them talking about it, making fun of "Sarah's mosquito bites," and "Jenny's milk jugs."

She had seen a picture online, loading painfully slowly, one little strip of the woman's face being added every minute or so, until finally, she was revealed from the top down, her bare breasts large and tanned and perfect and hairless. A man had sent her the picture in a chatroom. He had asked, "Is this what you look like?" Gloria had written back, "As if your tiny crooked dick could get that." Then she had signed off and they had howled in laughter.

But no, hers had not. "Put a little hair on your chest," one of her mother's boyfriends had told her once, a landscaper with calloused fingers that she found comforting and attractive. He had passed her a small thimbleful of whiskey when she was sick. "And cure your throat too."

"Hopefully it'll just do the one thing," her mother had said, laughing.

"What, make a man of her?" he had asked, feigning innocence.

Her mother had laughed and hit his arm playfully.

Well, it's not a fucking joke, mom, Lucy thought.

That night Lucy had stood in front of the stupid antique bathroom mirror with a pair of tweezers and taken one of the long hairs and pulled at it. "Youch! Fuck!" She hadn't pulled hard enough and the skin had lifted out as if it were hooked. She tried again, and this time it felt like barbs releasing. She looked at all the many that were left, little black rings, like eyelashes, around her areolae. "No way, that shit hurts."

She thought the spot would bleed, but it didn't.

So, she left them, but was always nervous they would be seen through some slip of her tank top or dress, or that they would be visible through an especially sheer shirt, little bumps of black beneath the fabric, pushing up against it. She was sure people knew, even as her bras were padded for safety.

That night, after meeting Nick, she decided to look it up to see whether other women had them. She read that it was common, that thirty percent of women had them, and that in extreme cases it meant that you were "hirsute" because of PCOS. She also read that many of the women were embarrassed by it, even though people said they shouldn't be. A woman wrote about making love in the dark, and not wanting to take her shirt off in front of her boyfriend. The advice columnist told her that if this boyfriend of hers wanted to get into her pants, he'd want her anyway and wouldn't care about the hair on her nipples. She thought of Nicholas looking at them in that intense way and saying something, something like what? "Nice hair?" The image of her sitting topless in front of him made her shiver. His cold unreadable eyes on her, his messy bangs obscuring what he thought. What would happen next she couldn't fully imagine, but the idea of the reality of it made her nervous and sick and excited. She lay back, reached down to her crotch, and rubbed at the excitement, moved it in circles until it swelled and burst in a long shudder.

Afterward, she lay back on her covers, spread her arms out, and let her stomach empty as the sick nervousness turned into something like helplessness and fear. Vulnerability. She twisted back and forth and moaned like a sick little kid, frustrated and stuck with her illness. When Nick's face appeared to her, she hated it, and flung angry darts at him.

The next day she ran into them again outside the Campus Center.

"Where's Bella," she asked.

"Forget that slut," Stephanie said. "She's crazy."

"Why is she crazy?"

"No reason; she just is."

Later Nicholas told her that Stephanie had taken Bella to see a guy Stephanie was interested in. They had all been drinking peach Schnapps and Bella had gotten very rowdy and started teasing the boys by lifting her shirt, which had led to a game of truth or dare, and every time the boys got a turn they chose dare and off came a piece of her clothing. Stephanie left because the boys wanted her to take off her clothes too. Supposedly Bella had been topless and in her underwear by the time Stephanie left and who knows what happened after that. Bella didn't come back to the room that night, and in the morning when she showed up she had said nothing, until, as if to break the silence, she blurted out that men were pigs. Stephanie told her that she was a pig and so that was that. "Three little piggies," he said, and smiled cynically.

Lucy didn't know what to say. It was shocking to her that someone would just take off all their clothes in front of two other people they didn't even know. They were drunk and that's why, but Bella might never even see those boys again, so why would she show them something so special? And she was so quiet! It was probably her only way to get their attention. But it made her itch because showing them her body wasn't actually showing them herself. It had nothing to do with it. They didn't even know her or like her or anything. The hot itchy sensation ran up her body as she kept picturing the two boys on the bed, a pilly blue comforter over it, and Bella standing in front of them lifting off her

The Sunfish

shirt, her bright white naked body revealed as the specialness dropped from it.

She thought about it all that night and it hung over her like a specter the whole next week, dark and shadowy.

She saw Nicholas more and more and began calling him Nick in her head, as her own little term of endearment. She thought that maybe, over time, as they got closer, he would let her call him this, and she would be the only one. She learned that he was at college because his father wanted him there but he was sick of being forced to do stuff. "The fuck does he care what I do? He's never cared before and now he wants me to go to college. Fuck him. But whatever, he's paying. I just don't like getting pushed around. You ever get pushed around?"

"Yeah, I guess so, I don't know. I just always went off by myself." She didn't want to tell him how much the others had pushed her around because he might start to think of her through the eyes of her high school classmates. Especially Stephen. She didn't want to be his joke too. They were sitting on their bench in the shadow of the oaks near the large steps that led up into the quad, smoking cigarettes. Admitting it to him would be like curling down on the grass in front of the bench. She'd be like a worm in her denim pants and blue sweatshirt. He would see the whole sequence of her life, peer right down through the past year and all the ones before to witness the scenes of her humiliation lined up until she got tinier and tinier wriggling there on the ground before him and he wouldn't want to see her at all. Instead, she sat next to him pulling on her cigarette with her eyebrows in an attentive furrow pointed at the shadow play on the grass, allowed to be a person just like him who had shown up new from somewhere else.

Not that it seemed like Nicholas had really heard her. There was only a small nod, as if he were still talking to his father in an angry room inside his head. He spat and pulled at a small piece of tobacco on his lips.

"We're going to a show later," Nicholas said. "Some band that Steph loves."

Being with this new little group, with Stephanie and Nicholas, was like having this brittle glassy exterior along her front, made up of every word and interaction, and always in danger of breaking. It made her on edge even as it excited her.

"Oh, can I come? I'd love to come."

"Desperate much? Yeah, you can come. That's why I told you about it."

Maybe she just didn't understand Nicholas properly. Maybe he did like spending time with her. He was always just so on edge or blunt, or cynical. She never knew really what he wanted. It just didn't seem possible that he could actually want her, Lucy.

And yet, they went to the concert. All she remembered was that the venue was in an old rundown brick building and that everything inside was painted black. That they wore bracelets that were pink, which meant that they couldn't order alcohol, and that the volume was so loud that the guitars seemed to screech back and forth across a thin wire in her skull. Hearing the actual notes was almost impossible. She left with her ears ringing. Steph didn't seem to mind at all, as if she had been at a different concert. She was elated. "Wasn't that the sickest show ever? They were so sick. I love those guys. Sick. God, I loved them. SO good!" Then she lifted her arms and screamed, threw her head back at the night with the streetlights lighting the whole scene. Nicholas looked over at Lucy and smiled like it was a kind of joke, her reaction. She had to wonder, did he live life or just observe it? Did he love anything?

When she was back in her room she kept thinking about that smile. They had been lagging behind Steph who was plowing through the night in her excitement and they had smiled at it, at her, together. Together. Yes. She gripped her hands tight, pressed one palm to the other as if they were joined. A rush went through her.

"If you're waiting for Nick to make the first move you can forget about it," Steph said the next day as they were walking to the cafeteria.

"The first move?"

"Don't act like you don't know or whatever. All cute and innocent. It's not cute. And Nick's not going to make the first move."

"What do you mean?"

"He's shy! Nick is the shyest person in the whole entire world."

"Nick? He's not shy. He's—"

"Is too shy. Super shy. Yeah, probably you think he's all dark and cool and cynical and sarcastic and all that. But believe me. I went to high school with Nick. He is shy. He'll never do anything, even if he wants to. Sooo, if you want something to happen, you have to do it."

"I don't want anything to happen."

"You don't?" Steph stopped walking, her face furrowed in shock.

"No."

"Really? Are you sure? I thought that was what this was all about."

"Well, it's not."

Or at least she definitely wasn't going to say it was to Steph, or to anyone else. If Nick was so shy then she was so shy too. They could both be the shyest people in the world. She wasn't all out and forward the way Steph was. Plus, she had liked just being friends. She liked being one of three, doing things together, for it not to be called anything.

But now she felt terrible. Steph might tell Nick and then everything would be ruined. She was nervous all through dinner. "Aren't you going to eat?" Nick asked. She nodded, but kept pushing the food around. A bite of the greasy pizza would get shocked the moment it landed in her stomach, like her lining was electrified. She didn't know what to do. Nick was normal, and Steph seemed normal too, but she couldn't tell. It was like they were in suspension. Steph had been surprised. She would tell Nick for sure. Everything was being ruined.

And it was. Nick didn't talk to her the same way the next day. He wouldn't look at her, and he said almost nothing. Then he didn't talk to her at all anymore, not for a whole week. Finally, she got up the courage. She sent him a text.

"Why aren't you talking to me?" She waited a whole hour. Finally: "I am talking to you."

Ugh, what was that supposed to mean? He wasn't being honest.

"Not the normal way."
"Everything's normal."
"Nothing's normal."
"I just didn't want to bother you, I guess."
"Bother?"
"Nvm."
"You're not bothering!"

But he didn't write back. She saw him from a distance and when he noticed her he turned and walked the other direction along a concrete corridor outside the library. His body was all in shadow.

The Sunfish

She wrote to him again. "Talk to me Nick or I'll kill myself."

"Yeah right. You'd never do it."

He was right, but she needed him to see how upset she was. She went to his room and knocked on his door. His roommate Dan was inside, in his gray cardigan. He was always wearing a gray cardigan and he was short and pretty fat and had red hair and a beard and a gingham buttonup, open at the collar. He looked like a kid trying to become an old man. But he was friendly and funny. "I need to see Nicholas," she told him.

Dan looked back into the room, which she noticed was empty. "You could try to make him appear," he said.

For a moment she imagined a hologram of Nick standing next to his bed in front of the shaded window, frozen in a column of purple light.

"Could I wait here until he does?"

"Of course," he said. "But there's one condition. I have this little bottle of Jägermeister here and I will let you stay if you help me drink it."

She didn't want to be drunk but she also didn't want to sit there quietly with Dan. And maybe it would help to have some alcohol in her.

"Okay."

Dan grinned and very small, very white teeth appeared in his beard. Baby teeth, in a perfect row, that someone had painted with white-out. It was the only thing that made him look young.

He got two Dixie cups from the top shelf of his wardrobe and poured the thick brown liquid into the cups. "Just like cough syrup," he said. "Have you ever had this before?"

"Not that I can remember. No, I don't think so."

"You would remember." He gave her a meaningful look, and winked, like an old man to a child. It was weird.

She began to sip but he stopped her, held his cup out, and she bumped her waxy rim against his, crinkling it just a little. They smiled at each other like they were doing something bad. Man was she high strung. She was sitting perfectly straight on the bed and imagining that at any moment Nicholas would come in and his tired eyes would land on her and waken in surprise. What would he think of her sitting on his bed? He might tell her to get out. He might just turn around and walk away. She would have to say something quick, or do something to keep him from running, to fix it, to fix everything, to show him that Steph had been all wrong.

"Stop thinking so much and drink," Dan said. "He'll be back. Don't worry. I know you're probably not used to sitting around and drinking with a fat ugly Irish guy but that's your afternoon, so just let it be."

"You're not ugly," she said, facing him.

"I am ugly. I'm definitely not good-looking, but neither is Nick. We're both ugly sonsabitches." He began to laugh and looked like a much older man again, but it was as if he was trying to be older so the laugh sounded a little off, fake.

"Nick is not ugly," she said, resolute.

She had never even considered that this might be the case. He was just Nick, with his long hair always in his eyes and his droopy clothes. And maybe yes, his face wasn't like an actor's but it was *his* face, long, a little crooked, like someone had bent it accidentally while they were working on it. A lawnmower blade warped by a stone. He was stooped over a little, looking up at things sideways, like his cynical observations of the world came out of that crook in his face, that bent part. *That* was Nick. Nick!

The Sunfish

"He is too ugly. That's why we're two lonely guys sitting here in our dorm room together on our computers or hanging out with other losers who don't know they're losers, or are trying not to be, or have given up or whatever. Point is, we're all ugly, baby. Think about it. I mean, most people are ugly. They're old, or fat, or just kind of washed-out. Especially middle-aged people. Almost none of them look good. There are really only a few beautiful people, if you think about it, a few rare ones. And these we worship and these we think should be what everyone else should look like. And it's stupid, because none of us do or can. Most people are just kinda crappy-looking. And then, I guess, as a counter balance to the beautiful ones, there are also the really ugly ones."

"You're depressing."

"No, I'm not; I'm truthful. The truth makes everything more easy. Watch: you too, Lucy, are ugly. I know I'm not supposed to say that to a girl, but it's true. You are ugly."

A familiar emotion pierced up from the bottom of her stomach into her chest. The shocking thing was that he was actually saying it to her. Rarely had people actually said it. They would come to the brink and then stop, and laugh, and peer over at her to see how she would react, or they would call her a horse. But he just said it and then sat there all calm as he regarded her, seemingly uninterested in her reaction. She wanted to hit him, to send him through the wall, to make him disappear the same way she wanted to make Nick appear. But there he was, looking at her intently, sitting in his chair, his fat belly bulging out over his lap through the cardigan that he had now unbuttoned, the gingham shirt hugging it tightly, strapped down over his belly.

"You're ugly," she said. "You're fat and ugly."

"I know. I just told you that."

"You can't just call me ugly when you're ugly too."

"Why not? That's the point I'm making. It's the truth. The truth feels good. You should like the truth. I know I'm fat and ugly. In twenty years when I'm married it won't matter. I'll just look like every other middle-aged guy. But right now, I'm fat and I'm ugly and that's how it is. You at least are not fat. Look, I bet your stomach doesn't even fold over like this:" He took a big gulp of his Jaeger and lifted his shirt. There was a surgical scar running along the side of his stomach. He grabbed that line and lifted it, so the white fleshy stretch-marked mass was uncovered. "I sweat a lot under there, believe me. But that's how it is. I go to the gym sometimes, but nothing really changes. I'd have to do something really drastic to get that to go away, but I don't care enough. I'd be ugly anyway."

She wondered all of a sudden if she should tell him about the line of hair running down from her belly button, about the hair on her breasts, the spiky rings around her areolas.

"My body betrays me all the time too," she said.

"I don't doubt it," he said, and didn't seem particularly interested to hear more.

"In weird places."

"It's always in weird places. It's always in the worst places, right? It's like our bodies hate us."

"I have hair on my breasts," she said.

He turned to her. They were silent, looking at each other. "Well, you've got my attention," he said. "I may be ugly but I am a man."

"But that's the problem. A man would not want to see this."

"Maybe, but I am an ugly man. Here, take more, take more of this." He reached the bottle toward her cup, which still had a small sip in it.

The Sunfish

"Now you just want to make me show you."

"Yes, that is exactly what I want. That is what we are doing here. We are ugly people and I'm willing to bet you have never had a conversation like this before. I am willing to bet that there has never been anybody in your life, ever, that has actually talked to you about something that you probably think about every day. Probably spend more of your time thinking about than anything else."

"That is not true!"

"It is true," he said. "It means everything."

She considered this as a low current rose in her body, starting in her legs, numbing them with fear. The expectation of what happiness could be like had continually fallen like a floor dropping farther and farther down as if it were crashing through a building so that she could see a different image of herself as it broke through each floor: huddled in her little dark dorm room, intently staring at the nature channel, thinking about being ugly; skulking across the quad, her head down or bent to the side as she avoided people's eyes, people who could see that she was ugly; appraising herself in the mirror, poking and stretching; perched on a chair bright with shame as a small group peeped over at her from their huddle, laughing and assessing; winding down a street, anonymous in a crowd of people, like at the beginning of a movie, just that when the camera zoomed down it rushed right past her, avoided her for the prettier girl who played the main character, who shoved her out of the shot. That was what her life looked like, a girl trying to get into the shot she wasn't cast for.

She grabbed the cup and drank. Her heart was pounding. The bottom hem of her shirt and the tight fit of her bra were glowing with possibility. It could have been this, it could have been anything. She saw a crazy hairy banshee of a woman, a tarantula, clothes off, ripping and dancing through the room, jumping on all the pink hairless things and devouring them. She drank. Cough syrup. Medicine. She put the cup on the bed where it tipped over onto Nick's comforter for lack of support.

"Thadda girl," Dan said.

She fixed him with an earnest look like a doctor explaining a procedure. "I am going to show you and you have to be honest, honest like always."

"I will be honest."

She lifted her shirt up just enough that the line of hair from her belly button showed. He grunted, nodded understanding. Prompted by this, she lifted her shirt the rest of the way up to her shoulders so that her black bra was exposed. Then she grabbed the top of the bra and pulled it down. It pinched at her sternum but she didn't care. She pulled it down and watched as her breasts, sprinkled with acne and white as cream, came into view. Then her pink nipples were out, surrounded by their small ring of dark hair. She looked at them for a long moment and then she looked slowly up at Dan. He was examining them as thoughtfully as she was. He was not moving.

"What do you think?" she whispered. His eyes flicked up to hers and then back at her breasts. His hand moved across his chin.

"This is what I think," he said. He was taking his time. "This is what I think. Initially, I was prepared for something much worse. Yes, there are hairs there but I have them too. I know women aren't supposed to but I bet you many of them have it. I think that, knowing they are there, I mean, once you've seen them, honestly, then you know they're there and you don't think about them. In truth, this is the first time I have ever seen a woman's breasts, not counting my sister's, which was an accident, and I think that yours are very nice. I think you have very good breasts."

It occurred to her that he might be excited. So, for just a moment, she lowered the bra farther to let her breasts spill forward and out into his gaze and full visibility. He inclined almost imperceptibly toward her.

"I take it back," Dan said.

"Take what back?" she asked as her heart constricted, her breasts suddenly foreign to her, displayed there on the open shell of her bra pads.

"I take it back. You are not ugly. I see you differently now. You are not completely ugly."

The honesty that had been in his eyes, the atmosphere of shared understanding and commonality in the room, was siphoned from the air and a tightness gripped her throat. A panic to conceal herself from his eyes jolted through her as the door opened and Nick walked in. She flapped her bra up just as his eyes jumped from her face and dropped to her chest where one of her nipples still hung over the top lip of the bra, stuck there. The horror of what she'd done found her. She gripped her bra, readjusted it, tried to push it over what had happened to conceal and take it back. It had been innocent. Scientific. But now Dan's inky desire clouded the room and Nick's bent face straightened into a blade that cut through the murk right into her. What she had meant to fix was broken by the even bigger wrong she had done. She had broken it; she had broken everything.

"I'm so sorry Nick, I'm so sorry. I didn't mean to. I don't know how it happened. I'm so sorry."

He just lifted his hands helplessly toward her as she ran by him.

She streaked back across the campus past the bench under the oaks where they had smoked their cigarettes, past the paths to the cafeteria, the places they had been, each like a zap, a jumpstart clipped to her heart. The brick walls of the buildings loomed indifferent, blank, and the warm landmarks of her campus receded into anonymity. She had lost each one and could never get any of them back.

She made it to her room, slammed the door shut, and threw herself on the bed where she flailed, tangled herself in the blankets, kicked at them, gulped at the air, lay still, moaned, then kicked out at nothing. She cried. Big sobs broke through her body. "Little piggies," Nick had said about Bella. "Little piggies."

A weak light filtered in through the blinds. She could hear people walking by on the path outside, the indistinct sound of their voices going to class. She tried to bite away her crying but it wouldn't stop. She wanted to wail and bunched her blanket up in front of her face and used it to clog up every ugly sound coming out of her.

Nick was gone and she had made him go away. She thought of his face, the shock, the helplessness, how it had straightened into rage. She thought of how it was all gone now, her one shot. She left her body and looked down at herself lying on the tiny bed, a poor worm-like creature in a school with all these people that didn't know her at all, that had no idea. A pink worm in a pile of dirt. And the only person who had kind of begun to know her was Nick. A pulsing hatred for Dan began to beat in her chest. Dan in his stupid chair talking to her about ugliness and his strange poisonous view of the world and his terrible cardigan and fat belly. She couldn't believe she had shown him. What she had done. Was that what he had been after the whole time?

She wanted to howl. She couldn't believe that he had been the person this had all happened with. It was supposed to be Nick. It was Nick she had imagined in her room, the light being crowded out by an intimate darkness, shushed away as they stood together, came toward one another in the full glow of her computer's underwater screensaver—.

But none of it now. She turned and tossed and rolled and grabbed her blankets until the violence went out of her.

In a fit of insanity, she called her mother.

"Oh darling, is it a boy? Is that what's happened? It's so painful isn't it? I've had, oh gosh, you couldn't count the heartbreaks."

"This isn't about you, mom."

"Oh I know, it's just that, if you only knew how much more there was to come—"

"Not helping."

"No, just that, you know, you'll get through it. Just be strong; be brave."

"Yep, I'll just feel completely different than how I feel now."

"Oh honey, I know, I just, you have to go get out somewhere. Forget him for a minute. Go get out of your skin. Just get out there for a minute. He's not worth all this, I'm sure."

"Okay, I'll just forget him then." She flipped her phone shut. When it rang again, she ignored it. "Plus, he's not the one that's the problem. I'm the problem," she said to herself. "I'm the one he's probably forgetting about."

She stared at the ceiling, flicked on the T.V. It was the middle of an episode of *Blue Planet*. A rerun. She turned it off, then on again. They were out in the open ocean. David Attenborough was talking about large kelp floats and the life that gathered there. Then the camera went down far below the kelp float and found the sunfish moving slowly toward the surface. It looked more like a banged-up silver dollar with a fin on its top and bottom. A big flat plate of a fish. The sunfish came slowly under the kelp float and Mr. Attenborough explained that she was coming there to visit the half-moons, the little fish that stayed under the float. Lucy joined her there. Together they were coming to the half-moons, hoping that they would slowly eat away the hanging parasites that had attached themselves to their bodies, as though she were rising out of the bed, pulling the blanket around her, floating out through the door and laying her body flat against the grass of the quad. The sun fish, gulping through its narrow open mouth, lay sideways in a position of surrender, barely moving, and let the half-moons eat and peck at the parasites. All the fish came to her, tugging, pulling, prying, taking all those parasites away, tugging the blanket loose from her shoulders and pulling the shirt from her torso as the voices in the quad called above her. Then, to get even more clean, she rose all the way to the surface where the gulls streaked, bobbed, and landed, freed herself from the black clasp of her bra, from all that covered her, so that again, she lay herself flat against the water as the sun streamed down warm over her silver body and the gulls with their tiny feet landed on her to peck away the parasites until they were all off and she was clean again. Everyone was there. All the gulls. Everyone had come to help.

ONE-EYED BOY

Part One: The Logging Accident

As HE WAITED for Oliver to pick him up, Luke nodded off inside the dirty, glassed-in front porch of the house on Madison he was renting with a bunch of other guys from college. He had landed a summer internship at News Chanel 5, one of the larger local networks, and had only been there a few weeks when the cameraman he was shadowing got into a car accident, a bad one. Because they were low on camera people, Luke was offered the opportunity to film a few segments for Oliver, who was a reporter. So, there he was, waiting to get picked up for his first shot at being a cameraman, just like the cameraman who had showed up to the scene of his sister's death two years before. He liked filming, loved the camera and everything he could do with it, but he also wanted to get inside one of those newsrooms to see how they operated, how it was that they could pry their way into people's private pain.

Luke hadn't slept most of that night, which wasn't much of a change over the last two years. All he could do was stare helplessly out at the dim light filtering through the ivy growing on the brick wall of the house next to his window as he waited for the yellow strobe lights of the streetsweepers to revolve in quiet circles through his room as the first sign that morning was on its way, that his vigil was ending, that his hope for sleep was lost and he could give up trying, which was when, in relief, he finally did fall asleep, only to be woken moments later by his alarm.

He had put on some of his nicer clothes, thinking he should probably dress up a little: black slacks, a black button up shirt, a thick red tie the color of wine (his only one), and his black zip-up sweatshirt. He didn't have any dress shoes so he just wore his black Vans with the tan soles. He made a cup of coffee. He took a Danish that he'd swiped from some big lecture event the night before at the college where he'd done tech support. He sat outside to wait. He'd only rented in the house because he needed a place to crash for the summer and there was an ad for a room on one of the bulletin boards in his dorm. All the guys that lived there were already friends, and since he didn't know any of them he just spent most of his time alone in his room.

And now he was out on the porch, dozing off, half in and out of sleep, sitting on a crummy folding chair and leaning his elbow on the dirty sill right next to a plastic bottle cap with three cigarette butts squished inside of it. He was gone enough not to notice his ride pull up along the curb, until the horn went off and he swung awake and knocked his coffee off the sill. "Fuck," he said, his pants covered with with coffee. "Goddammit," he said, and dabbed at it with his hands before giving up and running out to the black SUV with the News Chanel 5 decal on the side.

"Caught you napping, huh?" Oliver asked as he got in. He was clearly happy with himself, his eyes all crinkled into a self-satisfied grin at the corners.

"Guess so," Luke said.

"The news waits for no man," Oliver said, as he put the car in gear.

"Right," Luke said.

Luke pulled the belt across his chest and adjusted the small bundle of the Hi8, the Sony Handycam he stashed away in his sweatshirt pocket. It was his own personal camcorder, the one he brought everywhere, the one he probably wasn't actually allowed to bring with him to work. Still, his thumb ran over the red record button and flicked the silver lock switch open and closed as he fought the urge to take it out, pry the little flip screen open on the left-hand side, and train it directly on the man in the seat next to him. The video, he thought, would expose Oliver the way video always did.

Oliver was big and took up a lot of space in the car, as if his body spread out farther than his seat. He had gray hair at his temples, which gave him the look of an airline pilot in his aviators and the blue cardigan over his shirt and tie. He also had that weary look of the weight of responsibility legible in each pilot's face, which, for Oliver, most likely came from having to report every bad thing that dumped itself at his feet as if the world were some kind of truck constantly emptying its sadness and tragedy in his front yard.

"So, who died?" Oliver asked.

"What?" Luke asked. How had he heard about his sister's death?

"Your clothes. It's like you're dressed for a funeral."

"Oh, oh no, I don't know, just what I had I guess."

"Uh huh. You should think about making some upgrades there, man in black."

The houses on Madison started flicking by, old brownstones mostly stooped in decay that got nicer and nicer the farther up the hill they got.

"All right. First stop, the hospital," Oliver said, and pointed his thumb back at a bouquet of flowers standing in a white bucket on the back seat. "We'll visit Greg and get you set up with his gear."

Greg was Oliver's regular cameraman; they'd been working together for close to ten years. Greg sported a long thin ponytail and wore faded baseball hats that said things like Black Dog or Block Island, as if he only bought hats on vacation. In his spare time, he had explained to Luke how he built furniture in his garage. The top of his right thumb had been zinged off by a table saw.

"Is it weird for you to have someone new come and do the filming?" Luke asked. He had the urge to take out the camcorder to film his response.

"Gotta roll with the punches, kid," Oliver said, though he didn't sound totally convinced of his own stupid phrase.

At the hospital, Luke followed Oliver through the parking garage, up the elevators, and to a counter where they checked in. A little while later a nurse took them to Greg's room. Greg's face was bandaged up and what was visible of it was bruised. A ponytail hung over one shoulder as if there was a ferret hiding somewhere in his pillow. His leg hung in a sling from the ceiling.

"Tough break," Oliver said, as he placed the flowers on the small nightstand.

"That better not be a joke about my leg," Greg said.

"What? No. What kind of person would do something like that?"

"The bad kind," Greg said.

"But not the bad joke kind, come on."

"Ha," Greg said, and raised a tired hand. "You're here for the keys to the van, right?"

"We are. Seeing you was just a necessary inconvenience."

"God, I'm gonna miss this," he said. "Luke, are you sure you wanna take my spot?"

"He's counting on you to heal fast," Oliver said.

Luke didn't say anything and just kept his hands in his pockets and rocked on his heels. Greg pointed to a faded canvas duffel bag in the corner that contained the keys and then gave an overly detailed explanation of how to handle the equipment. Luke nodded, even though he knew all of that already. He was a film student, he worked in the AV office, and he was pretty sure no one at the news station could teach him anything about equipment he didn't already know. But that wasn't why he was there anyway, though why he was there still wasn't totally clear to him. He did have things to learn, he did want experience, but he was also sure he'd uncover some kind of corruption. It was like seeing someone you'd had about forty heated imagined interactions with, but once they were in front of you it became clear that they didn't remember you at all. They just behaved normally, like normal people. Of course, you got thrown off by that so you just acted normal too, and soon you were talking and everything seemed nice enough but at some point you knew you'd have to actually say something, do something, and the whole pretense would shatter. It all made him a little queasy.

"Lucky break for you," Oliver said, as Luke pulled the camera equipment from Greg's van in the parking lot of the news office.

"Tough for him, lucky for me," Luke said.

"He jokes!" Oliver said, and chuckled to himself as he wandered off to the curb. His cardigan was unzipped and he placed his hands on his hips. He hummed to himself and gazed out across the highway as if he was scanning off into the distance in some heroic newsman's stance. The wind lifted and dropped his thin dark parted hair like a leaf just clinging to its branch. Presumably he was wondering where his next story was coming from, what it was, and where he'd have to go to hunt it down and pin it to the wall.

"Done yet?" Oliver asked, as if he could tell that he was being watched.

"Yeah, sorry, just about."

Oliver turned, came up next to him, and grabbed a case with lighting equipment in it. "It's good you're observant. That will help you in this business."

Luke didn't know what to say to that. He was embarrassed that he'd been caught observing him, but as he grabbed the rest of the stuff and lugged it to the open back of Oliver's SUV, he thought that Oliver probably liked it, having an audience, someone watching and chronicling his movements, trying to understand the complexity of him, the newsman. Oliver would probably start performing now, regardless of whether the camera ever came out. People always did that, once they knew there was an audience, a real one, no matter how small.

"So, what's today's story?" Luke asked, as he got in.

"Logging accident," Oliver said, and grinned at him. "Guy lost his son."

A shot of nerves cut right through Luke's middle. He was on his way to do just what the news people had done to him, to his parents: to go blow up the scene of his heartbreak. How could this happen on the first assignment? He thought they'd only get to something like that eventually. A clear constellation of connection formed between him and the father, brittle with nerves. He gripped at the hard rectangle of the camcorder in his pocket.

Luke had received the camcorder as a Christmas present and initially it meant nothing to him. He didn't even ask for it. He thought his dad had probably just walked into a Radio Shack and figured his son would think that something like a camera, a big expensive piece of tech, would be really cool. After opening his present, he had turned the camera on, flipped open the small screen on the left side, and followed it around the wrapping-paper-littered living room and panned it across his father, mother, and sister on the couch. In the little screen they each looked gray, like the whole mood had gone somber. He did very little with it after that until his sister died later that year. He went back then and opened the video, replaying again and again the slow pan from the presents to his sister on the couch. She covered her face with one hand, her hair spilling out around it, her legs pulled up in front of her body. There was no sound.

The next morning, he took the camera out again, flipped the screen open, and followed it out of the house. He trained the eye of the lens low on the gravel drive, on the small dirt path out back, shot it up at tree trunks until he let it get lost in a ruffle of leaves at the crown so the screen was sun-blinded. He left it there, trained into the bright blinking whiteness until he lost time.

Later, he brought it out to the fields, dragged it across the line of the horizon, over each edge of mountain, thumbnail of barn, then back to the ground, inches from his feet. Near and far. The camera was like an eager, well-calibrated machine. Its eye pointed wherever he wanted: zoom in, focus, zoom out. Plus, it had tunnel vision. It blocked out everything that was peripheral, focused only on what was in front of it. He began to like the idea that the camera captured what was in its eye, took a copy of it, and put it into the small box inside of itself. One frame was linked to the next, and none of them were lost.

At night, in the darkness of his room, it was as if the camera was still over his eye. Often, he couldn't tell if he was awake or asleep, if he was still in the flow of his thoughts or taken over by dreams. The camera's eye would sway along a pockmarked brick wall, find a deer in a field, zoom in on its face, on its big dark watery watchful eye. The deer would frighten, scatter, and he'd see the fires in the field, the vague shapes of people drinking and laughing around them. He'd catch Cody's face lit up in the flickering night: long, dark hair, Black Flag shirt, tattoos on his arms and calves, big white teeth in a wide mouth, and his eyes—afraid, guilty. Cody.

"That motherfucker," he whispered. A stab of guilt followed, then weight and darkness pressed on top of him like the whoosh and thump of the airbag, the crash of glass. Whiplash. An electric emptiness in his stomach, clenched. The dark airbag grew to the size of a cloud so he was choked under it. He jumped out of the bed, swatted at the dark airbag, screamed. When he found his bed again he sat on the edge and panted.

His father would open the door then and ask, "Everything all right?" His face gray, tired—gentle and helpless.

"Yeah," Luke said. What could his father do anyway but nod, press his lips together, and slowly back out.

The camera gave him vertigo, the feeling of being top-heavy. His vision projected just inches out from his face. It made his head reel, as though the weight in his brain were shifting and throwing him one way and then the other. In his half sleep, once he was back in bed, people visited him like phantoms: Cody, the others at the party, and the white light of his camera, which grew in brightness. He followed it through his dreams. Whatever it trained on froze and got poisoned in its radioactive light. The last thing it saw was his sister, just disappearing around the corner of a doorframe in their old living room. It caught her hand, the rest of her long braid, parts of her back. He knew how the story ended. The next morning she was dead and Cody with her, the car flung off into a cornfield.

***

The logging accident was part of a larger series the channel was doing on workplace safety. Their job was to go and interview the father of the victim. According to Oliver, a branch had fallen unexpectedly, hit the front of a tractor, which swerved violently. The tractor had been holding a tree trunk, which swung across and hit this man's son in the head. The son was sent backwards down a small ravine. When they scrambled down to find him his skull had been crushed on a stone. When the paramedics lifted him, the stone had been covered in his blood.

They pulled up a long dirt drive lined by crumbling stone walls to a lot with a small brown cabin at the end of it. Large sheds holding firewood and covering tractors and A.T.V.s made it a kind of compound. Two large brown dogs ran out barking to greet them. A giant stack of freshly cut logs lay on the far side of the compound where it looked like a big section of forest had been cleared, as if they were making room for another plot, or trying to let more light in. Luke wondered if his son had been helping him clear it.

Luke retreated behind Oliver as he knocked. A bleary-eyed man squinted up at them as the door opened, his face stubbled with gray hair, as Oliver began to explain why they were there. Visible through the door was a small kitchenette at the back of the room with a counter of plywood supported by two-by-fours that held a coffee maker, a wooden dish rack, and a large metal slop sink, the kind you might find in a restaurant. The man let them in, stepping back warily with his large hand on the door, as if another part of him wanted to close them back out. Luke dropped his bag on a card table in the kitchen as Oliver moved toward the far corner of the room where a couch faced a very large television. This is where they would interview him, the television like a large black mass behind the man. Soon the screen would broadcast his own sad story on the news.

The other corner of the cabin held what looked like a makeshift bedroom, with a small cot, a ramshackle shelf that held a few books, and a self-assembled white particle board wardrobe that likely still contained the son's clothes. They would have been living tightly pressed together, father and son. There were two doors against the wall on the right from the door, both of which were partly open to a barely discernible darkness beyond. Luke set up quickly, made sure his light wouldn't be visible in the reflection of the television screen, and only while he was filming did he actually take the time to look over. One was a bathroom, and the other must have been a bedroom. He saw the large shadow of what looked like the corner of a bed. This was where the man would sleep, where he would have to dream.

The man began telling his story. "Aaron had just moved back in with me this last spring. And, and, we were beginning to make some changes here at the house, get some of them trees cut—it was what he was doing anyhow, so he had the will and the know-how, and lord knows I needed the help, and now, this, this accident. I, I don't know." The man broke off. Luke zoomed in slowly, the key light bright on the father in his wooden chair as tears slowly made their way down his face. The man never wiped them.

They gathered in the white of his large mustache, got muddled on his lips, fell to his chin and hung there before they dropped off. His red face looked far too exposed in the white light, like an escaping prisoner caught by the spotlight from the guard tower.

The heat crept up Luke's pant legs, then up inside his shirt. The tight room, the dark wood logs stacked one on top of the other with a gray substance between them, a kind of cement, suffocated the air. Father and son must have sat here every morning with their breakfasts, and at night too, on the couch, watching the television, barely talking until the son went off to his cot to read his worn copy of *Siddhartha*, to look through a guidebook of the PCT.

"Lost Marcy two years before, and you know, it wasn't long after that Aaron came back. Thought, you know, he'd keep his old man company. I kept telling him I was fine, fine out here, but he didn't listen in the end. Was a fireman out in California, putting out wildfires, and in the winter he'd ski—amazing skier Aaron, so fast. We thought he'd go to the Olympics when he was younger. Mountain bum!" His face broke into a big coughing laugh. "That's what I called him, 'Mountain Bum!'" He almost screamed it through the cough. Luke zoomed out.

"It's clear that you loved your son very much and we are so sorry for all you have lost. Do you have any concerns over the safety standards of the company he worked for? Do you believe that this branch falling was just, as they say, an accident?"

The man just sat there for a moment. The story was no longer about his son, or his grief. It was about an agenda. About blame. About lawsuits. And buried beneath that, it seemed, the question was about whether or not he was angry, whether he wanted to strike out at the people, at the world that had taken his son. Or that's how it seemed to Luke anyway, as he filmed. The man blinked up into the light and said, "I don't know anything about that. I don't pretend to know much about all that legal stuff, or the business, I don't pretend to know."

"And do you think," continued Oliver, "that the company could have done more to vet their staff? I read that the man operating the tractor was inexperienced, just a few months on the job."

"Now I don't like to blame anyone, okay. Aaron was new to the job too, but he knew what he was doing. They all did. They're good boys. They did what they did. My son, he knew what was what. He wouldn't have been doing it if he thought it was unsafe, and that's all I'm saying about it. That's it. Nothing more. You won't get anything more from me."

"I understand," Oliver said.

"I do not think you do," the man said. He turned his face away and held one hand claw-like over it. He did not say anything else and he did not move.

It was clear that they should leave.

On the way back down the dirt road Oliver was silent but unfazed.

"He didn't seem very happy with us," Luke said, something like quiet drumming nausea beating in his stomach.

"He doesn't have to be. We have to tell a story and he can't decide what story that is."

"Yeah. I don't think he wants us to tell it though."

"He's just sad. He wants us to run some memorial piece on his son."

"Yeah, probably. He didn't like it when you started asking about safety."

"He's saving it for the lawsuit or he's a sucker and that company's gonna run right over him. Either way, we got what we wanted."

"An angry old man?"

"Ha, yeah, actually. Viewers will see the pain. They'll know the company fucked up."

"Do you think they did?"

"Maybe. It doesn't really matter. Sometimes shit happens. The blame isn't always clear, but we want it to be, right?"

Luke had to agree with that. "He didn't want to blame that tractor operator."

"No, but like I said, lawsuit. Or he's a coward. If someone killed my son I'd be pissed. If I had any kids, that is."

"Yeah," Luke said. "I guess I'd be pissed too."

They reviewed the tape in the cramped screening room at the studio, surrounded by black, equipment-stuffed shelves. They watched the camera zoom in, linger as a tear slowly made its way down the man's face, and then back off as Oliver began to ask another question.

"You did good here," Oliver said. "You have the sense."

"I still feel bad for him," Luke said.

"Don't feel too bad," he said, getting up, "or you'll never get through it here. This shit happens all day. It's life. It's part of it. You just take the pictures." He slapped the door frame twice, looked past Luke's head at some blank space where his convictions lived, and walked out, holding his blue cup. Easy as that.

Luke went out to see his father that evening. The sun was still high in the sky and he rocked back and forth on the hard blue seat of a city bus as he made his way out to the suburbs. He pulled the cord and got off at an apartment complex that was a Tetris-like system of brick buildings with rectangular porches and grids of parking beneath. His father was in the galley kitchen pouring a bag of stir fry into a hot wok of sesame oil. The frozen noodles and vegetables steamed as they hit the pan. A twinge registered in Luke's stomach, watching his father bend over the stove and imagining the poverty of his thought process as he walked through the grocery store to choose this meal: something simple, easy to make, with a few vegetables. Something that would fill him up enough that he wouldn't have to make more. And something Luke might want.

They ate mostly in silence after Luke caught him up about the bare details of the internship. They were still pretty new to this. His father had only moved out that spring. Luke left out the crucial detail from that day's story, saying only that they had investigated a logging safety issue. Before leaving, Luke came out of the bathroom to find his father eased back in the big recliner facing the window through which the apartment was lit in a greenish late-afternoon aquarium light. His father's face looked old for the first time, as though the life in it had retreated and left a gray mask of itself trained stiffly on the window. He could have been dead. When his father noticed him, he didn't have the energy to completely hide this blank staring and faltered as if there wasn't enough life in him to lift that clay death mask off with a weak smile.

"Leaving so soon?" he asked, as if it were a kind of joke between them.

When Luke got home that night there was a party gearing up at the house. His roommates had opened the backstairs to the unit above so partiers could shove and maneuver between both. Luke slipped into his room and locked the door. Once inside he positioned himself in suspended vigilance on the bed as the rush and clatter grew at the front door, people invading the hall, yelling, laughing, steps rushing by his room, his panic pumping up, the idea that at any moment someone would try the handle to force their way in to smoke or to crush up some pills. They'd expose him on the bed, the dark whole of his loneliness. When the first knocks came he lay rigid on the bed and said nothing. "Probably a closet dude. They locked it 'cause there's valuables in there or something." There was a hesitant silence after that. But soon there was another knock, and this time he said, "Busy!" like it was a bathroom. "Yo, share what you got man."

"Be out in a minute!" he said. He heard the person muttering but couldn't tell if he'd left. Soon there was more banging. "Someone's getting laid in there bro," he heard a husky voice say. Then his roommate Ryan walked by and said, "Just leave it man, that's Luke's room. He likes to be left alone." But this was unbearable too, a dark ping of terror went off that he had been located, recognized. Whoever was out there started banging at the door and yelling at him to come out. "Party with us dude!"

It was worse staying in the room and there was nowhere else to go, so he came out with his camera up over his eye and it was like panning down a gallery. People parted for him in the hallway, turned to see the camera. They'd either avoid it, strike a pose, or stick out their tongues. He went through untouched, the lens like a submarine window between him and the crush of bodies talking and holding beer cans and solo cups and swimming toward each other through the crowd. When an elbow knocked the camera from his face he scrambled to lift it back up as if his mask had been knocked off.

He guided the camera to a heated game of beer pong and caught the ball bouncing from a rim and then splashing into a beer. He zoomed in close on a game of flip cup, turned to slow-mo as one fell and clattered on the ground. He accidentally lingered too long on a girl lost in thought leaning against the fridge. She caught him and stared directly down the lens before walking away. She was replaced by two girls in fluorescent tube tops who pouted at the lens, blew kisses and turned and stuck their asses out. When he panned to another set of girls one of them walked over and said, "This isn't Girls Gone Wild," and half-lifted her shirt before she pushed him out the door. He found the smokers out on the dark back porch and filmed the smoke pouring out of their mouths like ink. He went up the back stairs to see the small red flare of a glass pipe, and waited for a cloud to move across the moon in a reverent shot through a window.

He found his roommate, Craig, a short blond kid with stoner-spiked hair, bent close to a girl, talking, his hand up on the wall above her head, holding a beer. When they noticed the camera, they got this conspiratorial look, communicated something through it, and then Craig bent in, hesitated, and kissed her. With the camera on them, they began kissing each other harder, moved into the shadowy opening of a closet door, feeling against the dark coats, full into the performance. Craig lifted her up so she could straddle his hips. At that point Luke backed off, zoomed out, and when she noticed that he'd stepped back she called after him as if he'd broken the contract. "Hey," she said, and without the camera it was if she'd suddenly woken up, remembered where she was, glanced at Craig with embarrassed self-consciousness, and walked back up the hallway without him.

"What the hell man?" Craig hissed, but Luke just backed away into the other room.

A girl grabbed his arm, pulled him into the small upstairs kitchen and spoke with drunk earnestness into the camera, inches from the screen: "I am Melissa, and I am drunk, and I love this fucking party, and this weird fucking camera guy, and I am here to tell you that Albany fucking ruuuules!" And as the party wore on, girls lifted their shirts as he went by, yelling, "Tape this camera guy!" and if they got braver, they lifted their bras too, so the guys around them would yell "Whoa! Hey! Don't stop!" or "Shake them things!" and they'd wiggle them and go "Woo," and then everyone else would go "Woo."

And that's when the girl in the tight white shirt under the neon Budweiser sign nudged her friends and lifted her shirt. He was struck, and lowered the camera to look at her. She had a long braid draped over her shoulder. Her friends glared at him sideways. "Umm, what are you doing?" The girl hadn't immediately noticed but there he was, the camera sinking until it was in both his hands, clutched at his stomach. Her hands were still up, the hem of her shirt curled in her fingers. They caught each other's eyes and she mouthed, "What?" before she pulled her shirt down. But he couldn't answer. She must have seen it. Something like recognition in his face. The triangulation of the camera, her top, and his eyes. She was suddenly far too herself, too real. It was as if he had known her forever. Confusion registered in her face and she moved to cover herself back up. "Freak," she said, and flicked the braid from her shoulder before her hand rose to cover her face and she ducked out of the room. In that motion the fragile architecture of what he had seen broke apart. That ancient recognition. Her friends followed her, one with both hands on the other's hips, as though they were in a conga line of concern. "The fuck, dude?" a couple guys asked, like they might step in to fuck up whatever he'd fucked up. "The hell did you do?"

"I don't know," he mumbled. But he did. Of course he did. He had lowered the camera.

He escaped, sluiced through the crowded hallway, pushed the rubbery cap back onto his lens, and slumped in the corner of a couch next to a couple who was in a heated political debate. He hoped that no one was in his room going through his stuff, but he just knew that there were people sitting on his bed, talking, smoking, lifting books and clothes and cushions as if they would find some shameful evidence of his loneliness in there, something he couldn't even predict, and they'd hold it up to him when he came back in, and laugh. He crouched further into the dark. Outside, the shadowy branches of a tree moved across the window pane and a sense of separateness grew between him and the world, both the tree outside and the apartment inside, and all the people in it, and all the people outside of it, all through the city, all the way up to the college and the news station and every single thing he'd have to go and film in his life.

The day after the party, his roommates remembered that he had been there to film it all. "Let's get some party footage, bro," his roommates said. "Let's get some titties. I know you got titties. I wanna see those Albany titties baby." But Luke mumbled and said he hadn't edited anything, or labeled it, and wasn't sure where it was. Luke never showed his videos to anyone. Most of them were not meant to be seen. They were meant to be kept. The point was to get the footage, to capture it, not to let it back out. That was not what he was there for. He didn't want anyone to see what his eye noticed. What he looked for, what he saw. It would be like giving them access to his insides. "Awe, come on bro, just show us a little. Fuck." He just shook his head. He wasn't even looking at them. He hadn't gone through that party looking to film titties. If he showed them, it would seem like he had been, like that was the point. A block against showing them rose up in his body like a sheet of gray blunted metal, a barrier to the images and scenes he had captured, which needed to live in a private darkness inside the camera and the small boxes of footage he stored on the top shelf of his closet. "He just wants that shit for himself. I bet he rubs one out to those titties every night." Luke didn't look up or defend himself. "Just likes to watch what he can't have," another said. This should have hurt, and he guessed that in some way it probably did. Maybe that's why, later, he projected a bit of the footage against the wall in the living room for his roommates, but only three minutes, and only a little splice up. It ended with a shot of titties. Frozen on them. Since that's what they wanted.

He felt dirty for doing it, like he had spat some corrupted ink on the long white-lit tapestry of projection he had filmed for the last year and half, a collection of images whose meaning he did not yet know and whose sequence he was not yet ready to curate into a story that someone should actually see. Now it grew in that white projected light like an oily cancerous tumor.

"You the man, Luke," his roommates said.

Bobby, the one nearest him, leaned back and slapped him on the shoulder with his massive arm. It nearly knocked him from the edge of the couch where he had perched himself in a gesture of half-leaving. "We'll get you some of those soon my man," he said. Luke laughed noncommittally, gave a half-hearted "Yeah," which made Bobby look back up at him, a smile flickering across his broad good-looking face as if it were waiting for him to send a knowing signal back, which didn't come. Bobby was the head of the apartment, the one they all listened to, not just because he was by far the biggest of them—his muscles bulging loose ropes under the skin—but because he was the one they gathered around every time he was out in the living room. It just felt good to be near him and almost desolate to be anywhere else in the house when Bobby was out of his room, doing something, anything, in the kitchen, out on the porch. There was always company around him, giving him a hand, just hanging out to watch, whatever. If anyone was his opposite, his opposing force in the house, it was Luke, who Bobby was now studying, the expression on his face dropping to something that Luke couldn't quite read—sympathy maybe?—to the point where he had to say something. The look was too much, too close, too full of seeing.

"What's the matter?" Luke asked.

"Nothing's the matter," Bobby said, his big brown eyes still working something out.

"I'm sorry you're so fucked up, Luke," he said finally. "Really sorry."

Luke laughed a kind of broken laugh. The other roommates started yelling at Bobby. "That's so mean, dude!" They said. "Yeah, Luke's not fucked up," they said. "He just showed us titties, right?"

But Bobby persisted. "No, this kid's dealing with some shit. He's fucked up; that's the truth."

Luke got off the armrest, dodged Bobby's arm as it reached out to pull him back, and rushed to his room. He closed the door, lay down on his bed, and stared up at the ceiling. The sounds of the roommates arguing and laughing reached him as a thick ugly bubble of tears worked its way up from his stomach into his throat, where it hung, threatening to burst. Luke kept it there, twisting his face into something that might look like crying. The bubble wouldn't release its insides, its torrent, unless he allowed it to, but he failed to cry. He placed his forearm over his eyeballs and lay still. He should have stayed. Bobby was trying to help him, probably.

He pictured himself wedged on the couch happily ensconced between Bobby and the other roommates and half jerked himself up to go out there. But he fell back again. He saw himself in the darkness on his bed, a forearm over his eyes, then out there on the couch, settling next to body, and this image flickered in and out, between rooms, and the more he jumped back and forth, the greater the distance between the rooms became, and the more paralyzed he was to move.

Soon the images returned. Walls, and a face, a doorframe, and eventually, the swinging braid that swung up and then away, swung, and swung again, like a second hand stuck in its continual ticking, caught by the white light.

Part Two: The Naked Break-In

During the period of his initial obsession with the camera, Luke spent a lot of time going over to his girlfriend's house. When he got there, he'd flip the camera open and climb the stairs to the small bedroom at the far end of the carpeted hall. It was past her parents' bedroom suite and had a jet tub that he dreamed of using with Emily on some weekend when the house would be all theirs. When he got to her room he'd focus the lens on the door knob. He'd film his hand as he twisted it open, released it, then opened it again, then closed it again, over and over.

Once he finally stepped into her room, he'd train the camera on her shoulder, her hair, to watch it slide down her upper arm when she bent over her homework until it finally fell free. "Get out of here," she'd yell once the camera had been trained on this curtain of hair for long enough that she said he was being a "Camera creep."

Later she undressed for him as he filmed her standing next to her bed, facing him, the camera pointed at her from his chair by the window. She had gotten used to the camera being there like a third presence in the room, attached to him, and sometimes she'd flirt with it, as she did then. She would shimmy her underwear down a little and he would make a face like he didn't think she'd go farther, like he couldn't believe she was doing it at all, and then farther down she went. She would look at him and then look at the camera, which he held just to the side of his face, as though they were two different entities. When she looked at the camera, it was like each level that her underwear lowered was one more notch deposited in its box, collecting the stages of her undress. Then she would look at him again, and the connection would return, their eyes sending the tension of the moment back and forth. As she slid her underwear down, it was for him first, and then for the camera, a kind of second person she was teasing him with, until he disappeared behind the lens and the show continued through it, of the neatly shaved little triangle of her bush being exposed. By the time she had lowered her underwear far enough to reveal everything, his eyes had melded with the lens, and both of them watched as her underwear was freed from its final hitch and dropped down the length of her bare white legs to the green-carpeted floor.

He continued to film her as she climbed up on the bed on all fours, looked back at him with a grin that was a mixture of mischievousness and doubt, as though she were willing herself into playfulness with her ass in the air. As he followed her, it was unclear who she was looking at, him, or the camera, or both of them together. Lost behind the lens, her body became smooth, synthetic. He watched his hand reach for it in the gray of the little flip out screen, saw it touch her left hip, and felt his insides constrict with a buzzing nervous elated kind of energy. He was both watching and doing. The smoothness of her skin was under his fingertips, and the naked body of a girl was on the screen, being touched.

As he clambered up behind her, his knee slipped off the springy edge of the mattress and the camera jerked free of his face and he tipped forward, close enough to her lower back to kiss it. A few tiny moles were sprinkled across the skin there, and the pores pixelated it in a network of pinpricks. He raised himself and saw how from above she was so skinny, so pale, so like an animal exposed in some vulnerability in the wild, caught, that he felt torn between throwing the camera off into the corner of the room to hug her, and quickly bringing it back up to his face so the vulnerability and imperfections of her body would morph back to the smooth plastic representation of nakedness on the screen.

She peered over her shoulder and found his eyes with a look that attempted to pull out what was inside of him, the tenacious sticking closeness of his feelings, which were all lodged in his chest. She was stretching them toward her like a thick dark sap. She was searching him, scanning for intimacy, for connection, holding his look with a directness that locked onto his eyes, followed each tiny movement there. He raised the camera to capture her face, and saw, just before he was lost behind the lens, a moment of confusion and hurt trail across her eyes.

The rest was inevitable, how she became passive, lay on her back as he lowered himself over her and his disembodied hand coasted over the smooth naked front of her body as the lens turned her anonymous.

"I have to talk to you," she told him in the early morning before school about a week later, "but not with that thing on." She reached out and slapped it shut and held it down in his lap, her hand forcing the camera there. All of a sudden she was crying. "I wanted to end it before, you know, before your sister, but I didn't have time. There just wasn't the right moment. And then after, you know, I couldn't leave then, could I? So, I just stayed around. But I can't anymore; I can't. I tried. I did. I tried." The words swung across him like a boom over a boat deck, the blow knocked him right across his chest so he couldn't breathe. Her hands released the camera in his lap and he made no effort to lift it. He decided to let her see him perfectly clearly sitting cross-legged opposite her, stunned, the great wall of dark open inside him. He intended to cry, to let his body be wracked with sobs so that she could see him, could see all of him. Clearly.

But it didn't happen, he couldn't make it come. Instead, he sat there, perfectly still, blankly staring at her.

"Please, please just say something! Please, I'm so sorry, I'm so, so, sorry."

His hand twitched to reach for her, but then he realized that she was gone, not his to touch. He put it back in his lap, and stared at a spot where the skin of her knee was visible through a small tear in her jeans.

Afterward, they drove to school together and he filmed her as she walked away from him in the school parking lot. The camera did not budge. He trained it on her skinny body, this thin form in high-water jeans that exposed her ankles and the pink socks sticking out above her black Converse as she walked to the end of the lot, turned behind a school bus and re-appeared much later as a silhouette that made its way slowly and steadily toward the school building into which it disappeared. The long shot, it was called, in college.

***

There was another story to cover.

This time he hadn't fallen asleep on the porch. Instead, he had brought his Discman out, put his headphones on, and listened to Rage's *Evil Empire* to get himself hyped up. *Rally round the family . . . with a pocket full of shells.*

"So, what's this story all about?" Luke asked, as he got in.

"A Naked Break-In," Oliver said. "Should be a good one. Teenagers do the stupidest shit."

"I wouldn't know," Luke said.

"All of them except you of course, I should have said."

"Only for two more months anyway."

"Plenty of time to make mistakes."

"Ha."

Mostly they drove in silence that inflated the tension in the car with each slow breath. Luke would cast about for things to say, but Oliver didn't seem to mind the silence. He just drove on without any music on or anything and spaced out as he looked at the road. Every now and again Luke would think of something to ask, but it occurred to him that Oliver never really asked him anything about himself, even though he was a journalist. He guessed it was because Oliver didn't think there was a story to get out of him.

Oliver had this handmade cup that he kept on the wide lid of the center console even though there was a cup holder just below it near the gearshift. The coffee would slosh around as they drove and whirlpool after they hit a tight corner. It stressed Luke out, but Oliver didn't even seem to notice. He'd just reach a blind hand out for it, find the little notch for his thumb on the top of the handle and rub it absentmindedly before he'd lift it and give it a loud suck.

"So, what's the story with the cup?"

"I made it myself in this pottery class I signed up for while I was trying to find interesting hobbies during a period of meaninglessness in my life."

"Oh. Uh, it's really good," Luke said. It actually was. Smooth and evenly thrown, fired in a speckled blue glaze with a white stripe at the bottom.

"I'm kidding. What do you think, I'm in some kind of a midlife crisis or something?"

"Oh, I don't know."

"My mother made it."

"Ah."

"Aren't you going to ask if she was in a crisis?"

"Um."

"Well, she wasn't, really. Ah, maybe she was." He went into a blank space, as if he had left the car and was seeing something overlaid on the highway. His hand felt around for the cup, grabbed it, raised it, then lowered it without drinking. In a quiet, more sincere voice, he said, "After her second husband died she got into making ceramics. Ceramics and religion, for some reason. Jehovah's witnesses came to her door one day and instead of closing it, like she usually did, she sat and listened, then went to a meeting, and pretty soon she was sliding the literature across the table at me."

"Did you read it?"

"Ha, me? No, she only did that once. She only had to try that once."

"Hm."

They reached the turnoff for the parkway and Oliver flipped the blinker.

"I think she wanted certainty, you know. They just told her what she had to do and that was enough. If she did it, she'd get in. Who wouldn't want that?"

"Yeah. Not you though, huh?"

"In my job, you'd be stupid to think it went that way."

Luke nodded, then nodded again. It seemed like kind of a grandiose thing to say. "But you do have to take the assignments you get," Luke said. "Right?"

Like a twitch, Oliver's shoulder and right hand cocked toward Luke like a spasm immediately reigned in. The violence in it held back.

"I take the assignments 'cause that's the work," he said in slow, constrained intervals. "What I find when I get out there, in the world, that's the mess, that's where there aren't any easy answers."

"That's true, that's true," Luke said too quickly. He sensed that the power of Oliver's presence could expand, like it could slide him out the door as easily as wiping something off the dash, a crumb or a bug or a cup of coffee sloshing with liquid.

They came to the tolls. Oliver slowed, opened the window, handed the ticket over and counted the 35 cents out in his large soft palm. A teenaged girl waited in the window, sharp strands of pink hair descending from her visor on either side of her face.

"Here you go," Oliver said. "Have a nice one."

"Thank you," the girl said. She took the money, scanned it, then raised the gate to let them pass.

"You don't want to get EZPass?" Luke said.

"No, I like talking to actual people."

"Is that why you're in journalism?"

"Ha! Maybe. Mostly people don't like what I talk to them about."

"Yeah, but you like it."

"I guess. I like pressing people a little, finding out what they think."

He lifted the cup and sucked. "Yup, that's where it gets interesting. But the trick is not to think about it too much. Actually, a pretty good general principle in life. Probably the opposite of what they're teaching you at that college of yours, right?"

"Yes, definitely."

"Ha!" Oliver said. "Well, welcome to the real world."

The day after Luke's sister's death the camera crew showed up. They heard that there would be a memorial at the site of the crash. The crew had already been there the night before, gotten the footage of the car in the cornfield. They weren't in time to catch the emergency vehicles taking the bodies out on stretchers though. Luke hadn't been either. They only met his sister at the hospital where she was already unconscious and later bled out. It had taken Cody three days to die. He had come back to consciousness twice, long enough to ask about Catherine, to find out that she had died, that if he lived he would be charged with her death for driving under the influence.

It was easy to find the spot of the crash. There was a massive gash in the even rows of corn where the car had gone over the edge, rolled, and then plowed the stalks over. According to the officers who interviewed Cody, he had been trying to avoid a deer.

Kids who were at that same party were now at the site, and some teachers from school, and some of his parents' friends. Some people brought candles, flowers, stupid stuffed animals. When the news crew showed up the reporter started asking for interviews, going from group to group in her black high heels and blazer and long blond hair tied in a ponytail down her back.

Her friends were so ready to give them. They formed a circle around the speakers while the reporter held out her microphone. "She was such a bright light," they said, "and her smile could light up a room," and "she was the most generous person I ever knew, so funny, so kind." Luke listened as they turned her into a superlative. It was like they didn't know her at all. He kept thinking of that time she'd grabbed his hair and swung his head back and forth and said, "Do what I say, puppet, do what I say." For some reason that had been the thing he couldn't get out of his head, even though, almost always, she had been just about the best big sister he could have asked for. But he wasn't going to tell them that story and at the same time, not telling it also seemed dishonest. He wouldn't say anything at all.

When the reporter got to his father he just waved her away. She was undeterred and went up to his mother, who also turned her back. The reporter asked, "Don't you want your daughter's story told? This is your chance to remember her, publicly." The cameraman was right behind her, filming right over her shoulder.

"You think this is the story I want told?" his mother said.

The reporter gripped her mic, took a step back and asked, "Don't you want to pay a tribute, tell everyone what she meant to you?"

"Oh leave off," his mother said. It was his father who, later, approached the reporter and spoke into the microphone about how special his daughter had been, how good at track and field, how talented with a paint brush, how she had loved animals. It was also, Luke thought, the thing that broke his marriage.

"And do you think it was this love of animals that led to the car swerving? Do you think she was trying to get the driver to avoid the deer?"

His father looked so shocked, so taken aback, that he just finally walked away.

But the farmer, they got him talking, the one that owned the cornfield. They saw it all when the story ran, when their neighbor recorded it in case they'd want it as a memory. For a week the tape sat on the counter with a white label along the side where the neighbor had written in black sharpie: "News Story," as if the vagueness of the language would cover up what was inside it.

"It's not the first time someone's gone off the road here," the farmer said, "and it won't be the last. I keep telling the town to put a guardrail in there but they don't listen."

"And these drunk kids, they just don't know," his wife said. "Such a shame that they have to die just so things can change. But they won't."

"And the damage to the field," the farmer said. But Cody's family, they paid for that. An undisclosed amount in court. But how were they supposed to pay for the damage to Luke's family? There was no amount that would actually change what had happened.

Finally, at the scene, the reporter had turned to Luke. "And I hear you are the younger brother of the deceased. You must be in so much pain. What would you like to tell us about your sister, how would you like to remember her today?" Luke stared back at her. The questions were by far the most direct things that anyone had said to him since his sister had died. It was as if the reporter had reached her hand inside of him and started grabbing at one organ of pain after another. No one had asked him something that direct since, either. It was shocking, in this moment, that it came from a stranger, a powerful and intense stranger, this journalist with the long serious face, heavily made up, blue eyes looking right at him as if she were waiting for him to stare back, to assert himself, to challenge her, to press everything inside of him out into the open.

"Don't film me," was all he could manage to say.

"Our son never agreed to an interview," his father said, quietly.

"Are you sure you wouldn't like to say something?" The reporter asked. "This is your one chance."

He shook his head, looked down at his hands, and wondered if he was making some kind of mistake. If maybe he should. His emotions curled together in his stomach, twisted. He didn't know what to do.

Even after his denial, the camera didn't back off. As he stood next to his parents in the memorial circle, Emily stiff on the other side of him, Luke asked again for them not to film him. He didn't want them to see what was on his face, the desperation of his conflicted feelings, how he had to squeeze his eyes together so his frustrated tears wouldn't come out, how he hated them for not letting him just think about his sister.

"We want to be sensitive to what you're going through," the reporter said, "but this is a public place. We can film what we want. We're the news."

"Don't film him if he doesn't want it," one of his sister's friends, Rebecca, said. When the camera didn't stop she stood in front of him and the bright light from the camera crew was splintered by her long dark hair on either side of her head. It was the image that stayed with him the most from that night, the dark spot of her head, and the blinding light breaking all around it, streaming through each strand of her hair.

And later he could hear the reporter saying, "And tonight, a family in grief." But he didn't listen to the rest as the spotlight stained them all white.

***

They pulled into the driveway of the house of "The Naked Break-In" and Oliver filled him in. A teenager had apparently gotten drunk at a sleepover, gone out to a soccer field with his friends, had gotten lost on his way back, and just walked into the wrong house thinking it was his friend's. The owner had kicked him out, but he kept trying to get in, thinking it was his friend's dad playing a joke on him. Finally, he undressed and fell asleep on a wicker couch on the back porch. The man had called the cops, who finally took him away in just his underwear.

"Isn't the title of this story a little misleading?" Luke asked. "I mean, after all, he only got undressed once he stopped trying to break in."

"I don't know that there's really any big difference. Point is, he tried to break and he got naked. And anyway, it sounds better right?"

"Yeah, I guess."

The house they had arrived at looked like a big box covered in cedar shingles set back in the woods with stairs leading up to a deck and the front door.

"You think they'll do the interview?" Luke asked.

"They always do the interview, one way or another. You'll learn that." Luke wasn't sure. He hadn't given one.

"You don't think they'll be embarrassed?"

"Who knows. They might think it's funny. But if they're embarrassed, we'll have to do some convincing."

They walked up the steps and Oliver motioned for him to put the camera down.

A teenager came to the door. Skinny, good-looking, dark hair. But he looked a little too young to be out drinking. Fourteen maybe. But who knew.

"Are you Marshall," Oliver asked, in a friendly tone, with thinly veiled menace.

"No, I'm Michael."

"Do all your names start with M?"

"Only me and Marshall."

"Where is Marshall?"

"He's not here."

They heard a woman's voice somewhere in the room behind.

"My mom wants to know who's at the door."

"Tell her it's Channel 5 News. We just want to ask her a few questions about Marshall."

His face broke into a smile.

"It's the news," he said, shouting over his shoulder. "They want to know about Marshall." He turned back to them, grinning now as if they were all in on the joke. They heard the mother's voice again and Michael reluctantly walked away from the door.

"He would have told us everything we ever wanted to know," Oliver said in a low voice.

Luke nodded, and smiled a little in spite of himself.

A man appeared in the hall but did not approach the door. He just watched. Then a woman walked past him. She had blond hair that it was obvious she had just brushed. She took off a paint-splotched apron and placed it on a chair before she came up.

"I don't want any interview," the woman said, in what was surprisingly a German or Scandinavian accent.

"We just want to ask you a few questions, that's all."

"I don't want any questions. We're all the time asking questions now too."

"Maybe we can answer some of them together."

She just stopped and looked at him. Luke could tell that even Oliver knew he'd said the wrong thing. Condescension never works.

"Look, if you don't want to answer questions, that's fine, but we'll post his picture on the news, and we'll run the story anyway. You either get a say in how it's told or you don't."

"I don't want you running his picture."

"But that's what we'll do."

"I won't be giving one to you."

"We'll get one. We'll call his friends, his teachers; we'll go down to the school and open yearbooks. We'll find a picture.

It's not hard. Not nowadays. You do the interview and we won't run the picture."

She looked Oliver straight in the eyes. There was something violent and desperate in her. She wavered at the door. Luke began to feel slightly sick; thin sweat broke out along his neck, poked through his pores like needles. This woman, it seemed to him, was not used to her name, or her family's, being run through the mud. This wasn't the amusing stunt of a teenager to her. He could see it in the way she carried herself. This woman was far above Oliver and because Luke was standing out there on the deck with him, this woman was now far above him too.

The woman turned, walked down the hall, spoke briefly with the man, also skinny like the son, dark, handsome, obviously the father, and then returned to the door.

"Come in. We'll make a quick interview."

The room they were in was large with vaulted ceilings, unlike the logger's. It had an open concept with a kitchen, a dining room table, and a living room. There was no television. There were books, large shelves overflowing, and an upright piano. There were also windows, big windows, and sliding glass doors that led out to a large deck in the back. Large abstract paintings hung on most of the walls. Presumably, she had made them.

When Luke came in he turned the camera on, shooting from the crook of his arm, holding the large camera nonchalantly, even though it took some effort and he could feel the muscles in his elbow tightening with its weight. He began to scan the room, to pause on the table, on a painting of streaked textured reds, browns, and yellows, and on a bookshelf overflowing with papers. A gentle hand touched his shoulder and he turned and saw the man. His eyes sat back inside of purple-lined sockets, as though they were in a cave, and from that darkness looked down at him. In a soft voice that was incredibly sure of itself, the man said, "Not of the house. Only the interview."

"I'm just carrying it, I'm not—."

"Not of the house." The man's grip on his shoulder tensed for a moment. He wasn't stupid.

Shocked over being caught, and tense with the sense of his own wrongdoing, Luke lowered the camera and turned it off.

The man backed softly away and Oliver waved him over near the piano, which sat catercorner to a couch full of papers, on which there was just enough room for one person to sit.

"I'm sorry," the woman said. "It's all my husband's teaching things. They're everywhere."

She began to lift them and place them on a coffee table. Oliver started helping her but she shushed him away. When Luke turned around he saw that the man was still watching, and did nothing to help sort his own things. Luke began to feel mildly afraid, or as if he were a sort of virus in the house, an unwanted guest who didn't know when to leave and who continued on in this unwanted behavior.

The woman sat down on the piano bench, and to get close enough, Luke had to step over a cello, which was lying nearby, as though it had just recently been picked up and played.

"That is my son's cello," the woman said. "Marshall's."

Oliver shot him a glance from the couch, and for the first time Luke saw something like doubt in his eyes. These people hadn't been exactly what he had expected. Luke imagined the boy, Marshall, an older facsimile of his brother, sitting at his music stand and practicing, his dark-haired father at the piano, gently yelling out the beat, nodding for him to come in, as the boy looked with concentration at the notes, worked his fingers along the neck, and moved his bow steadily back and forth to bring the notes out.

Luke made a motion to move the cello but hesitated. It felt wrong to touch it, and when he turned he saw the man still looking at him, and again making no motion to help. So, Luke stood cramped against it and set up his tripod, shone the light directly at the woman, and the whole time the cello was right behind his heels and he was afraid of snapping its neck, of the clang of strings and the bridge breaking when he accidentally stepped back over it. Marshall would come home, Luke would be at fault, and there was no money in his bank account to pay for it.

The light was too close on the woman. It turned her face completely white and made her look as though she were in the floodlights of some desperate search team. He wanted, but couldn't, to step back. He knew that she would look overexposed on film, the dark of the upright piano behind her would be made even darker. He could sense their intrusion; the falling natural light of two triangular windows high up on the wall slanted their mote-stocked rays down over her, as the camera trained its bleached eye on her.

"Tell us how you're handling this, how you're feeling about what has happened," Oliver was asking.

"My son, he is ashamed," she said, numerous times, as Luke trained the white light on her. "We are all ashamed. And we feel only utter thankfulness that the owner of that house knew it was only a teenager, knew that he was not violent, and that he did not use his gun."

"Did you know that he had a gun, was that mentioned?"

"No, no, we just feel, we feel tremendously lucky, that nothing bad has happened, and we are ashamed, we are regretful, that this has happened, that our son was drinking and did not know when to stop, where was his friend's house."

"And your son's friend's parents. Have you spoken to them? It seems like a real lapse in supervision, right?"

"We have spoken, but our conversation, that will remain between us only."

Oliver nodded. "So you did speak?"

"We have spoken."

"And your son, has he struggled with alcohol use before?"

The assumption in the question seemed to shock her. "Struggled? No, this was a young man who has made a mistake. There is no struggle with alcohol. No."

It occurred to Luke that this was a strategy Oliver used, to ask a much more extreme question to get a response out of his interviewee.

"Just kids having fun then?"

She did not seem to like that question either and was struggling to find a response.

Instead, Oliver cut the interview short and thanked her. "I really appreciate you taking the time today."

"Yes," she said, her face rigid, her hands folded in her lap. When he stood up to go, she rose as well, both hands tight at her sides. Oliver began to extend his hand, seemed to think better of it, and turned toward the door. Luke snapped the record button off, lowered the camera, got the light, and freed himself. Oliver too, seemed in a bit of a rush to get back out, though it wasn't as obvious, and Luke wondered later whether he had imagined it, whether he had wanted it to be true.

As they left, there was a new car in the driveway, a crappy gray Honda Civic all rusted out along the wheel wells, the kind a teenager might drive. Oliver didn't seem to notice it, or ignored it on purpose. He just opened the back for Luke and then walked right up to his door and got in. But Luke studied the car as he loaded the camera equipment in, heard the engine clicking as it cooled. Marshall must have snuck in through some back door. When he looked at the house a face appeared in a back window and Luke was sure it was Marshall. A face similar to his younger brother's. Marshall stared at him through the shadowy window as if he was watching to see what they would do with his story, with him.

When he got back into the car, Oliver didn't seem fazed at all. He was writing something on a notepad and when he finished he said, "Another interview in the bag." Then he pulled the gear into drive and they moved slowly away from the house, Luke tense in the seat beside him.

After they had interviewed the mother, they went to the "scene of the crime," where the man whose house Marshall tried and failed to break into showed them a cardboard box full of Marshall's clothes. He stood out on his porch in gray felt slippers and a plaid bathrobe. A messy wisp of dark hair sat on his head as if someone had taped it there. "Collected these off the back porch," he said, "though this hat was right on the fence post there by the front walk." He lifted a green beanie out of the box. "He must have just been in the undressing mood the moment he got in my yard." His eyes wrinkled into something like a smile and Oliver winked back at him as he took the box.

As they walked down the steps Oliver said in a low voice, "Lay some of his clothes along the walk here, as if he was just pulling them off as he went. Start with the hat on the fencepost there."

He held the box out to him. Luke hesitated.

"But he only got undressed on the back porch."

"Does it matter?"

"It would to me."

"Well, we're not filming in the back and we need to tell this story."

Luke looked at him uncertainly, a trapped anger kindling in frustration.

Oliver shoved the box into his chest and said, "Trust me. I know how to do this stuff. We'll have a better story. Just get it done."

He walked down the path and spun his hand in the air as if he were motioning for a helicopter to take off. He didn't even check to see if Luke was doing it.

Luke looked down at the collection of clothes stuffed into the box. It was as if Marshall had been standing there on the walk and all of a sudden evaporated, transported back to that window at his house. These clothes were all that was left, a scattering of items that, put together, would recreate him. Luke turned one way, then the other, then looked backed down at the box, the remnants. He was stuck. "Fuck," he said.

He pictured Marshall watching him as he took the sweatshirt from the box, held it out in front of him, then lifted it up as if he were taking it off. He threw it on the ground. He got the pants next and turned one leg inside out as if they'd been taken off in a clumsy drunken hurry, bouncing on one leg. The two black socks he threw haphazardly on the brick walkway. The white shirt with the Champion logo he left on the bottom steps of the porch so the camera could zoom in on it. From a distance it looked a little like crime scene tape, only that it had been filled in with white. He approached the front gate and imagined himself in a fog, lifting the hat from his head, and placing it there, almost like a benediction.

One-Eyed Boy

When he was done he was strangely pleased by this little reconstruction he had created, as if it were a play, all the props lined up down the row of the walk.

The socks though, all bunched up on the walk, looked pathetic in their sense of betrayal.

Luke got his camera, shot some B-roll, and then watched through the heavy lens as Oliver narrated the break-in, lifted Marshall's hat from the fencepost, dangled it in his fingers, and pointed back to the sweatshirt lying near the path. Luke followed this up to the front steps where the white shirt lay like innocent proof. When he zoomed back out, he found Oliver's face smiling at the camera, as if to say "Look at this idiot. Classic."

He felt complicit.

Once they'd filmed the bit, Oliver said, "Let's go down to the precinct and make sure we're not missing anything."

In the parking lot, Oliver hailed an officer just pulling in for his night shift. "Were you on last night for the 'Naked Break-In?'" Oliver asked, raising both hands spookily.

"Haha, yeah. What a mess. I can't talk about it on the record, but man, that kid was blotto. Like, we had to restrain him. He kept trying to sneak out. Like, we'd turn around and he'd be crawling under a table toward the door and we'd have to say, 'Hey there, get back here!' and he'd pretend not to hear. Or he didn't think we were real or something. Eventually it just got old so we had to restrain him. Threw him in a chair and cuffed him to the wall. Problem was, once he was cuffed to the wall, he started puking. Luckily the mother showed up around that time, 2:15 a.m. I'd say, approximately, and she cleaned it up, and I have to say, that was an uncomfortable scene, this kid watching his mom clean up his vomit and asking what the fuck she was doing there. I mean, he was out of it. She clearly, you know, she clearly did not take that shit lightly. White as a sheet. Just, oh man. I feel bad 'cause I bet that kid got what was coming to him once he sobered up."

"You and me both, brother," Oliver said, and winked. Luke stopped listening after that. It was clear they weren't going to put any of this in the story, weren't going to interview the officer. He went and sat on the rear bumper while Oliver finished up the conversation. He heard them laughing.

On the drive home they sat in silence as the highway blurred by them. They had well over an hour before they were back in the city.

"There was a woman, a reporter, who worked for your channel. She was blond, and um, tall. Serious. What happened to her?"

"Oh, Gina? Yeah, she quit. Got sick of it, I think."

"Really, why?"

"Who knows. She was pretty burned out, I think. She was intense, you know, so everything she did she just went all in on. Super successful that way. But I don't know, she just lost the taste for it I guess."

"I wonder why."

"Yeah, we were never that close. Actually, opened up a lot of doors for me. I got a lot more stories once she was gone, and they were good ones too. She tended to get the good ones because the higher-ups knew she'd deliver. Maybe she got sick of that, you know. I did learn a lot by watching her though. Probably could have learned a lot more if we weren't always competing for stories, haha. If I were smart I would have shadowed her, but I guess I just thought she was the competition. Meanwhile, she didn't even want to play anymore. Just goes to show you." There was a silence. "Why do you ask?"

"She did my sister's story."

"Your sister's?"

"When she died."

"What?!"

It felt good to say this, like a vengeance, like yes, he had a story too, and it was bad, and Oliver's news station, it was involved. "Yeah, when my sister died. Got into an accident. Her boyfriend crashed into a cornfield."

"Shit. I don't remember that one."

"I do."

Oliver looked at him for a long time then, his eye flicking back and forth between Luke and the road.

"I bet you do."

Luke nodded.

"She do it right?" Oliver asked.

Luke shook his head, "No."

"Huh," Oliver said.

"Well maybe that's why she quit."

There was another silence out of which the sarcasm in the remark landed.

"Shit. Sorry. I don't know why I said that. Just slipped out I guess."

"Maybe she should have," Luke said. But even saying that felt like he was absolving Oliver of just making another insensitive quip, this time about his sister's life.

But it did keep him from asking any more questions, like why it was that Luke had ended up working at the station if he didn't think they'd done it right. In all likelihood, though, Oliver was beginning to put it together.

***

When he got home that night Bobby was in the kitchen so Luke tried to avoid him.

"Hey wait," Bobby said. He held up the orange juice carton. "Want some?"

By instinct, Luke began shaking his head, but stopped.

"Can't make up your mind, huh?"

"Guess not."

"Hey, listen man. I'm sorry about the other night. I didn't mean to call you out like that. I just feel like you're struggling sometimes, or you've got some shit going on, you know. I care, actually. Really. Seriously. I'm not trying to be a dick."

Luke stood there in a kind of frozen paralysis of need and fear. "It's no problem," he said. It was all he could say. If he said anymore it would all just spill out of him. Telling Oliver about his sister's story had made it all tremulous, like something was cracking, like he was chipping away at some massive thing that couldn't be unloaded. But still, if he said it, it would join with the tremendous calm of Bobby pouring orange juice.

"My sister died," Luke said, picking at the fraying edges of his sweatshirt cuffs.

Bobby put the carton aside, sighed, and took him in with concern. The track lights from the ceiling caught the tiny hairs of his buzzed head and turned them bright. He crossed his arms, ready to listen. Luke's chin began to quiver. He was sure that he wouldn't be able to say anything, that nothing would come out. Bobby's kindness was too big.

Finally, Bobby took his glass from the counter and said, "Here man, here, have some of this, drink some of this." Again, he waited, and as Luke sipped he thought of the way

Marshall's face had looked at him out of that window, fearful, and how he had just made it worse for him, the same way the news had made it worse for Luke after his sister died. But it all seemed too complicated to explain, so when he lowered the glass he just said, "Thanks."

Bobby nodded, waited, one big bicep squeezed by the fist beneath it.

"How long ago?"

"A couple years."

"Hmm." Finally, Bobby just took over, said what everybody said when they talked about death. They told one of their own stories, which was always the same, a pet, a grandparent, a distant cousin. "You know, my grandma died, it was really tough. I loved my grandma," Bobby said. As he began telling him what it had been like going to her house, and how she had looked later in the nursing home, and what she had taught him about being a person. But even though this was the same old story, Luke was listening as if he were separated from his body, coaching himself from a few feet away to nod, to lean in, to really look at Bobby. It was important to do this right, to do this the way Bobby would have done it, and to have Bobby like him, even though it probably wouldn't work. There was too much torn-up ground inside of Luke.

Luke couldn't find anything to say when Bobby finished, just looked up at him in helplessness as tears began to ring his eyes.

"Hey, hey, don't worry man. It's cool. That was a long time ago. Listen, I get it if you don't want to talk, or can't or whatever, but you should come watch a movie with us. You know, come join us for once."

Luke shook his head and said "Thanks for the juice," before he turned out of the kitchen.

He got back to his room and stood inside the door. He didn't even have a chair in his room, just the bed. He was always in the bed. Just lying there.

There was a knock and the door opened.

"Actually, it wasn't an offer. This is an intervention." Bobby grabbed him around his middle, lifted him up, and carried him into the hallway.

"Hey!" Luke said.

"Don't struggle."

"Fine." He went slack and Bobby rag-dolled him into the living room. "Look who decided to join us," Ryan said, the kind of kid that hated it when people didn't join the party, have another drink, go as wild and as hard as he wanted.

"He's just gonna hang with the boys for a while," Bobby said. "Aren't you?"

"I guess."

"That's right," Bobby said, and put one of his big arms over his shoulder so he was trapped into the corner of the couch. "You're not allowed to leave, sorry."

"Okay," Luke said. And then he let out a big sob. He fought against the next one, the swell, and coughed it back.

"It's all right man," Bobby said. "We're here. You can cry."

"Yeah man," they said. "Just cry it out bro."

But he couldn't. The sob came and then the others got all blocked up behind it and he coughed and wiped at his eyes and couldn't do anymore.

"His sister died a couple years ago," Bobby explained.

"Oh my God. So sorry dude, so, so sorry," they said and then he wiped at his eyes again and hiccupped and said it was all right, it was all right. "We can watch the movie now," he said, and somehow, having it out in the house, he couldn't tell if it would be more awkward now or less. Whether the tension was out of the air and he could just move in and out of rooms, join them on the couch, or whether it would be even more constricted, whether they wouldn't know what to say to him anymore, and he'd be even more locked away in his bedroom. So, he just kept sitting there, his chin quivering, and stared straight ahead at the screen as a car raced down a road and a tree was struck with lightning and the car reversed and the Bruckheimer Production logo came up.

Late that night, his camera kept catching the boy, Marshall, running naked in a field. His dark form was streaking across the grass like the shadow of a wild animal, like a deer. And then his white light found him, it found him right there in the field where his sister's car had crashed, and when it caught him he turned, shocked, as though the light were cold. His skin was white in the light and his eyes were wild and manic. Then he turned and bounded off into the shadow of the trees at the edge of the field and Luke's light couldn't find him anywhere, though he had already caught him, trapped in the cone of light from which he would never escape.

***

The next day was the championship game of the Women's World Cup. Team USA had made it to the final. Oliver had invited Luke over to watch. "They'll play our bit after the game, so we can hang out, watch, and hopefully celebrate with 'The Naked Break-In.'" He chuckled. "Should be a good one. Plus, you can meet my wife."

"You're married?" Luke was shocked. He had never even considered it. He somehow thought Oliver would have girlfriends, maybe, but never a wife. He had pictured Oliver at bars on weekends, meeting women with whom he talked in his confident way, able to impress them with his intensity and his stories. He'd get somewhere, but never very far past the first night, or the second or third. And if things did go farther, invariably he'd get bored, or blow up, or be insensitive. The fact that he had a wife wiped out this whole side of Oliver that Luke had believed was there. Just as immediately a new thought knifed in: he must have regular affairs.

The shock of this made such strong sense that he immediately had to tell himself it wasn't true or else he wouldn't have been able to stay in the conversation.

Oliver smiled at him, held up his hand with the wedding ring on it. "Shocked that a guy like me could have a wife?" He was smiling. "You know, for a cameraman, and a good one at that, you're really not very observant."

Luke pinched out an embarrassed smile at the hand held out in front of his face.

"But maybe the problem is that you're not a journalist. The first thing you learn as a journalist is not to let your," and here he took on a high-minded tone, "preconceptions cloud your judgment." He was grinning.

"I had no preconceptions," Luke said. "I just didn't see."

"You keep telling yourself that."

"Well, I look forward to meeting her."

When he showed up at the house it was Nancy who answered, wearing a white shirt tucked into jeans. Her hair was shoulder length, light brown, and straight. "Oliver's just getting the snacks ready," she said. "He's been looking forward to this. Come on in!"

"Welcome to mi casa!" Oliver said from the large kitchen island where he was pouring chips into a bowl.

"Thanks," Luke said.

"Here, grab this." Luke took the bowl while Oliver carried the tray of snacks. "You want a beer, honey," Nancy asked. When Luke realized she was talking to him he looked over at Oliver who pretended to ignore him.

"Um, sure, thanks."

"You got it." She carried two Coors Lite bottles by the neck out to the large carpeted living room, which looked out on a big deck. Once they were settled on the couch she said, "Enjoy boys," and rubbed Oliver's shoulders. "Ooh yeah, baby," he said, and she slapped him lightly on the head and walked away.

As the game went on, Nancy kept calling Oliver into the kitchen and he would reappear with new platters of food. She pressed bottles of beer into Luke's hand whenever his got empty. By halftime there were three bottles of Coors Lite on the coffee table in front of him. They were treating him like a guest, an adult. He tried to focus on the game, to follow the movement of the ball between all the tiny players on the screen, but again and again his mind was torn back to the previous day, to staging the scene, to the woman in the living room, to Oliver laughing with that officer.

Nancy tried to get him to take off his sweatshirt, to make himself at home, but he said he was all set, and Oliver told her that he was always "all set," when it came to that sweatshirt. "The thing practically lives on him; it's like his second skin, or his business suit, or his life suit, who knows. Anyway, it'll be four thousand degrees and he'll still keep it on and just smile as if we're in the arctic when I tell him to take it off." Nancy waved her husband's comments away as if to tell Luke not to worry about it, which he tried not to do, unzipping the sweatshirt and cradling the bulge of his camera in the front right pocket so that it wasn't visible.

Luke had also worn his News Channel 5 baseball hat, which Oliver had given him the day of the Naked Break-In, to make him a "Company Man."

"At least he's got the hat though. That's a look that will never go out of style."

Now and again Oliver would flip up to channel 5 during commercial breaks to see if there was a news preview. As the game concluded with the final ninety minutes scoreless, they caught it perfectly. A news brief came on and the announcer's voice said, "Coming up on News Channel 5, 'The Naked Break-In!'" The camera flipped to show Marshall's mother speaking in the bright white light of his camera, her face pale. "I feel utter thankfulness," she was saying, her strong accent seeming even stronger in the spotlight, in the throng of American voices around it. The word "utter" sounded like "uttah."

"Is it always like this?" Luke asked as the game clock approached its second overtime.

"What, the game? No, man, this is a special game. It's incredible. Overtime! In the championship game! It's amazing."

"No, I know that, it's awesome, I mean the news. Reporting. What we're doing. Is this an unusual week?"

"Unusual? No, not really. A little intense maybe. But it always gets intense. Is that what you mean? Or do you feel bad for that woman with the naked break-in? Don't. We did nothing wrong there."

"Well, we did force them to do the interview. They didn't have to."

"We did what we had to do to get the interview."

Luke's heart was beating faster and the blood beginning to move out into his arms.

"We didn't have to spread his clothes all over the walk though."

"Hey, you did that," Oliver said, grinning.

"I wouldn't have."

"But you did, didn't you? Plus, it made the story better. Stop worrying about it. It's not like we changed what happened."

But he was worried about it. And not just that. It was the titties on the screen without the context of the party, it was the way the news reporter had a smile on her face, just barely visible, when she stood in front of the crash site with his sister's boyfriend's silver Acura half out of the ditch and the black cornfield behind it. It was the way her smile was just the same when she was reporting on a local election victory, on a heartfelt story of an owner reunited with his dog after many years. It was the way the smile never changed, just barely there, no matter what the story was. It was the way Oliver's face had that same smile when he lifted Marshall's hat off that lamppost, only exaggerated, it was even the same feeling he'd had when he had finished placing those clothes all over the walk. It was the way the officer laughed about the story when he was retelling it. It was a smile that glided right over the people in the stories, turned them small, indistinguishable.

Oliver was watching him, one arm stuck out along the top of the couch, like a sight through which his eyes aimed.

"It just didn't feel right. Any of it. Like we weren't supposed to be there," Luke said, pushing the words out through the roiling tingling blood in his arms.

Oliver considered him for a long moment, as if to decide whether he was being insulted or not.

Finally, Oliver turned back to the T.V. and just responded to his initial question: "No, not super unusual. Most days it's reporting on the popularity of Girl Scout cookies and traffic pattern changes to increase safety, or the breaking of ground of some new building, or the excitement people have for the holidays and exactly how much shopping they're doing. But the thing is, in most of these stories, there's tragedy somewhere. Either it's in the banality of the story, or it's in the thing that led to the change, or it's the change itself, which mostly comes with some kind of violence, or some kind of fucked something. A kid hit on a crosswalk. An overdose. An accident. Mostly that's the news. Fuckups and violence." Then he looked over at Luke and said, "Listen, if you want to get into this, you're going to have to have a thick skin. Either for all the boredom and fluff stories, or for the ones that don't feel good. Most of this stuff doesn't feel good, one way or the other, and you're going to have to decide if you want to be a part of that. I don't know what happened with your sister's story, or why that made you want to join the news, but clearly it did." He was looking at him straight through that sight again. "Just remember though, it's our job to tell the story, and to make it good. We're not out there actually killing people. All that bad shit has already happened by the time we show up."

Oliver's eyes had become too intense for Luke to face.

As if he were talking to a squirrel out on the deck, Luke said, "Yeah, we're making it worse, we are killing them afterwards, after they're already dead. We're killing them. That's what we're doing. We're not telling their stories, we're killing their stories." Luke's body, his bloodstream, was full of something so boiling that he wanted to hurl his camera, lift the table, the drinks, he wanted to wing them at Oliver and his big comfortable body on the couch. He didn't even know what he was saying, just that he had to disagree, just that it felt like killing, or something else, some kind of wrongness.

Nancy came in then and Luke stared straight at the television, aware of a violence in the air that was directed his way. If he looked at the T.V. he wouldn't have to look at anything else, at the violence emanating from Oliver. The game had gone to a penalty shootout and Nancy squeezed in next to Oliver on the couch, saying "Scoot!" He grumbled and moved to the side, then asked if she had brought more chips. He was acting, playing the entitled man, trying to cover up the intensity in the room.

"They're in the kitchen hun," she said. "You know where they are. My women are about to deliver us a World Cup!"

"Says the woman who doesn't like sports."

"Oh shush, this is exciting. The women are gonna win it long before the men ever do. Just you watch."

And sure enough, they did. A player on Team USA scored the winning goal. She ran down the field and then slid on her knees and tore her shirt off over her head. Her teammates ran out to crowd her. "We won!" Nancy said, raising her hands like the player had. "The women won! We won! Yes!" Luke was trying to smile, just the way that Oliver had kept up his act. He didn't want Nancy to see that he was upset. Luke wanted to celebrate with her and kept looking at the woman on the screen, a player named Brandi Chastain, kept seeing her there on her knees in her sports bra, a world champion, and he imagined the cameraman running across the field toward her with the camera heavy and shaky over his shoulder to catch her in this moment where the story was totally and completely hers. A perfect moment.

Soon Oliver would flip over to News Channel 5 to watch their bit and Luke suddenly knew that he couldn't stay to see it. The familiar sickness went through him again. He'd have to leave. He kept looking at Brandi Chastain's face, all the cameras on her, her moment of ecstasy.

He got up and started walking away.

"Hey! Where're you going?" Oliver said, a little too much uncontrolled anger in his voice.

"Oh, just to the bathroom," Luke said, without turning around. "I've been holding it for a while. I just wanted to see the ending."

He could sense Oliver staring at him over the back of the couch, figuring out if he was being lied to. But Luke didn't turn around, just heard him say, "Well, hurry up, we're almost on. And that's the real show."

But Luke didn't wait to see the rest. He got upstairs, walked past the small bathroom in the hall to the front door, lifted the gold lever and slowly pulled it open. When he did, the plastic along the bottom gave a soft whoosh as the air released. When he got outside he realized he'd forgotten his hat. He couldn't go back in though; the door was locked and he'd have to ring the bell and he was afraid of ever seeing Oliver again.

He kept walking up the slope of the paved driveway and then stopped midway, took his camera from the pocket of his sweatshirt, flipped open the screen on the side, and hit record. Step by step, he began to back up out of the driveway, watching as the camera caught Oliver's beige house with its vinyl siding and stone-facade entryway, the big two-door garage with the Chevy Suburban hidden inside it, and the incremental backward movement of his feet taking him away from the house until he made it out past the driveway, turned, and walked toward the bus stop with his camera rolling, his one eye lit up on the world.

ACKNOWLEDGMENTS

So many people have touched this book in some form or another. I worked on these stories off and on for well over a decade, and during that time I showed them to trusted family members, teachers, colleagues, and friends. Their input was invaluable and truly taught me that a book is not made in isolation, but in community.

I would like to begin by thanking my family, who have always, from the start, supported me in my writing and never doubted that it was a worthwhile pursuit. How lucky I am. They also saw many early drafts of these stories and were always kind in their assessments and gentle in their recommendations. My father, especially, spent a great deal of time on these stories, both in reading and editing them, and in allowing me to talk about them over coffee.

I have been so fortunate to belong to a variety of writing communities, first at Emerson College in the undergraduate WLP program (Writing, Literature, and Publishing), where I met friends I still rely on today. Theadora Siranian has been a stalwart friend and inspiring creative force who spent a whole summer diligently reading over drafts of these stories, which helped me to make it over the final hurdle.

At Warren Wilson's MFA Program for Writers I had encouragement from all angles. Michael Parker was the first person to set eyes on my title story, which, at that point, I had no idea would become a book. Karen Tucker has been an incredible friend and trusted reader of my work, Katie Runde helped in figuring out how to pitch this collection, and my whole Warren Wilson family, especially Christian Gullete, Laura Van Prooyen, James Herndon, and so many others who were always there in support. You know who you are. I was also lucky to receive the Levis Prize from Friends of Writers, which helped me in the completion of this book. Many thanks to Melanie Hatter for choosing my manuscript and speaking about it so kindly.

My colleagues at Berkshire Community College who were part of the Works in Progress Group saw many of these stories in their embarrassing early stages and gave me insightful feedback that was always constructive in nature. I'm so thankful for their voices. Nicole Mooney, Julianna Spallholz, Nell McCabe, Charles Park, Lauren Goodman and many others.

Among my friends, I am so lucky to have brilliant readers who are always interested to read my work, even if it is long. Gavriel Cohen read many early versions of these stories and provided fantastic Feedback. Helena Zay, as well, supported me in the early stages of this book and through my time at Warren Wilson. Emma Sawyer was a consistent voice of support and insight and helped me to see my characters in a new light.

Finally, my partner, Toula Taliadoros, has been my rock, supporting my writing and defending it from all comers and willingly sitting with a pen and a hard copy to give me her feedback, which I have come to trust and rely on deeply. I am so grateful.

This book wouldn't exist without Alan Good taking a chance on it and bringing it into the world through Malarkey

Books. I am so thankful that he saw something in it and chose to dedicate his time and energy to making edits and seeing it through all of the phases of production. I feel so lucky. Thank you also to Angelo Maneage for the incredible cover art. He really got what this book was all about.

Finally, these stories are created by the life around me, which is created by all those people I am connected with. Thank you for being part of my life!

Many thanks to the editors of the following journals for featuring stories from this collection, in somewhat altered form:

"Watch Me," in *Cottonwood*

"Mr. Perfect," in *Eunoia Review*

"Tornado Warning" and "Hank" in *Halfway Down the Stairs*

Other Titles from Malarkey

Faith, a novel by Itoro Bassey

The Life of the Party Is Harder to Find Until You're the Last One Around, poems by Adrian Sobol

Music Is Over, a novel by Ben Arzate

Toadstones, stories by Eric Williams

Deliver Thy Pigs, a novel by Joey Hedger

It Came From the Swamp, edited by Joey Poole

Pontoon, an anthology of fiction and poetry

What I Thought of Ain't Funny, edited by Caroljean Gavin

Guess What's Different, essays by Susan Triemert

White People on Vacation, a novel by Alex Miller

Your Favorite Poet, poems by Leigh Chadwick,

Sophomore Slump, poems by Leigh Chadwick

Man in a Cage, a novel by Patrick Nevins

Fearless, a novel by Benjamin Warner

Don Bronco's (Working Title) Shell, a novel? by Donald Ryan

Un-ruined, a novel by Roger Vaillancourt

Thunder From a Clear Blue Sky, a novel by Justin Bryant

Kill Radio, a novel by Lauren Bolger

The Muu-Antiques, a novel by Shome Dasgupta

Backmask, a novel by OF Cieri

Gloria Patri, a novel by Austin Ross

Where the Pavement Turns to Sand, stories by Sheldon Birnie
Still Alive, a novel by LJ Pemberton
I Blame Myself But Also You, stories by Spencer Fleury
Hope and Wild Panic, stories by Sean Ennis
Thumbsucker, poems by Kat Giordano
The Great Atlantic Highway & Other Stories, by Steve Gergley
Sleep Decades, stories by Israel A. Bonilla
Boxcutters, stories by John Chrostek
Hair Shirt, poems by Adrian Sobol

Death of Print Titles

Consumption & Other Vices, a novel by Tyler Dempsey
Awful People, a novel by Scott Mitchel May
Drift, a novel by Craig Rodgers
The Ghost of Mile 43, a novel by Craig Rodgers
One More Number, stories by Craig Rodgers
Francis Top's Grand Design, stories by Craig Rodgers
Francis Top's Lost Cipher, stories by Craig Rodgers
Detective Novel a novel by Craig Rodgers

malarkeybooks.com

www.ingramcontent.com/pod-product-compliance
Lightning Source LLC
LaVergne TN
LVHW091713070526
838199LV00050B/2384